POLKA DOTS AND MOONBEAMS

A Word in the Reader's Ear.

David Longridge is a writer with a wealth of experience and success in the Real World.

After school he worked for, and became, Chief Executive of Avis International, then second biggest car rental company in the World. That was followed by a long stint with international banks in the City of London. Throughout these times his inner creativity was released by his occasional playing the tenor sax, something he would love to have done professionally.

On retirement, he decided to release his creativity by writing books that were fictional, but in a historical setting of a period he loved.

'Polka Dots and Moonbeams' is his third novel, an extraordinary story that flips between the Parisienne fashion houses, the dark showbiz and drug-soaked world of Josephine Baker and the Vietnam War with the French in the 1950s. It was an extraordinary time, at the birth of our modern age, and Longridge has caught the mood, ambience, romance and urgency of that period as he always does in his novels. Through it all, like a river of molten gold, runs the love stories of people caught between the two sides as they fight to keep their lives normal while transiting through the violently opposing worlds of war and peace.

Tragedy and joy go hand in hand.

Eddy Shah. Media owner and novelist.

Polka Dots and Moonbeams

David Longridge

Matador
9 Priory Business Park,
Wistow Road, Kibworth Beauchamp,
Leicestershire. LE8 0RX
Tel: 0116 279 2299
Email: books@troubador.co.uk
Web: www.troubador.co.uk/matador
Twitter: @matadorbooks

ISBN: 978 1838593 124

British Library Cataloguing in Publication Data.
A catalogue record for this book is available from the British Library.

Typeset by Mach 3 Solutions Ltd (www.mach3solutions.co.uk)
Printed by TJ International Ltd, Padstow

Matador is an imprint of Troubador Publishing Ltd

To Francesca, Sebastian, William,
Alexander and Louisa

Vietnam as part of French Indochina, 1950–1954, made up of Tonkin, Annam, and Cochinchina

1

Justine feels Ka's hands through the lace, as they work on the bolero. The movement of the needle as it makes last-minute adjustments to how the material falls around her shoulders and down her back. No one else in the house works like Ka. Justine knows how dedicated she is. Late into the night before a show. Last night when most of the team were long gone, Ka was still at her desk in the *atelier flou*, the dressmaking workshop, hand stitching the final details. Concentration that is almost tangible. They are all like that, the finest of their kind in the Paris couture world. But Ka is the best. What's her story? Why is she here, why in France?

On an ordinary day, they gossip about work, about the other staff in Schiaparelli, about the clients. Justine has her secrets. Ka must have hers, more than she reveals. She'll talk about today, not yesterday. How she studies French literature, even a little about her social life in the Vietnamese community. Yet nothing about her former life. Justine can't blame her. She herself never says anything about what happened to her. After all, everyone in Paris of her age has a story. Some are true, some false. Just good enough to get away with. To stay clean. Not to be tarred with the brush of collaboration, nor the horror of the camps.

'Nearly time,' says Ka. 'You okay?'

Justine is silent, her thoughts to herself. Why is she going through with this?

Ka knows. She's the only one in the salon who knows what Justine's going to do.

'Five minutes,' the *guardienne* calls out. Justine looks around the salon, converted to a workroom for the day. It's from here that they will be launched onto the runway.

Janice glances across at them, smiles, or is it almost a sneer. 'Marcel's here.'

Had to be, thinks Justine. The money behind Christian Dior.

'You know I worked for Dior, before I came to Schiap last year,' says Ka. 'A totally new house. The New Look put them on the map. Monsieur Boussac came in almost every day.'

'How did he find Dior?' asks Justine.

'First mannequin ready,' the *guardienne* interrupts. Justine's only showing one item in this collection. She knows she'll be last. The wedding dress. Never been a wedding dress like it. What inspiration, what daring. Made entirely from a lace veil. Front of the dress and the sleeves cover her from waist to neck. The back? There isn't a back. Except for the ribbon around the neck, holding up the front. There's nothing from head to her waist. Designed to surprise when the moment comes. When she enters, they'll just see the bolero, from shoulders almost to the tummy.

'Can I get you something? Why not sit down. I'll check you all over before you walk.'

'Just water, thanks, Ka.'

The music starts. Jazz guitar on its own, American dance music. Django. He's here. Heaven.

There goes the first mannequin, round the heavy drapes and out onto the floor, the runway. Clapping. Polite, for the first garment.

More clapping as the first girl finishes and Janice goes forward for her moment. Cries from the audience as she hits the runway. Justine's not surprised. She's showing off the latest incarnation of the 'lobster dress'. Full-length evening robe in white silk with wide shoulder straps and broad pink wasteband. From just below the waist almost to the hem, there is a lobster design sewn into the dress material, the fan tail at the top and giant claws plunging downwards, its pink body almost jumping outwards as the motion of the mannequin sweeps the dress across her legs.

The water arrives. 'Thank you, Ka. Just a sip. Talk to me about something.'

'If I were in your shoes, I would play with the audience, tease them before you shock them.'

'What do you mean?'

'In the way you walk. They'll see the bolero first. Underneath, your long concave back will rivet their attention, even though it's covered by the lace of the bolero. Build up their excitement.'

'The usual crowd,' says Justine. Anyone special?'

Ka laughs, in her musical way. 'Kept women, some of them. Limitless cash in exchange for who knows what. Mixed with an English duchess or two. Blue-haired madonnas from New York. The *grandes dames* of *Harper's* and *Vogue*. Then the special ones, they're the ones I like. The Begum Aga Kahn. She's here, loves her polka dot silk dresses. Has them made in Paris, to wear at Ascot. And I'm sure I spotted a sketcher.'

Justine grins at Ka's last comment, knowing there are women with the skill to sketch the garment within the time the mannequin appeared and vanished, for sale to the top New York labels on Seventh Avenue. 'Yes, we need them all,' Justine says emphatically, as she stands up.

Ka walks around her, tucks and pulls, misses nothing. 'Perfect,' she says. 'So in a moment, they'll all know your secret.' She touches softly Justine's hands. 'Show them. They must see to believe.'

'*Robe de mariée,*' the voice commands. It's Justine's time at last. Animated murmuring filters through from the audience. The collection's gone well. Justine looks across at Django as the drapes part. His sleek black hair shining under the chandeliers. A wonderful smile of encouragement. *I can't give you anything but love* starts its wonderful refrain, as the two good fingers of his left hand move across the six wires of his guitar.

American dance music, she adores it, makes her move provocatively. Timing's going to be the key. Halfway along the outbound trip, that's the moment. The first half of the room will see, the other half won't until she turns at the end and heads back.

Another four paces. Effortlessly the bolero is off her shoulders, her back naked. Sudden gasps from those behind her. Then silence, everyone dead quiet. Just the music. She's almost at the end. Swivels round. Justine heads back the way she came. The other half of the room see her back. What's on their faces? Disbelief, horror, admiration? Almost at the end, as she's about to disappear, people cry out. How did it happen to her? Why is she showing it to them? What is she telling them? People on their feet, not knowing how to react, yet driven by compulsion. Compulsion to express their emotion.

'What the hell was that, Christian?' Marcel Boussac turns to his designer, seated beside him. Hardly noticed when they crept into the back row just before the start of the show.

'Never seen anything like it,' says Dior. 'Those wounds were brutal. Healed, but the strokes have cut deep, won't ever disappear. Poor kid. She's been thrashed terribly at some stage. In the war, I suppose.'

'She's making a statement,' says Boussac.

On the other side of Boussac, a familiar face turns towards him.

'You're right,' she says to him, before rising and addressing everyone in the room. 'My friends, Justine told me she had something to tell you, and this was her way of doing it. In tomorrow's edition of *Le Monde*, you can read what she told me.'

~~~⊙~~~

The *petites mains* seamstresses, the fitters, the mannequins, all face her. A few saw her on the runway, keeping out of sight but peeping through the drapes. Even the *arpettes*, the lowest form of life, who pick up and tidy up. They must have informed the others. Some already know about her back, seen it fleetingly from time to time since she returned to Schiap. Even though she keeps it covered as much as possible. The boss knows, of course. Also, Giselle who looked after her way back on the first day she joined Schiap. Today Giselle is *première main*, head of the *flou atelier*. She kept Justine away from designs where the back of the garment was open. Until today.

Several of her workmates come forward, kisses on both cheeks, showing emotion, tears.

Ka is beside her. Justine feels the gentle hand against her waist. A movement to adjust the garment, but she knows it's more than that. An intimacy, awareness of the bond between them.

~~~⊙~~~

It's almost dark. The narrow street is badly lit. Ka stops outside an ancient apartment house, just off the rue du Bac. She can hear the nuns singing in the convent nearby. A small hatch in the door slides sideways to reveal an Asian face. Nothing is said. The door just opens, and Ka goes in.

2

Paris, Latin Quarter, the next day.

Justine waited for the faint knock on her door. The sound of the water-driven elevator and its door flaps told her the knock was coming. To be sure, as she opened the door of her apartment on the chain, there was the diminutive seamstress smiling at her. Unlatched, the door swung open and Ka was up against her, a kiss on one cheek, then the other, and back to the first. In one hand was a bunch of small autumn roses, in the other a copy of *Le Monde*.

'Here, Mademoiselle Justine, a little gift for the star. The star of Schiap's autumn collection.' The musical laugh filled the air as Justine took the roses. 'You shouldn't waste your money, Ka. My success, if you can call it that, is also yours.' She paused before asking, 'What are people saying about yesterday's show? You have your ear to the ground, and not just at Schiap. The Maison Dior as well, I suspect.' As she was speaking, she was filling a jug and arranging the roses.

'They know you were telling the world something when you showed your beautiful back, and the way the torturers left you. They weren't sure what. So, as we agreed, I helped them.'

'How did you put it?' said Justine.

'I told them it was a wake-up call, to the wickedness in the post-war world of Paris. The pain of the hungry and the sick, with no money for anything. The pain of those who lost their closest in the camps. The pain of the destitute mother with

12

her sick child, seeing the spoilt of the city in their beautiful clothes.'

'Yes,' exclaimed Justine, taking Ka to her and giving her a long embrace. She felt the small but beautifully formed body, warm against hers. 'Brilliant, we must fight for equality, for fairness, and equal opportunity. Only *Le Monde* knew, I gave my friend there an interview the day before.'

'That's why you have a copy already,' said Ka, looking at the newspaper lying on the sofa.

'Just what I wanted,' said Justine. 'Now the message is out.'

'Sounds like you're becoming a Communist,' said Ka, in a teasing voice.

'Not a Communist, just a Socialist,' said Justine. 'A follower of Léon Blum.' She paused. 'I know he just died, but his spirit will live for ever in me. Those Pétainist bastards sent him to Buchenwald. He was one of the French politicians who didn't support Pétain becoming President when Germany overran France.'

'So, what's your next step?'

'I met Blum several times after I returned to Paris. He was Jewish, of course. That's the other reason Pétain and Laval were after him. You wouldn't know, Ka, but my parents were Jews. They escaped from Berlin in the thirties, moving their wine business to Bordeaux. That's where I came from when I joined Schiap in '41.'

There was a pause, a loaded silence. Then Ka almost whispered, 'Something terrible happened to you, didn't it, Mademoiselle Justine.'

Justine nodded as Ka went on. 'You never tell me about the war, about what happened to you, Justine.'

'I know. I can't. But then, you never tell me your background. Why you live in France.'

There was another heavy silence.

Justine finally said, 'Let's not go there.' She saw Ka's eyes return to the headline of *Le Monde* lying on a chair in the corner of the room. 'You realise what that means, don't you?'

'What, the disaster threatening on Route Coloniale 4?' asked Ka.

'It means that Ho Chi Minh and his Viets are no longer a band of guerrillas. They have become an army. This client on my list at Schiap, the one you're working on the cocktail dress for, her husband's a senior civil servant. They have a son out there. She said the same that's in today's *Monde*.'

'They were talking about it at work,' said Ka. 'The Viets now have infantry divisions and artillery, like in the war in Europe.'

Silence for a few moments. Then Justine said, 'It could be the worst catastrophe ever in France's colonial wars. Already thousands are killed or missing. The government is being pressed by the military to send conscripts to Indochina.'

Ka murmured, 'So, what will that mean?'

'To me, it means Ho Chi Minh will win in the end,' said Justine. 'France can't afford an army big enough to defeat the Viets. It would bankrupt her.' She headed for the stove and the coffee tin.

'The public won't have it,' said Ka. 'Conscripts being sent down there.' She paused. 'What will you do, with your political friends?'

'I'll tell you what we'll do. We're going to march, that's what I'm going to do next. About the situation in Indochina, Vietnam in particular. People here are angry. Why are they angry? For two reasons, the continuing loss of young Frenchmen dying in the brutal fighting, and the enormous cost of the war. Money that could improve the life of ordinary people here in France.'

Ka's face tensed up. 'Mademoiselle Justine, that's a red-hot subject, especially for us Vietnamese in Paris.'

'I understand that,' said Justine. She knew this was a difficult subject for Ka and her community. If the French withdrew, the lives of people like Ka's family would be destroyed by Ho Chi Minh. The French were hanging on for now with the arms and aircraft being poured into Saigon by the Americans. Justine sipped her tea. The Americans. They didn't support colonialism, but they'd look the other way and help the French if it meant halting the spread of Communism. The whole American nation was going mad with fear of the Red Menace, just look at the madness of the McCarthy hearings, shaking up Hollywood to see if any Communist sympathisers might fall out into the open.

'But it can't go on as it is now,' said Justine. 'We need a voice in France to change things. For that we need money.' She drew herself up, looking intensely at her friend and workmate. 'I have something to ask you, Ka.'

The Vietnamese woman went tense, on guard, seemingly fearful of what was coming next.

Justine took a deep breath. 'Ka, people at work say you have certain private arrangements with some of the firm's clients. I don't want to know the details. I just don't want to see you hurt, my darling.'

Ka remained silent. She felt there was more to come.

Justine continued. 'This client I was talking about just now, let's call her Madame X. She's the wife of a government official. He could never afford Schiaparelli clothes for her. But she's also the daughter of a rich businessman. People say he made a fortune making flamethrowers for the German army during Occupation. Now he has a licence from the Americans to supply something called napalm.'

Ka repeated the word, softly. 'Napalm, I know it. Terrible weapon. Gasoline in jellied form. When dropped from an aircraft it devastates in fire all around it. Sticks to bodies and burns more slowly than gasoline itself. Terrorises the enemy. Nothing lives.' She paused, as if for effect. 'Some say French bombers drop it on the Viets.'

'Precisely,' said Justine. 'Now, the point is, Madame X has a problem. An opium problem. Seems it stems from her husband being introduced to the drug in Saigon, and him encouraging her to indulge in it.'

'Nothing that unusual,' said Ka, cautiously.

'Ka, I have a plan. Part of me says I shouldn't involve you. But I felt you should know, since there's more to this than satisfying people's craving for the drug.' She paused. 'It involves politics. Politics and the war. You'll have heard of the Montagnards.'

'Yes. They inhabit the central Highlands and the mountains in north-west Tonkin, along Vietnam's border with China.'

Justine went on. 'Well, these Montagnards, and particularly the Meos from Laos, control the opium trade up there. It's big, and the story is that Ho Chi Minh wants to get hold of it. The profits are huge, just what he needs to buy arms for General Giap's army and rice for the troops. They're frequently short of food.'

'I know,' said Ka. 'But why are you telling me this?'

Justine looked at her Vietnamese friend, wondering how direct to be. She must test her, be sure Ka would remain loyal. 'Because, my darling, there's a fortune to be made. You and I could have a part of that fortune. I have tried to raise the money I need. Money to print newsletters and leaflets, to buy advertising space, to pay lawyers' fees. If necessary, to form a new political party. But no one wants to put up the money.'

Silence from Ka. A long silence. Then she seemed to decide. 'What would you want me to do?'

'Ka, you would have to think about using the channels I suspect you are already in touch with.' Justine paused. 'Or whether you and I should set up our own pipeline.'

'What do you mean, pipeline?'

'I mean that, together, we would make contact with those in Vietnam who are buying opium from the Meos. We would offer to import a certain amount of it directly into France. You and I would supply it to wealthy clients.'

'Like clients of Schiap, and their friends,' interrupted Ka, softly.

'Yes, that's it,' whispered Justine.

Silence again. Justine could see that Ka was struggling, undecided whether she should open up to her.

Finally Ka said, 'I already have a supplier. He's a wicked man. You don't want to have anything to do with him. He'd kill me if he discovered I was double-crossing him by going into business with you.'

Justine was half expecting this response. 'Ka, my darling, I'll tell you something about myself. Then you can make up your mind. In the war, I was a secret service agent. I signed what the British call their Official Secrets Act. So I can't tell you anything about what I did for the Allies.'

'I understand, Justine.'

'The point I'm making is that I was trained. Trained not only in espionage, I was trained to protect myself, and others. If necessary, to kill people. In cold blood.'

'And they caught you,' said Ka, fast on the uptake, as always. 'The marks on your back. That's where they beat you, terribly.'

'Yes,' whispered Justine. 'And then they threw me into a concentration camp.' A pause. 'What I'm telling you is that I can look after you, protect you.'

Ka smiled, 'So, you're my big sister.' A pause. 'Let me tell you about this man. His name is Bao, he's Vietnamese, a killer.'

Justine thought for a moment. 'Ka, we have a choice. We could go together to Bao, and offer to join with him. On the other hand, I already have a friend in Saigon, an ex-RAF pilot, who might help. And a friend at the *piscine*.'

'What's the *piscine*?'

'Headquarters of the French secret service, here in Paris.'

'Oh,' said Ka.

'Going with Bao would be easier than setting up our own pipeline in competition. Or we could compete with him, without him knowing. If he found out and threatened you, I would deal with him.'

'Hold on, Justine, Bao's a gangster. We'd end up in the Seine.' She paused. 'What are we going to do with all this money, if we can stay alive?'

'I've told you. I would spend it on the cause I'm passionate about. The political movement I'm involved in. No one else is going to finance me. That's why I came up with the idea.'

Ka looked at Justine in some surprise. 'So you're really serious about French politics. You followers of Léon Blum.'

'We have a plan, either to influence existing socialist deputies, or to form our own party. We have to fight the Communists as well as the right. That needs lots of money.' Justine paused, and smiled at her friend. 'And you, Ka. With your share, you'll be able to buy the freedom of your family in Hanoi. To have the best treatment for your brother. To escape from Bao.'

'I realise that, Justine. But what about the danger? And the morality of what you're proposing? Opium is not the end of it all. There is a place in Marseille, Bao told me, where the opium is refined into morphine and heroin. It is sent to the United States, and sold on the streets. You must have heard that addicts die from it.'

'That's a judgement each of us has to make. I'm prepared to take the risk. I would only bring in opium. Opium smoking is not illegal in France.'

Ka looked unhappy, uncertain.

Justine thought about her own convictions. 'Ka, I didn't suddenly decide to go into politics. It was a number of things, but one in particular, which led me there. Let me tell you.'

'Go on then,' said Ka, a little flippantly. But she was clearly intrigued, curious as to how someone like Justine could have reached this conclusion.

'It was three years ago, the war a fresh memory. Still those long lists of names in the papers, on the posters in the streets, of loved ones missing and sought by their families hoping for survivors from the camps in Germany and Poland. I was living then in a poor part of Montmartre. My tenement block housed destitute people of all ages, people literally starving. Just above my studio was a young mother and her daughter. I didn't know their history, only that they lived off nothing, in just the one room.'

Ka could sense the emotion welling up inside Justine, and placed a hand over hers. 'Go on,' she said.

Justine made an effort to hide her feelings. 'We became friends, and I gave them the odd thing, a baguette, a block of soap, whatever. The daughter, about six years old, seemed to take to me. Perhaps it was the lovely clothes I would sometimes wear back from work. Schiap let us do that, although I was paid virtually nothing. Two or three times a week, the mother asked if her daughter could stay the night with me. I used to play simple card games and read with her, before she curled up on a small bed alongside mine.

'The mother went out on the streets, not the best streets in Paris, not where the well-off men went. She would bring one back, on the nights she went out. Sometimes they gave her a rough time. You could hear it going on above. That's how she made enough for the two of them to live. I know she dreaded it.'

Ka sighed. Then she leant across and put her arms around her friend, feeling the emotion.

Justine went on. 'I saw terrible things every day in Buchenwald. Yet somehow, the plight of this mother and her daughter was different. There was no hope, no break, no help from the state. Then a terrible thing happened. I heard the coughing coming from above, in the mornings. It was tuberculosis. They came and took the mother away. The daughter clung on to me when she was preparing to leave. I felt the desperation in the way her hands clung to mine. I didn't know what to do. My work dominated my life. There were no allowances for staff with problems. You either reported on time for work, or you were out.'

'Still that way,' said Ka.

'She had no shoes,' said Justine, her voice breaking. 'I cooked her meal that evening, then took her out and bought her a dress, wool cardigan, and pair of sandals.' She paused, collecting herself together. 'In the morning, she came on the bus with me to Place Vendôme. I hardly knew what I was doing. The little girl came into the staff entrance holding my hand. That dragon at the guichet, behind the glass panel, looked down at her as though I had a bag of rubbish with me. Her mother died in the night, I told the woman. I said I was going to see Giselle, who was already *première main* by then. The woman said nothing. I walked on.'

'I must have still been at Dior then,' said Ka. 'I didn't know about this. What happened?'

'Heads rose from the work stations as we marched through the *atelier flou*. Giselle was astonished. I explained what had happened, that I had a client to see and that I couldn't leave the girl behind. Giselle was amazing. She asked the little girl if she liked clothes. Then she took her by the hand, telling me to get ready for the client and other commitments, that she would look after the girl.

'*Incroyable*,' said Ka.

'It was. At lunchtime, Giselle found me, and the two of us took the girl out to lunch.'

'So, what then did you do?' asked Ka.

'I found her a home, friends of my family in Bordeaux. My mother and father were just back from England,' said Justine. 'That's cutting the story short. The authorities tried to help but there was no money, anywhere. I learnt how destitute children are provided for, or are not. It opened my eyes.'

'So, that made you start thinking.'

'Yes, Ka. I was conscious for some time before all that, of how so many people were surviving from day to day with no hope of improving their lives. But the mother and daughter shook me, woke me up to the burning need to do something. The political parties all said a lot about the problem but did little. I worked out early on that Communism was not the solution. It would lead us back into an autocracy, take away the freedom we'd fought for.'

'I witnessed an incident that made me stop and think,' said Ka.

'What was that?'

Ka explained it was just after she joined Dior, when his New Look was launched. The publicity people took two of the mannequins and some others, including Ka, to the heart of working-class Paris. They wanted to show off the clothes against a backdrop of ordinary Paris life. They chose Montmartre, coincidentally. Children on the streets without shoes. Out-of-work men back after four years in forced labour camps in Germany, leaning against street walls. No money anywhere.

Ka recounted how the mannequins changed into the fabulous New Look clothes in a bar, and walked around in the small square as photographers took their shots. There was a muttering from people in the street, a derisory cheer or two. Suddenly, three women ran out of a tenement block, howling in fury. They tried to tear the clothes off the mannequins. They couldn't bear the inequality it showed off.

'Oh, that's what it's all about,' gasped Justine. 'I'm determined to put that right. I know it'll be a long struggle. My political movement will liberate the destitute. We're the future of this country.'

Ka could see the passion in her. 'Okay,' she said. 'You're clearly convinced, and I trust you. As long as we don't involve Bao.' She hesitated, then whispered, 'How do we start?'

Justine was thinking. 'We need a cover. A legitimate business that would pass public scrutiny. Ideally, it should be close to the real activity. Such as importation of morphine paste for use in the pharmaceutical industry, as a painkiller.'

'I see,' said Ka. 'Maybe I can find out what comes into France from Vietnam, like that. I have my Vietnamese friends here in Paris.'

'Yes, good idea. I'll make my own inquiries.' Justine was thinking of her friend at the *piscine*.

3

On deck earlier that morning, the fresh morning air was a delight as they steamed past the Mekong Delta. Now Theresa felt the heat of the mainland pulsating from the banks of the Saigon river as they headed for the city's port. The sweet scent of oleander reminded her of the many stories she'd picked up since they sailed from Marseille. How the flower was delicious to smell, like apricots, but could be deadly to eat. Soon, as they began to edge into the port, it was cooking smells that took over, above all the soya.

All about them were small narrow boats piled with vegetables and fruit in small heaps, each making its way under two long paddles worked by women in their conical hats. When they came close to the small craft, the women looked up at the passengers and called out their merchandise and prices. One woman with her child on board offered Theresa rambutans, mangosteens and lychees. Both were smiling at her and waving.

The skyline gave way to warehouses and wharves close by along the banks of the busy river. Here and there, a large freighter passed them on its way to the ocean, a reminder that much of Vietnam's own transport is by sea, up and down the coastline of a very narrow country.

'At least you can read what they write, even if you can't speak Vietnamese,' said her nursing friend Denise standing alongside and pointing to the signs over warehouses along the wharf. 'Unlike those over there, in Chinese characters. There are plenty of Chinese in Saigon. But the Vietnamese were taught to write our way by a French missionary priest centuries ago, did you know that?'

Theresa marvelled at the never ending list of facts Denise would roll out day and night. Induction into the Legion nursing service brought them together two years before. Both were already experienced nurses. Theresa, from her time in Libya and Italy in the war. She said little to her friend about that time. After all, a German in the forces of France soon after the war ended was odd to say the least. Except in the French Foreign Legion.

'Why did you volunteer to come out here?' said Denise suddenly. She'd asked the question often, sensing that there was something Theresa was holding back on. So, she tried again.

'Just exotic feelings about the East,' replied Theresa, stretching her tall slim body, arms in the air. 'More and more Legion units are being posted here from France and North Africa, you know that.' She kept the real reason to herself. She would inquire discreetly when the right moment came. Didn't want her superiors to get the wrong idea. But she knew that Leo was out here somewhere. Her senses softened when she thought of him. That day in the desert when the paratrooper introduced himself, one of the legendary Fallschirmjäger.

'We have to look out for the white kepis, don't we,' laughed Denise. 'What will our friendly legionnaires be like? If you ask me, they must all be spoilt by the gorgeous Vietnamese women everyone talks about.'

'I know. We won't get a chance, except invitations to stiff military parties.'

The Legion Captain strode into the room, walked to the table, and looked around the dozen nursing staff facing him. There was a hush among the girls. His face broke into a broad smile. I like him, thought Theresa.

'My name is de Rochefort. I'm here to welcome you and help you settle in. This is a base hospital, serving French forces in Cochin China. That's the traditional name for the south of Vietnam. You'll find everything here strange. Take your time to get used to it all. You'll be here for a month or so. We're still in the monsoon period, and nothing new is likely to happen in the south while everything's still waterlogged.' He was silent for a moment and his manner changed, almost as though he'd been given sudden bad news.

'There's a different picture in the north, in Tonkin as it's called. A violent attack by the Vietminh on French forces is under way on the Route Coloniale 4, the highway north-west of Hanoi. We've suffered severe losses already.' He walked over to a large wall map of Vietnam, and pointed out the line of a road running from north of Hanoi towards the western frontier with Laos. 'The Battle of Route Coloniale 4, the press are calling it. RC4 is this road across the far north of Tonkin, close to the frontier with China. Some of the worst wounded are arriving here, brought in by air.' He paused again. Theresa wondered whether he was gauging their reaction when confronted with tragedy.

Captain de Rochefort continued. 'The truth of this war is that France alone is holding back the forces of Communism in South East Asia. Like the Americans and the United Nations are doing in Korea. Some politicians in Paris think we shouldn't be committing such large forces, depleting the nation's resources. The Americans send us equipment, but Washington is full of anti-colonialists. They'd like to see the French and the British stripped of their empires. Meanwhile, Ho Chi Minh and his General Giap can draw on Communist China for training their army and providing it with weapons.'

He looked around the room. He caught Theresa's eye, then moved on. 'So much for the challenge ahead of you. The good news is that we provide transport most evenings to Saigon city centre. There should be plenty of opportunity to explore, as long as you don't wander into prohibited areas. Now, what about some questions?'

Denise put her hand up. 'How will the locals regard us, Captain?'

'The *colons,* that's what we call the French settlers out here, will love you. They're desperate for reassurance that the French won't pull out. But the Vietnamese down here in the south are ambivalent. Most want independence, a Vietnam free from French control. That's what Ho Chi Minh is fighting for. There have been atrocities in the south, even though the main action is in the north.'

－◦─◈─◦─

Theresa was about to leave the room, when Captain de Rochefort appeared beside her. 'Nurse Krüger, let's have a drink together this evening. I see from the notes on the new arrivals that you have an interesting background,' he said, smiling.

Theresa was immediately on guard. What did he know? Mustn't show anxiety. 'But of course, Captain.'

'Nearby the officers' mess, there's a coffee house for all ranks. I'll be there at seven.'

She nodded and turned away. This was going to be challenging. How much did he know, her war service perhaps? Not her real secret, there's no way he could know that. She'd only told one person, and that was a long time ago.

Back in her room, she took off her smart Legion uniform dress, and showered. She would have to get used to this humidity. The fan hanging from the ceiling helped, but not that much. She pushed back the mosquito netting around her bed and flopped down on her back, staring into space. They say the Legion collects people of strange backgrounds. Not many could match hers.

At 7 o'clock precisely, Theresa entered the coffee house. He's sure to know I'm a German, so I might as well behave like one.

'Mademoiselle Krüger, welcome to our den. There's no opium here of course, but otherwise the ambience is about right,' he said as he smoothed out a cushion beside him. He still wore his white uniform, she was in a khaki gabardine jacket and skirt.

The Vietnamese waiter appeared, and Theresa ordered a citron pressé, the Captain a Scotch Perrier.

The questions came, about the voyage, how she found her new accommodation. But clearly he was leading up to something very different. They stopped talking for a moment. Must be wondering how to start, she thought, and she looked steadily at him, trying to show encouragement and not frighten him off. Not that he looked that sort. This guy was young, but clearly with a ton of wartime experience behind him.

'Look, forgive me, but I'm intrigued as to how you were able to sign up for the Legion's nursing service. Given that you were a Luftwaffe nurse in the war. Not that that's anything to be ashamed of.'

Theresa laughed, a little nervously. 'Thanks. Well, actually I served most of the time alongside the Fallschirmjäger, the parachute troops. First in the Libyan desert, and then in Italy.'

The Captain remained silent for what seemed an age. Then the bombshell. 'I have a great friend, we were at school together.

Fought on opposite sides in the war in Europe. I was in the French Foreign Legion, he in the Fallschirmjäger. Now he's out here.'

'Oh,' was all Theresa could say, a feeling of wonder and fore-boding spreading through her. Should she ask the next, obvious question? Or just leave it there, and move on? She couldn't stop herself. 'Strange, I wonder if I know the name.'

'It's Leo Beckendorf.'

Silence. She may be giving herself away, but couldn't pretend not to know him. That would be madness. She'd come all this way to find him. Yet, it was Leo who knew the real truth about her. 'Yes, Leo Beckendorf. I knew him.' It was almost a whisper.

Another silence, broken by the Captain. 'Look, Theresa, I'm going to use your first name, if I may. Mine is Henri. You see, I know what happened to Leo at the end of the war in Europe. I don't know what your relationship was with him, if any. That's none of my business. But if you want to meet him again some time, I might be able to help.'

Theresa tried to hide her emotion. 'Certainly, I would love to see him again.' Another pause. 'Could I ask what happened to him?'

Henri leant back into the cushions. He seemed to be playing for time, perhaps deciding how much to say. Then it all came out. How he'd heard that Leo was taken prisoner close to Bastogne during Hitler's last daring gamble in the Ardennes. Henri's meeting with von der Heydte, Leo's commander, in Stuttgart after the German surrender. Their discussion about Leo's application to join the French Foreign Legion, the FFL.

'Do you know what Leo is doing in Vietnam?' asked Theresa.

Henri waited, clearly considering his response. 'Leo was an intelligence officer in the Fallschirmjäger. He has skills which we badly need out here. He was taken on in the FFL after the war as a legionnaire. Had to start at the bottom, having been a Major in the German parachute troops. We were forming a parachute battalion in the Legion. He was just what we wanted. Now he's a *sous-officier*, normally the highest rank a foreigner can attain in the FFL. Yet he's just been offered a commission in the French army because of the contribution he's already made, and the potential he offers us. A remarkable story.'

She tried not to appear overly interested, but knew Henri would notice how intensely she was following every word. Should have expected something like that, she told herself, having known Leo so well. What was his attitude going to be when she appeared on the scene? In 1945 he disappeared into the Legion. He didn't come looking for her, at least he never made contact. Clearly he wanted a clean break and soldiering was all he knew. Could she throw herself at him after all that?

Theresa was brought back to earth when Henri suddenly said, 'Right now, Leo's in the war zone in the north, what I was talking to you about this afternoon.'

'You mean,' said Theresa quietly, 'the Viet attack on the RC4?'

'He's on a rescue mission. It's going to be tough.' He paused, then put his hand on her arm. 'Theresa, you're a grown-up girl. You've been through a lot in your life already. You probably knew Leo when he was in the German parachute division defending Cassino against the Allies. He'll come through.'

4

'Sergeant Beckendorf, thank you for responding so rapidly. We have an emergency on our hands,' said the Colonel as Leo entered the map room. 'You will know that two companies of your Battalion dropped over That Khé a week ago, to help against Viet attacks on our strongpoints along the highway RC4. The Colonial Parachute Commando went with them.'

'Yes, sir.' Leo was at attention in front of Colonel Jean Gilles, commander of parachute forces. Beside the Colonel was a young officer Leo knew and thought highly of.

'The escape group, heading south from Cao Bang down the highway, has met the Bayard rescue group advancing north from That Khé. The bad news is that they've been ambushed by massive Viet forces.'

'Sounds serious, sir.'

'They are trapped, and continue to take heavy casualties.' Looking towards the officer beside him, the Colonel added, 'I want Lieutenant Loth to lead your Company in the drop over RC4, to help the combined force defend itself.'

'I presume we go in straight away, sir.'

'The Company will, Sergeant. However, we know you're about to be posted to France and St Cyr. I congratulate you on your pending commission. You have every right to proceed to France next week as planned.'

Leo froze to the spot. The drop about to take place sounded as close to a suicide mission as you could get. It was straightforward for him to stick to the reassignment to France. Not a question of saving his skin by doing so. His senses went numb, but his mind continued to work. 'That's impossible, sir, under the circumstances you have just described. My regiment's existence is at stake. I have to join them.'

'Sergeant Beckendorf, thank you,' said Colonel Gilles.

'Thank you, sir,' said Leo.

Lieutenant Loth, some years younger than Leo and in his first war, smiled and spontaneously shook Leo's hand. Both he and the Colonel knew that an ex-officer in the German parachute forces was an asset of immeasurable value.

Leo knew there was another more difficult decision bearing down on him. Going to the French military academy, St Cyr, was the stepping stone to being offered a commission in the French army. To achieve that goal, he would almost certainly have to change his nationality from German to French. Could he really bring himself to do that?

5

Ka was used to the man sitting opposite, across the table. A hard man, she assumed from Hanoi. Her life was falling under his control, as she depended on him. She wasn't comfortable in the world of the black market, which was his world. That wasn't all. The merchandise he dealt in was in a different league from penicillin and gasoline. Those were controlled or rationed goods. No, he was into more exotic substances. Above all, opium.

She watched him carefully. There were stories about what he could do to anyone he suspected might be double-crossing him. More than one damaged body floating in the Seine the next morning was evidence of his way of making people talk. Ka knew she must obey him, dependent as she was on his protection. Not protection of herself, but the safety of her family. The reality was that her parents depended on his money. To provide for their sick son in Hanoi. Ka's brother, much younger than her, was afflicted with palsy, a muscular disease which needed constant attention and treatment.

Their first encounter was soon after she arrived in France. Back in Hanoi, her parents faced financial difficulty because of the cost of their son's much needed treatment. They relied on Ka to send them cash, which she didn't have. A Vietnamese friend said she knew of a money lender. The friend introduced her to Bao. He questioned her about her work as a seamstress.

How she was trained at the best house in Hanoi and found work in haute couture in Paris.

Bao agreed to deliver the funds directly to the family in Hanoi. She must repay him out of her earnings every month. Her salary wasn't enough to meet his demands and he suggested she should become a link between him and any client she could find who wanted opium. That was risky, she could lose her job if her employer found out. The reality was that her parents depended on the money.

Ka didn't know how to begin. She couldn't ask clients whether they smoked opium. Then came a lucky break. A wealthy client on whose costumes Ka worked, was with her behind the screen on one visit and talked about her leisure time with girlfriends. She let slip that some of her friends smoked opium. Ka took the opportunity to say she knew where to find it, and that was the beginning of her business relationship with Bao.

Ka waited for Bao to speak. She knew him just by that name. Which after all, she reasoned, in Vietnamese meant protection.

'So, Ka, show me your order sheet. You move in high circles.' He coughed as he drew on a fresh cigarette and laughed at the same time.

'I have to be careful, Bao. My best clients are rich and powerful women, and their friends. Some pay on the spot. Others pretend they've left their money in another handbag. If I tell you that, to explain why the takings I pass to you are short, you don't believe me.' She didn't say it, but this was the terror she lived with. All right, she enjoyed her job at Schiaparelli, and it connected her to the clients of the house. But could she go on forever scared she would be exposed in some way or, worse still, be accused by Bao of double-crossing?

'Ah, Ka, you're learning. I have the power of life and death over your family. Never forget that. In exchange, I'm generous with the cash I give you to supplement what you earn at Schiap.'

Generous, she thought to herself with bitterness. He asks me every question imaginable about my life and the cost of how I live. He adds it up, and then halves it. One day, I will … She put the idea out of her mind.

6

Henri looked around the room. Still the same after so many years. Suddenly back home thanks to a plane ticket from a friend in Saigon and a few days' leave. His twin sister Françoise on the floor, reading a magazine, just like when he was back on holiday from school before the war. His English mother gently playing 'Claire de Lune' on the piano by the window. The Debussy notes ebbed and flowed like a tide across the room. Sometimes joyful, sometimes sad. Like life in those crazy years since he and Françoise both finished school.

His gaze fell on his father, so much older and long retired from his practice as *expert-comptable*. So well connected he was. Henri knew his father's accounting work for the Cour des Comptes led him to finding the job for Françoise in Vichy. That's when her life as a spy began.

All four of them together in the old home, the perfect way to celebrate his and Françoise's birthday.

'Where's Justine?' Henri called out to his sister, thinking of her great friend at school in Bordeaux, and after. They'd said enough for him to figure out most of what the two got up to in the conflict, secret as it was.

Françoise explained that her old friend was back in the fashion industry, now a top mannequin with her own list of clients. That she would be seeing her next week.

'Is she married?' asked Henri.

'No, not the sort. Frankly, I'm not sure she will ever recover.'

From Buchenwald, Henri said to himself.

Françoise swung over to face him, both arms behind her on the floor. 'They did terrible things to her. Not just in Buchenwald. At Natzweiler-Struthof, they were about to kill her and put her in the camp oven.'

'You got her out of there, I remember.'

Françoise said nothing for some time, then expressed her view that Justine was a convinced socialist, in some sort of movement. They were followers of Léon Blum. No one spoke. The de Rocheforts were a strong Catholic family, always wary of the left. Françoise and Henri were brought up that way.

'Do you have to go back to Saigon, Henri?' her mother exclaimed. 'That war out there is a disaster.'

Monsieur de Rochefort appeared to wake up with a start. 'A Captain in the French Foreign Legion expects to be in places like Indochina. That's what the Legion's for.'

Henri went over and gave his mother a hug. 'At least we can communicate, unlike my days in Africa.'

His father looked around the room. 'They need a new Commander-in-Chief. Someone to combine the military and political jobs. With enough clout to bang heads together, and act without covering his backside from the politicos in Paris. Only one man, in my opinion.' They looked at him.

'Jean de Lattre de Tassigny. He not only has the prestige to shoulder everyone out of the way, he's clever. If anyone can take the war to the Viets, instead of waiting for them to pick us off at will, it's him.'

'He'd be mad to accept,' said Henri. Incidentally, I met his son, Bernard, in Hanoi the other day. Company Commander in a South Vietnamese formation. Tough and daring. Hope he lasts.' A pause, then Henri said to his sister, 'Françoise, don't you have any man lined up to keep you comfortable for life?' Everyone laughed. 'What about Bill Lomberg?' he added, thinking of his South African school friend, who joined the RAF just before the war.

Françoise was up on her feet. 'I couldn't tie him down when the war ended. Always off on some crazy project. The latest is flying Dakotas. There aren't enough French pilots in Tonkin. Based outside Hanoi, he drops paratroopers and supplies to the outlying posts. Keeps in touch with me, I'll say that.'

'I heard on the grapevine you're in the Sûreté or Deuxième Bureau,' said her brother.

'Not meant to talk about that. What about that other school friend of yours, Leo something?'

'Leo Beckendorf,' said Henri. 'He reached Major in the Fallschirmjäger, the German parachute troops, before being taken prisoner in the Ardennes in that final winter's battle.'

'He was at school with you in England, wasn't he, at St Gregory's? You brought him here to stay.'

'That's him. He decided to apply to us in the Legion just after the war ended. His parents were killed in a bombing raid on the town where they moved when the German foreign ministry was evacuated from Berlin. Had to start from the bottom, as a legionnaire. We wanted him because we were forming a Legion parachute battalion for Vietnam.'

Monsieur de Rochefort was listening. 'That's extraordinary, a German officer of his rank. How has he worked out?'

'Remarkably well. He's an intelligence expert. Now a *sous-officier*, and I think he was going to be offered a commission.'

'Was?' said Françoise.

Henri felt the others look up towards him.

'He was dropped on the Route Coloniale 4, in a rescue mission.'

Silence for a moment, before Monsieur de Rochefort spoke slowly. There was emotion in his voice that Françoise didn't remember hearing since the day the armistice with Germany was announced. Their father said, 'The RC4 debacle is the worst single disaster of France in any colonial war. The equivalent of when the British army was wiped out by the Zulus at Isandlwana.' He paused as they all stared at him. 'What happened to Beckendorf?'

'We don't know. His paras were part of the relief column under the command of Le Page. Only a few are finding their way back. Losses are at least four out of five.'

'Everyone pray for Leo tonight,' said Madame de Rochefort.

'And there's another odd thing that's happened,' said Henri.

'What's that?' asked Françoise.

'Well, a German woman, Theresa Krüger, arrived in Saigon the other day, on transfer from the Legion's base hospital in Algeria. I interviewed her on arrival. She served as a Luftwaffe nurse in the war. She was with the Fallschirmjäger in Libya, and knew Leo. I think there was a close friendship between them at the time. I've said I'll put them in touch.

'Heavens,' said Françoise. 'Does she know Leo is missing?'

'Yes,' said her brother.

7

Paris, 20th arrondissement, October 1950

The venerable green and cream bus Justine took from nearby Place Vendôme ground its way through the gears past Bastille, on the way east. Justine couldn't wait to see her old friend again. The bond between her and Françoise remained as strong as ever, even though their worlds were now a long way apart.

Leaving the bus in Boulevard Mortier, she found the bar easily, close to where Françoise said she worked. No sign of her as Justine sat down at a table inside, ordering a *demi pression*. Her thoughts went back to that night in '42 and their flight in the Lysander to London. The next day, those terribly English people at 50 Broadway beside St James's Park, and afterwards the training camp.

Suddenly a voice called out, 'Justine, darling, you look fabulous.'

She leapt to her feet. 'Françoise, I've missed you a lot,' as they gave one another a wonderful hug.

Françoise passed on love from her family in Bordeaux, and the waiter brought more beer and took their orders for *croque-monsieur*. They laughed and joked as they swapped news.

'He's a spook too,' said Justine, eying up and down a nondescript and rather dishevelled man who entered and flopped down on a stool at the bar, ordering a Scotch Perrier. 'Must have been on the night shift.'

'Justine, you know the unwritten rule between us. You don't talk about my job.'

'I know,' said Justine, 'but I want to let you into a secret, and maybe you can give me some advice.'

'I doubt it,' said Françoise, with a rather cynical laugh.

Justine knew she should go slowly. She'd start with politics. The revolution in employment laws started by the Front Populaire before the war. Followed by Pétain winding back on workers' rights. And now, the power of the Communists who took their orders from Stalin.

Françoise just nodded. 'That's okay so far. Can't argue with that.'

Justine continued. 'The other thing's the terrible strain on the country's finances of the war in Indochina. We can't go on kidding ourselves that we can beat the Viets. It may need a new socialist party to make these changes. We'll need money, lots of it.'

'What do you mean by we?'

'I want to be part of a new movement, but for that I'll need funds. If I can show I have access to money, people will listen to me. I'll have influence.'

'Okay, but what are you planning. Surely you get paid lots as a top mannequin?'

'You're joking. My pay is near breadline. It's slavery. Standing all day, waiting to be fitted, waiting for the maître to create on me. Mannequins do have their worshippers, most are kept by them. We can borrow beautiful clothes from the House, but not hot meals.'

'Oh, you surprise me. Anyway, what's your plan? I read that report in *Le Monde*. Why did you do it?'

'Because I had to. It was my only weapon, to express my passion that is.'

'You mean, about inequality?'

'It's worse than that. The eyes of the well-off in France are closed. They're either ignorant, or they don't want to know.'

'That's a bold statement. Why do you think that exposing what the Nazis did to you will solve the problem? Won't people just think you're drawing attention to yourself?'

'Well, I am. But not just me. It's not me in fact, it's to the cause, I want people to know what has to be changed.'

'Okay, but how will they know what it is you want?'

'I'm drawing attention to myself so I'll be given a hearing. So I can stand on a platform and people will listen to what I have to say.'

'And what do you plan to say? It's politics isn't it?'

'Yes.' Justine paused. 'France is a democracy again. It gives me the chance. I have no money, so I can't buy myself the people's attention. I must earn the public's attention.'

'Okay, but you can't do that alone. You have to belong to a party. You need organisation, and support.'

'I've thought about that. Trouble is, the Communists are the best organised, more powerful than the other parties. I'm working on it. In the meantime, I need the publicity.' Justine halted for a moment, to underline the point. 'I'm already fairly high profile in Paris haute couture, in the fashion magazines.'

Justine explained that Schiap paid her very little, but that was the nature of the game. They were a top house, and Elsa herself worked hard for France in America during the war. She might be Italian but her heart was always in France. She cared. She knew what Justine was doing. The house of Schiaparelli was a great start for her.

'You're taking on something awfully big,' said her friend. 'It'll be hellishly tough wherever you go in politics, left or right. You do have the stamina and won't give up. But you have to be sure.'

'I know that, Françoise. What I did at the dress show, what you read about, was to get noticed and talked about.'

'I understand. Let's stay close. Come to me when you have a problem, at least we can talk it over. We know a lot about everyone at the *piscine*. Much of it I can't tell you. But where our interests coincide, I can help.' She paused, 'So, let's get back to the plan.'

'Well, my darling, I do have a plan. Me and my Vietnamese friend …'

'Vietnamese friend?'

Justine thought. Mustn't give away Ka. She explained her friendship with her Vietnamese friend. Why that friend needed money also. Her family's problems in Hanoi, and her own connections with a gangster in Paris. Justine paused, looked around the room. 'There's a business opportunity too important to miss, Françoise.'

'And, what's that?'

'It involves importing basic ingredients for pain killing medicines, from Indochina.'

Silence. Françoise looked at her in a curious way. 'You need to watch out, Justine. I know a little about that world. You'll be rubbing shoulders with some dangerous characters. And you could easily cross the line and be in trouble with the law.'

Justine knew this was the moment to play her trump card. Yet she didn't want to alienate Françoise. Nor put her close friend in a position where she herself could be compromised.

Françoise took her friend's hand. 'There's something you're hiding. Isn't there, Justine?'

'Some information came to me. I can't tell you where from. It's that the French secret service, at least their operation in Saigon, are working with the *Bình Xuyên*.'

Justine watched for her friend's reaction. It was almost imperceptible but was there all the same. Was she startled by this revelation?

'That must come from your Vietnamese friend. What do you know about the *Bình Xuyên*?'

Justine explained. That way back the *Bình Xuyên* were a collection of gangs, river pirates, involved in kidnapping and protection money. Rather like Robin Hood, the English bandit, they robbed from the rich and distributed some of the takings to the ordinary people. After the war with the Japanese, they were recognised by Bao Dai as an independent force in his army. They went into prostitution and gambling. And they now controlled the opium world down there.

'Yes,' said Françoise. You've done your homework. Extraordinary that organised crime in Saigon is officially sanctioned by the Vietnamese authorities. Bao Dai calls himself Emperor of Vietnam, but actually spends most of his time on the Côte d'Azur. No one's meant to know, but we all do. That doesn't mean they're safe to deal with. Nor that you won't be arrested by ...'

'The Sûreté,' interjected Justine.

Françoise laughed. 'Don't expect me to save you if you are.' She hesitated, seemingly looking for words. 'Seriously, though, you are making a mistake, Justine. You have an excellent career in fashion. Why risk ruining it, being caught out doing something which might sound legal technically but which would lead you into criminal circles? You're likely to end up in disgrace, at best. Or you could go to prison. And, God help you, you could be killed.'

Justine hit back stubbornly. 'Françoise, neither of us took that line in 1942 when we agreed to go to London for our training. How would we have beaten the Nazis if we'd reacted in that fashion?'

'That wasn't the same thing. We were at war, France was occupied.'

'I've made up my mind,' said Justine. 'I won't blame you if you refuse to discuss the matter further, or say no if I ask for help.'

There was a long silence, broken by Françoise. 'There's a guy called Jean. Used to work for Colonel Passy.'

'The Passy in de Gaulle's Deuxième Bureau in London?'

'Yes. Jean's tough as hell, and ruthless. We still use him sometimes. Anyway, he has an import/export business in Saigon. The silk industry is a big client of his. He might be interested in doing business with you, might have some ideas how to ship the merchandise. He's in Paris as often as Saigon. I think he's here at the moment.'

'Françoise, you're an angel,' said Justine leaning forward and clasping her friend's hands.'

'Not sure whether Jews have angels, but the two of you should get on well.' They laughed.

'What's more, my darling, there's another motive in me recommending Jean.'

'Oh, what's that?'

'He might just save your life.'

<hr>

Afterwards, Justine felt apprehensive and yet more confident, if that was possible. Françoise's warnings made her stop and think through the risks more closely. But her earlier questions about her political ambitions made her re-assess issues she previously left parked in her mind. The challenges ahead of her now became clearer. What party should she join? What niche would she carve out for herself? Should she be studying something of value so she had more to offer? The fashion industry she knew something about. But there was not much else. What about health, social services, housing?

And that raised a burning question. Should she consider giving up modelling, her association with one of the greatest names in haute couture?

8

Route Coloniale 4, North Vietnam, October 1950

Leo stood ready, the blast of the slipstream roaring at him as the dispatcher opened the side door of the C47 Dakota. One last glance back at his platoon, lined up behind him. The best France had, part of 1 BEP – the French Foreign Legion's first parachute battalion. A grin and thumbs up to them. A final check of his harness connection to the static line running along the inside of the fuselage. The past flashed through Leo's mind as the red light came on. His first jump into enemy territory, Rotterdam 1940, then the mass drop on Crete in '41. On comes the green light, a shout of *allez* from the dispatcher as he slaps Leo on the back. Loss of breath from the blast of the slipstream as he's flung out and behind the plane, and the jerk as the canopy opens.

Then silence, just the disappearing drone of engines as the Dakotas head for home. Parachutes everywhere. Lieutenant Loth and his platoon would be among them. A comfort to have his machine carbine and ammunition with him this time. Not like Crete when the weapons were dropped from the Junkers trimotors in their own canisters. The massacre of his regiment by the New Zealanders as the Fallschirmjäger parachuted to the ground, and went looking for weapons canisters before they could arm themselves.

Must concentrate on this crucial mission. To rendezvous with the columns trapped on the RC4. Around him was the

Replacement Company of 1 BEP. He could have avoided taking part. His mates were down there, in desperate trouble, trying to break out. It must be hell for them. At the briefing before take-off from Haiphong, there was no argument over the objective. Bring fresh firepower to the survivors of a succession of catastrophic ambushes. The "Charton column" from the north of the highway, and the "Le Page column" from the south, now joined up but surrounded in a last stand. Essential that there be no deviation from the Drop Zone close by That Khé.

⊷⊨◉◉⊨⊶

There were the weak flares marking the DZ, a night operation when the fighting would have slackened to the occasional shell. God, please make this the perfect drop. Suddenly, Leo was on the ground, a tight grouping as the other paratroopers land nearby.

The two platoons rapidly came together, there was Lieutenant Loth. Ready for action inside ten minutes. Now came the march north to the Coc Xa gorge where the survivors were surrounded. As they approached, Captain Jeanpierre came towards them. Just the man to have held the survivors together. A thump of friendship across the shoulders.

He beckoned to them to follow him to a dugout forming 1 BEP's command post. Hastily constructed with excess soil heaped around it, and corrugated roofing camouflaged with small trees and undergrowth. Inside, Jeanpierre's first words were that their commanding officer, Major Segrétain, just died of his wounds, and he was now in command.

Jeanpierre explained that fifteen Viet battalions were pressing in on all sides, outnumbering the paras and colonial infantry four to one. 'They're surrounded by the Viets and the Coc Xa gorge,' said Jeanpierre. 'Only chance is to surprise them, let the bastards think we're in larger numbers than they thought. Force them to break off and re-group. That's the point we would lead a break-out and make a fighting retreat towards That Khé.'

Rain lashed down outside. Even in the dark, the mist seemed to be thickening.

'How are the survivors made up?' asked Leo.

'The largest part are the Moroccan Tabors. They've been fighting for days. Even their French NCOs are totally exhausted,' said Jeanpierre.

They rested until dawn, wrapped in their waterproofs on groundsheets. Just drifting in and out of sleep in their drowsiness. At the first suggestion of dawn, they assembled, prepared for the attack. More rain and fog, still no chance of calling up air support. No way fighter bombers would be able to operate in these conditions.

As they approached the gorge, they split into three columns of twelve men. They must achieve surprise by crawling up on the Viet mortar and machine gun positions from the rear. The firing was starting and the Viet positions could be located from the smoke puffs of the enemy's mortars. Leo and Loth split the columns in half, and each of them plus an NCO led the front teams, approaching at forty-five degrees to one another. Orders given to hold fire, they crawled forward as close to the Viets as possible before breaking cover. The aim was to take out six targets simultaneously. The other half of each column followed, either to finish the task or go for another Viet position.

A Viet rose suddenly in front of him. No shot, Leo drew his knife and plunged it into the man's abdomen. The target sank to his knees in silence. So far, so good. Enemy firing and mortar bombing were increasing. So many of them. Suddenly the amplifiers screamed out, urging the Moroccans to give up.

Leo knew Loth's approximate position. A flare went up, lighting the scene brilliantly. The French paras opened up on their selected targets. When one went silent, the next was attacked. Now the Viets realised the danger behind them, they tried to turn their mortars and machine guns around.

Leo's optimism from the first successful attacks gave way to horror as he saw what was happening on the edge of the gorge. Terrorised Moroccans were starting to jump over the edge. One of their NCOs, close to Leo, was trying to stop them. Leo tried to do the same. The men seemed possessed. As one went over, others followed.

Enemy fire on them was increasing. Leo and Loth signalled to one another. Nothing left but to break out and return to their starting point before the Viets came for them.

Captain Pierre Jeanpierre joined Leo and Loth. What to do next? 'Never seen it worse than this,' he said. 'No surrender, but only a few of us left and we must find a way out.'

'Perhaps a hundred remaining out of the five hundred in my drop and yours, sir,' replied Leo.

'I'm going to lead a group into the jungle and try to make That Khé,' shouted Jeanpierre above the din of machine gun and mortar fire.

'I'll come with you,' said Leo. You're right. Some men are giving up, worn out, desperate for food. Just putting down their rifles and holding out their hands. They say the Viets are offering them a ball of rice a day.'

They could hear the amplified shouts from the enemy's loudspeakers, '*rendez-vous, soldats français, vous êtes perdus*', give yourselves up French soldiers, you are lost.

Leo listened in disgust. Bastards, some might succumb to their taunts, to encouragement to hand themselves over, accepting that all is lost. Leo was not that way. Any chance of escape, however hopeless, was worth more.

'We'll have to lash the wounded to our backs, as we climb down the cliff face,' shouted Jeanpierre.

Leo just nodded. The consequences of leaving the wounded, the incapacitated behind were too terrible to think of. They would be gripped in the terror of vicious insects, scorpions, and snakes. Massive rats that would break through clothing to gnaw at flesh. He knew what must be done with the hopeless cases, the overdose of morphine.

The descent would be frightening, carrying their comrades. Then twenty kilometres through jungle, much of which could only be penetrated by machete.

To Leo, it was like a terrible dream. On autopilot most of the time. Jeanpierre a magnificent leader, brutal perhaps but someone the paras respected and followed. Leo forced himself forward with every step. Cutting and plunging through the undergrowth, the lightweight paratrooper's smock torn to ribbons. Swinging the machete left and right, hour after hour. Their sole radio transmitter used sparingly, given the danger of interception by the enemy. The knowledge that there were Viet agents with their radio transmitters in the villages. Villages which must be skirted as they trekked towards That Khé.

He came back to his senses in a hospital bed. Colonel Gilles was speaking to him, although the words meant little. 'Leo, you made it. Five hundred men out of both the Charton and Le

Page columns came in so far. Only one in ten of their original strength. There can't be more than a handful still to come.'

Leo's response was to mutter the only thing in his mind. 'First Parachute Battalion of the French Foreign Legion is wiped out.'

Jean Gilles touched his shoulder, saying simply, 'Fallschirmjäger, you did your duty.'

9

'Theresa, this is for you.' Denise handed her an envelope from the noticeboard at the entrance to their quarters. 'It looks important, from the outside.'

That's Denise, inquisitive as ever, thought Theresa, sliding out the note. She read the handwriting, it was from the Captain, Henri de Rochefort. 'Dear Theresa, I have just been notified by army headquarters in Hanoi that Sergeant Beckendorf of 1st Battalion REP is in Hanoi military hospital, recovering from his escape from the recent battle along the Route Coloniale 4. He is suffering only from minor injuries. I am sure you will be pleased with this news. I still intend to put you in touch with Sergeant Beckendorf when the opportunity presents itself. Yours sincerely, Henri de Rochefort.'

Overjoyed that he was okay, Theresa still worried how Leo would receive the news that she was in Vietnam. The space of six years since the war in Europe lay between them, there was no knowing how he would react. His sudden break with the past when he joined the Legion must have been a desire for just that. Wiping clean the slate, and starting again from ground zero, was a statement in itself. She must take account of that, and be cautious how she re-entered his life.

That was unnecessary. The voice brought back the past, suddenly, as she just finished her shift at the hospital a few days later and was about to climb into the truck taking her and the others back to their quarters. Almost like their first encounter in Libya, he was suddenly there, walking towards her.

'Hi, Theresa. Found you at last.'

That was the voice. There he was. Older, of course. Short in stature but tough-looking, still a paratrooper, although he wasn't wearing uniform. Just a khaki shirt and shorts.

'Thanks to Henri de Rochefort,' Leo said. 'He told me about you, just as I was offered some leave and a seat on the plane down from Hanoi.'

'Oh, Leo,' she spluttered, as he held out his hand. Then a peck on each cheek, as the other nurses looked on and no doubt whispered to one another. Theresa touched his arm and nudged him back towards the hospital building, waving the others towards the truck.

'I've borrowed a jeep,' he said. 'Let's go and have something to eat.'

She just nodded, a mixture of excitement and apprehension running through her. How can this be happening? He was only just released from hospital after the disaster of RC4. Everyone was talking about their enormous losses. The French press were raising all sorts of questions. She's mustn't mention it unless he does.

She snatched a few looks at him as they walked towards the hospital building. He still had a large plaster on his left cheek, and the backs of both hands were healing from what looked like lacerations. Probably other wounds I can't see, she thought. Hope he can drive properly.

They found the jeep. She noticed his kit was lying in the back. 'Would you like me to drive?' she asked.

'Thanks. I seem to be okay for the moment,' he replied. 'These things have such heavy steering. I messed up my hands when we escaped. Cutting our way through the jungle.'

'Oh,' said Theresa. She couldn't bring herself to ask anything, knew he must tell her what he wanted to.

Her mind jumped back to reality as Leo asked the way, and she guided him out onto the highway. 'Just follow the route marked Cap St Jacques. There's a good place for lunch about five kilometres from here, on the river.'

'Okay,' he said, turning and giving her a wonderful smile.

It was a veranda restaurant she'd been to before, with the other girls and their boyfriends.

Shade and a breeze were a relief from the relentless sun during the drive. They ordered drinks from an immaculately turned out waiter. 'Fish is the thing here,' she said, as menus were put in front of them.

She'd allowed an extra button of her blouse to stay undone. She felt his eyes on her. This was the test, she thought. Will I still attract him? Take it slowly.

'Tell me about your life out here,' she said once they were settled in, a bottle of Gordon's, lemonade and ice between them.

Leo explained his time since the war in Europe ended. How he became a legionnaire and was then promoted to NCO in the French Foreign Legion's first parachute battalion. The importance of the new airborne units in the fight against the Viets in the north. He didn't try to explain his decision to fight for the French. Those were times in Germany best forgotten.

She hoped it would be okay. That extraordinary feeling of togetherness seemed to be still alive between them.

'You managed to reach Paris after the war ended,' Leo suddenly said.

'Yes, a friend of my father in the US embassy fixed my papers. He knew about my change of name and why I was forced to take on another person's identity before applying to join the Luftwaffe early in the war. The American hospital in Neuilly invited me back to nurse there. A lucky break. My parents stayed on in Baltimore. He's still at a famous hospital there, a consultant professor in respiratory diseases.'

'I remember,' said Leo. 'And in mustard gas, I recall.'

Silence. Each thinking back to the extraordinary circumstances of early 1944.

Out of the blue, Leo suddenly said, 'I'm about to go to France, for officer's training at St Cyr.'

'What? We've just met up. I've been waiting six years.' As soon as she said it, Justine regretted jumping the gun. She could sense a train crash. I'm a fool. He'll disappear again, for good. Pull yourself together, make fun of it. 'Leo, I'm just joking. Fantastic that you're going to be an officer in the French army. How long will you be away?'

If he was upset at her reaction, he didn't show it. 'Six months, if all goes well. Might be less, they're getting through officers at an alarming rate out here. I don't think the French nation will put up with it for ever. But in the meantime, it's a case of every front line unit on constant call.'

She mustn't push her luck. Let him come to her. She wanted him, the feeling of desire was returning to her until it ached through her body. Maybe we can go somewhere before he leaves. I'll just play him along. 'Can we see something of one another before you go?'

Leo looked at her steadily, his expression softening as his hand closed over hers. 'I'd like that, very much, Theresa. There's so much to catch up on.' He looked at his watch. 'I'll run you back to your quarters.'

They climbed into the jeep. How does he really think, she wondered, as they bumped out onto the main road. Do we have a future together?

⟶⬧◉⬥⟵

The villa's owner was in France for some months, and he made the property available to visiting diplomats in Saigon. Leo heard about it through an army friend who knew it was empty for a couple of weeks. A cook and housekeeper were provided.

'Come and inspect the place with me,' said Leo over the phone to Theresa the following morning. 'I only heard about it after I dropped you off yesterday.'

Theresa was on early morning shift, and said she'd be free at lunchtime.

In a residential quarter of the city, it was easy to find. Trees and shrubs typical of that part of Vietnam were everywhere, and a lawn surrounded the house.

They shook hands with the Vietnamese housekeeper. 'Everything is prepared for you,' she said as they walked up onto the veranda of the single-storey timber building. She seemed to assume they would both be moving in, and Theresa wasn't going to correct her.

Leo confirmed he would be signing up for ten days, being on two weeks' convalescent leave.

The cook prepared them a light lunch, and Leo started to talk about a stroll into the city centre and some shopping.

Theresa knew she wanted to be alone with him. She stood up, and touched his arm, whispering 'Come with me Leo. You're supposed to be resting, recovering before they send you off to the rigours of Paris.'

'Actually, St Cyr is in Brittany,' said Leo.

She led him across the teak floor of the hall and into the large bedroom at the back of the house. Everything was immaculate with the faint smell of jasmine, mosquito netting tied back around the bed. She turned to face him and took him in her arms. It was going to be like their first night together at the Hotel Rose in the town of Cassino, ten years before.

10

Justine was standing ready as the *vendeuse* led in a tall graceful woman, her sleek black hair tied up at the back, and wearing an exquisite dark blue suit. A Schiaparelli suit, forever unique in that the large metal buttons were the work of Giacometti. Beautifully made up as she was, it was hard to tell her age. Perhaps around forty, this was the client they decided to call by the code name Madame X.

With a smile and quick shallow curtsy, the *vendeuse* withdrew. Justine showed Madame X round behind one of the magically decorated screens that were a feature of the client salon at Schiaparelli. The Schiap screens were sacrosanct, clients knew that behind these, any secrets could be safely divulged. That included malformations of the body or even face, which would become invisible after the Schiap tailors and seamstresses were finished. The place where beauty was created.

As Madame X sank into the cushion of a gilded chair, Justine pressed a buzzer and immediately Ka came in, carrying an almost finished cocktail dress.

'Would Madame like to try the dress on?' asked Justine. 'The tailor has made the changes we agreed on at the last fitting. You know Ka, she'll make any final adjustments.'

She took the day suit as Madame X disrobed, and Ka helped the client on with the dress. Shocking pink, long flared skirt, with a large bow at the apex of the neck. Both told Madame

X that with her dark features, she looked wonderful in it. Ka pinned up a tiny adjustment under a shoulder, and stepped back, satisfied.

'*Ravissant*,' exclaimed the client, as she posed before the tall mirror opposite, entranced by the result. Looking at both of them, she added, 'You must know well the tenth commandment according to Elsa Schiaparelli.' And all three of them intoned, 'Never fit the dress to the body, but train the body to fit the dress.' They all laughed.

'If you're happy, Madame, then it can be delivered to you tomorrow.' Ka knew this would be the start of the client's real ecstasy. The uniformed porter standing on her doormat, the box and its ribbons, how they would fall to the floor, the lid coming off and the mounds of light tissue, the moment she sees herself wearing the *modèle* in her own home, the rhapsody of confidence as she enters the salon at her friend's reception and the faces turn towards her.

Justine knew this was the right moment. 'While Ka helps you change back into your suit, Madame, perhaps we could continue our discussion of the other day on the needs of your friends,' said Justine, as calmly as if she was explaining what she would be shopping for that evening.

Madame X looked around her. Ka was placing the new dress on a stand. 'Yes, Mademoiselle Justine,' she said. 'As I told you when we last met, there are a number of us who meet to smoke opium or take laudanum. It's an important part of our lives, helps us to live through the problems we face every day. There are four of us, but we have links to others.'

'And you all want a steady supply,' said Justine.

'That's right. Along with secrecy. Going to a doctor or pharmacist could lead to rumours about us. Better that no one knows who we are.'

'That's where we can help,' said Justine, glancing across at Ka. 'The two of us are discreet, a barrier if you like, between the source and the client. And Ka knows where the best sources are.'

'I suppose you are referring to Indochina,' said Madame X, looking across at Ka.

Ka spoke softly, her voice intimate as though suggesting a conspiracy. 'Our aim is for you to be satisfied with the product, Madame. It's better you don't know how we arrange the supply, in the same way it is better Mademoiselle Justine and I do not know your friends.'

'Quite so,' said Madame X.

'Justine moved forward, handing the client a card bearing the telephone number of her apartment and a small leather bag. 'Let's start by us providing you with this sample, Madame. If you are happy with it, we can agree terms for a regular supply.'

As Madame X rose to depart, she said almost as an after-thought, 'Thank you both. Let's be careful. France is at a turning point. She has crucial decisions to take, in politics at home and militarily in Indochina. Trust no one. Those are my husband's words, and he is close to where the real power lies.'

Paris, 13th arrondissement

Ka was thinking of her family, above all her brother, as the Metro clattered into her destination. Gobelins, where her Vietnamese friends lived. The person she was seeking out belonged to a rare species in France, rare anywhere beyond the north of Tonkin. His family was from a tribe found among the north-west Highlands. Glun's father worked in the French administration, helping to construct military training camps. The Highland tribes were beginning to make themselves felt in the struggle against the Viets. As the privileged family that they were, the children went to a French school. The eldest, Glun, gained a place at the Sorbonne and was now a tutor there on Indochinese affairs. It was to him that Ka was heading.

----◦◦◦----

'What a treat, Ka,' said Glun as he watched the waiter put down between them one dish after another. Prawn pho, beef curry, caramel trout, banh mi, Vietnamese cooking brought them closer together, stranded as they were in the heart of the western world.

'How are things at the Sorbonne?' asked Ka, as she lifted a spring roll with her chopsticks. 'I envy the French literature degree course you took. My evening school is better than nothing, but often I have to work late at Schiap and miss out. I'm still a seamstress, you're now a tutor.'

They laughed together. 'All those beautiful people you must meet there,' joked Glun. 'Place Vendôme is just a dream to me.'

Ka knew Glun might be able to help her. Yet she was nervous, wondering how to raise the subject. Glun's family were Meo, a tribe originating from Laos and now loyal to the French. Very independent, they despised Ho Chi Minh's doctrines and resisted any Viet infiltration into their lives. Important for Ka was that she knew from Bao the Meos grew and harvested the opium poppy. From them flowed the crude opium supplies to the *Bình Xuyên* in the south, who refined it and handled the distribution to the opium dens and into the export market.

'Glun, I have something to ask. You might be able to help me.' Ka hesitated. 'It's a subject we must keep between the two of us.'

Glun looked up, putting down his chopsticks. 'Go ahead, Ka. You know we trust one another.'

'Well,' she whispered. 'You know about the Meo people, you're one of them. I'm told they're the source of most of the opium in Vietnam.' She stopped for a moment, then took the plunge. 'This friend of mine, well, she and I want to set up in business to import opium paste into France. For the pharmaceutical industry, to be used in the manufacture of painkillers, and the like.'

Silence for a moment. 'Go on,' he said.

'To be competitive, we want to buy directly from source.'

'Cut out the *Bình Xuyên*?' Glun was obviously surprised.

'Yes.'

'Remember that the activities of the *Bình Xuyên* are tolerated by the French administration. At least indirectly, through Bao Dai and his corrupt government in the south. So if you bypass the *Bình Xuyên*, you may find you've upset the French authorities as well.'

Glun was wise to point that out, Ka thought. 'You're right. We have to be sure we don't attract their attention.' And to herself, she added, we'll need to decide what is legal and what is not. 'Would you be able to help us, Glun?'

Glun was thinking. 'We'll see. But, what about our relationship, Ka. If I and my family organise the Vietnam end of the pipeline, should we not be entitled to half the proceeds?'

Ka was quick with her response. 'There would be three of us taking the risks and making the pipeline work through to receiving cash for the merchandise. If you were in partnership with me and my friend, and she's the one with the customer contacts, your share couldn't be more than a quarter. What's more, she would have the most to lose in terms of reputation, should something go wrong.'

'I see,' said Glun. 'Let's discuss that further when we have the pipeline outlined, and when I've met your friend.'

'Okay. If you could decide how you might organise things in Vietnam, then the three of us could meet and talk about the partnership.'

Ka left it to Glun's imagination to guess the extent the end user would be pharmaceutical companies, and where the rest of the merchandise would be heading. She didn't know the answer herself. Was Justine ready to cross the line and risk arrest if they were caught out? That might remain unsaid. But the three of them needed to know how far each one would go.

Enough said for the time being. 'Will you be returning to Hanoi at the end of the university year?' asked Ka.

'Probably. But I'll write home now, and start my inquiries. I'll have to watch out for the censors.' He paused. 'By the way, Ka. I'm not going to fall out with the law.'

'Surely that depends on whose law,' said Ka, half joking.

St Germain des Prés

Justine saw him spring from the table as she entered the brasserie. Looks like a hard and calculating man, short and probably in his forties, she thought. Eyes that roamed everywhere all the time, including over her.

'Mademoiselle Justine. Mannequin extraordinaire. I'm honoured to meet you.'

She shook his outstretched hand. 'You must be Monsieur Jean.'

'Françoise de Rochefort told me about you. She said you were with her in London back in '42.'

'Yes, I don't deny that,' responded Justine, her guard well up.

'I really missed out,' said Jean, a warm smile on his face. 'I was in Baker Street with Colonel Passy. We could have dined in splendour together if I'd known you were in town.'

Maybe he has a sense of humour after all, thought Justine, although her face remained blank. 'A lot of my time was spent on a moor in north Scotland, hardly ever in the Savoy Grill.' That memorable lunch with the two Rothschilds came back to her in a flash. A moment of luxury just after she arrived from France, just before they gave her the commando treatment at Arisaig. 'Thanks for agreeing to meet,' she said, glancing around the bar they were in, tucked away behind the great church of Saint-Sulpice. 'Françoise said you might be able to help me.'

'I'll be pleased to if I can. You must tell me what's on your mind. But first, a waiter,' and he clicked his fingers loud enough to be heard across the street. Menus in front of them, he said, 'What would you like to eat.'

'Mannequins don't eat,' Justine snapped back.

'Oh dear. Maybe some crudités?'

'Yes, grated carrot, please, and a glass of rouge.'

Justine met his gaze, and sort of smiled for the first time. 'I have a project which should make some money. You may think that being a mannequin is an exotic way of life, Monsieur. Actually, it's murder. No money, and you're not allowed to eat.'

Jean, his face lined and not much of his sandy hair left, didn't react.

'I want more excitement in my life.' She paused. 'By that I mean I'm willing to live more dangerously than I am now, if I can make some real money quickly.' She knew what he was thinking. 'I'm not for sale.'

'And I'm not a pimp,' he said with some humour. 'So, what's the project?'

'What if I said there's money to be made importing medicine from Indochina?' Justine whispered as she leant towards him.

'That sounds intriguing. What sort of medicine?'

'Painkillers, like morphine.' She noticed a slight tightening of the skin on his face, as she said the word.

'Well.' He hesitated for a moment. 'If you mean selling to the large pharmaceutical companies, that would be hard. They have their own links to Indochina, and arrangements in place.'

'I've assumed that. I'm thinking of the private market here for, let's say, opiates which help people to manage the pressures they face in their own lives.'

'Ah, now you're talking. I can see that's a growing market. It's not illegal, although in America there are moves to control opiates. When that happens, there will be fortunes to be made by those ready to break the law.'

'We don't have a legal problem in France. However, people who use opiates such as opium and laudanum are very private about their habit. They want guaranteed supply but don't want to go to their doctors for it.'

'I can see that,' said Jean. There was a pause in their conversation while the barman refilled her glass with rouge, and his with Pernod. He poured in some water, producing the familiar cloudy effect. Then he said, 'Mademoiselle Justine, there is one opportunity which anyone doing business with Vietnam should consider.'

'And what is that?' she responded.

'The official exchange rate over there, for piastres into the franc.'

'Oh,' said Justine. 'What's so special about that?'

Jean showed his pleasure at finding something important she didn't know about. He explained in simple terms that the French government fixed the exchange rate value of one piaster at 17 francs. That was about twice the market value of 8.50 francs. In other words, you could sell an item exported from Vietnam at a sale price of 100 piastres and be paid 1,700 francs by the importer in France.'

'So,' said Justine, slowly, 'the exporter in, say, Saigon would make a massive profit just on the exchange. Sounds too good to be true, or legal.'

'Well, it is true and legal, controlled by the Banque de l'Indochine, at least in theory. What's even happening now is that paper companies are issuing false invoices for goods which don't exist, and the profit on the currency exchange is made without any real transaction for goods or services. The Banque del'Indochine cannot check every transaction for its validity.'

'That's incredible,' said Justine.

'Yes, and no. The flip side is that Ho Chi Minh's lot are exploiting this opportunity too. It's said that the profits they make, using a friendly Chinese bank, go to purchase surplus American-made weapons in dollars.'

'With which they kill Frenchmen,' exclaimed Justine. 'Why does the French government over-value the piaster by such an amount?

'Because it acts as an incentive for French military and civilian personnel to go out to Indochina. It also keeps a lid on inflation in Vietnam, Cambodia and Laos. And, of course, everyone's into it, from Bao Dai and his Vietnamese government cronies in the south, to the politicians back at home.'

'The politicians?' said Justine. Something clicked in her brain when she heard that.

'I understand on good authority that the Gaullists used the method to fund their RPR party in the 1948 election.'

Justine's mind was whirling. Jean might just turn out to be the key to unlock her ambitions, to help her find the funding she needed to deliver her political ambitions.

After a moment, presumably to let all of this sink in, he said, 'Justine, how would you operate this sort of business?'

She knew she must take him into her confidence, if this introduction from her close friend Françoise was not to be wasted. 'Well, I and certain others have access to this market here in France. We're already in touch with people who use opium and laudanum. What we need is supply from, say, Haiphong. I do know about the *Bình Xuyên* in Saigon, and don't want to deal with them. Ideally, we should arrange supply from the north, away from the *Bình Xuyên* territory. One of my partners is investigating how we could link directly with the Meo tribe.'

'Sounds ambitious. What can I do to help?'

'In two ways, ideally. I know you have an import/export business in Vietnam. You could help in arranging transportation. Secondly, I want an adviser, Monsieur Jean. Someone I can come to any time to help solve a problem. Or obtain information.' She waited to measure the effect. There wasn't any. This man was what his background suggested, a true professional. 'It would be an undercover arrangement. I wouldn't disclose our connection to my other partners. What do you think?'

Jean laughed. 'Mademoiselle, I'd have thought you would be very good looking after yourself. But I'll give it a go. As far as helping you with arrangements in Vietnam, I would not want to take on the French government. By that I mean there is a cooperation between them and the *Bình Xuyên*.'

'Yes, I heard,' said Justine.

'If you wanted to bounce ideas off me, I'd be pleased to listen. Where do we meet, how do we keep in touch?'

'Here's my home number,' she said handing him her card. 'I'm at Schiaparelli during the day, 21 Place Vendôme, but that's only if there's a crisis. Let's say that if we can't reach one another for any reason, we'll leave a note with the proprietor of this bar. His name is Anton. I first met him in the canteen at,' she stopped herself. There was a silence.

'You were going to say,' said Jean, quietly.

'I was going to say at.' Again she hesitated. 'At Buchenwald.'

'At Buchenwald,' repeated Jean, slowly, with feeling.

11

It was late in a tiring day. A mixture of waiting, waiting, then sudden action. Showing new *modèles* to a highly discerning client. Then, waiting again. All the time, standing, standing. Suddenly, a call came to go and see Giselle, on the floor above. Giselle, the person who welcomed her on her first day at Schiap all those years ago. Now, she is *première main*, head of the *flou atelier*. Tall and refined, grey sleek hair tied up neatly behind the head, unflappable as always.

'Justine, my darling. You discussed with me the other day our clients in Indochina, mainly those from Saigon. There's always the problem of distance. You said we might visit them for a change, did you not?'

'Yes.' Justine tried not to sound breathless, this was the moment she'd been hoping for. 'They come a long way to see us.'

'We've been thinking about that distance problem, and have decided that we should go to them, for a change.'

This was it, thought Justine, daring not to say anything.

Giselle continued. 'The plan is for one of our mannequins and a *vendeuse* to visit Saigon. With them will travel at least one of our *tailleurs,* and a *modéliste* for the clients wanting an original design. They will take a selection of our latest *modèles*, and some accessories from the Schiap boutique.' She paused, smiling. 'Would you like to be the mannequin in the team?'

The words burst their way into Justine's mind. She didn't wait to consider.

'Yes, yes, Giselle. What a wonderful idea. I would love to. How long would I be away?'

~~•~✠~•~~

Justine and Ka were together in an eating haunt just off rue de la Paix. It was a favourite spot for people from Schiap, the atelier workers scraping together their meagre earnings, the mannequins dining off their grated carrot, vin rouge and piping hot coffee.

'Ka, would you believe it. Giselle has asked me to join a party from Schiap to go and visit Saigon.'

'What? You must be joking,' said Ka. 'All that way. It'll take you weeks.'

'No. we're going to fly.'

'In an aeroplane?'

'How else. By Air France flight DC499 from Paris to Saigon. We stop on the way in Bahrain and Karachi, to refuel.'

'Incredible.' Ka was clearly amazed.'

'Don't worry. Travelling there and back will take about five days. And we'll stay there about fifteen. So, three weeks altogether.'

'Oh. I suppose that's not bad.'

'And you know what it means, my darling Ka. It means I can try and tie down our pipeline. You mentioned that Glun is going next month to see his family in the north.'

'Yes,' said Ka. 'So, perhaps you can meet up with him. He's flying also, and therefore has to pass through Saigon.'

'That would fit really well.'

Justine looked around her. 'You know, Ka. I've been thinking. Maybe we should start with a single large shipment, if somehow we could finance it up front. That would give us working capital while we're setting up the regular flow of the medicine. Let's call it medicine whatever the actual merchandise is.'

'How do we get paid up front?'

'I've been thinking about that.' Justine paused. 'Why don't we ask Madame X and her friends to pay us in advance? Nothing to stop us explaining that we are setting up new supply arrangements for their benefit. That the way to secure a reasonable price is to order a significant amount up front.'

They swapped findings since the discussion with Madame X. Ka reported that her tutor friend Glun at the Sorbonne was writing to his family in Tonkin to see if the Meos would supply raw opium directly. That he was saving up to go out there during the university vacation. Justine talked about her lunch with Françoise, nearby the *piscine*. She kept to herself her later encounter with Jean. She did however explain the currency profits being made from the government's over-valuation of the piaster.

'I've been thinking about the person I call my other boss,' said Ka.

'That gangster Bao?'

'Yes. I saw him yesterday. He's putting the screws on me. Says I'm not finding him enough business.'

'From the clients wanting opium,' muttered Justine. 'Do you think he's guessed our intentions?'

'How can he, we haven't done anything yet.'

'I've been thinking about Madame X.' Justine paused. 'You know her husband's important in government, but has no real money. On the other hand, her father is wealthy. Maybe there's a deal to do, and ...'

Ka interrupted. 'Her father was a collaborator.'

'Precisely. So far, he enjoys protection from the government. He's on the inside, has some sort of licence from Dow Chemical, where the napalm comes from.'

Silence for a moment. Then Ka said, as though she was surprised, 'Are you thinking of blackmailing him? I don't think we should mix with those people. Let's do it on our own. What's the name of your friend in Saigon?'

There was no response from the other.

'Now, come on, Justine. Tell me about him, your RAF friend in Saigon.'

'Well, his name is Bill Lomberg. He used to fly agents in and out of France, before the Liberation. That's how I met him.'

'And,' said Ka, sensing there was a lot more.

'He took part in a spectacular raid on Amiens prison, to release resistants locked up there. The flak got him, and he baled out and escaped. Until the Milice raided a farm he was hiding in. The Gestapo accused him and other RAF crews of being 'terror flyers', and they ended up in Buchenwald concentration camp.'

'Where you were.'

'That's right. We got out of the place together, but that's another story. The important thing is that Bill's now a freelance pilot flying Dakotas from Saigon to the north. He could be a vital link for us.'

'Interesting,' said Ka. 'If we could bring him into what you call the pipeline, part of our transportation problem would be solved.' She hesitated for a moment. 'A lot will depend on whether Glun's family comes on side, and can set up the supply at source.'

'I intend to see Bill when I'm in Saigon. You're right, he might be a help for us getting the raw opium down from the Meos in the Highlands.'

'I'll see Glun again at the weekend, and make sure he understands how important it is.'

'Okay, I'll contact Bill. What I need is access to a teleprinter so we can exchange views and, when we start, track what's in the pipeline and where it's got to. I've an idea. I'll see what I can do.'

'If all that comes together,' said Ka, who was beginning to show some enthusiasm, 'then we only have the Saigon to France shipping to sort out.'

Justine was thinking of Jean. His export/import business would be shipping merchandise from Saigon to France. 'I think I might have the answer to that,' she murmured.

St Germain des Prés

Jean sat at the same table as a couple of days before. She felt his bear-like hands press against her arms, as he delivered kisses to both cheeks. 'It's late evening, and I bet you've eaten nothing all day,' he said. 'I propose we have them prepare a large omelette for the two of us. And what we save by not having a chateaubriand, we'll spend on a bottle of best red burgundy.'

'Now you're talking,' said Justine, acknowledging she was in good company, if not with the most attractive of men.

A pause while Jean sorted things out with the waiter. Then she said, 'Thanks for joining me, Jean. I have a couple of questions I want to put to you. One simple, the other not so, I suspect.'

'Can't wait to hear them.'

'Well, the simple one first. I need access to a teleprinter link to Saigon.'

'No problem. You can use the one in my Paris office. And the other?'

Justine hesitated. 'We think we may have identified a source for the medicine, and a way to have it brought to Saigon. The big question is, how do we transport it to France?'

'I would have to think about that. If the *Binh Xuyên* get a smell of competition, at best they would want a cut, at worst you would end up in a bag, tossed into the swamp. There are some hungry reptiles in there, just waiting to meet you.'

'You're trying to put the frights on me, Jean.'

'Somehow, you must have a cast-iron cover story. Maybe, climb on the back of someone else's merchandise which is shipped out regularly and without check. It's not illegal, but if you applied for an import permit, you'd probably not get it.'

'What about silk?' Justine blurted out.

'Why do you mention silk?'

'Because that's an important export from Indochina to France. We could slip our opium pouches in with the bales of shantung. Only the best,' she laughed. 'Françoise mentioned to me that you handled silk in your business.'

'Interesting,' said Jean. 'It'll be tricky, to ship it out securely and beyond the watchful eyes of the customs authorities.'

'I realise that.'

'I do business with the people who own the silk mills in Annam, the centre of Vietnam. I'll have to think about it.

'That's only part of the challenge,' said Justine. 'How does one retrieve the parcel at the other end, Marseille or wherever?' She paused, and drew herself up for effect. 'Incidentally, I'm going to Saigon.'

'You are what?' said Jean.

'I'm flying out to Saigon soon. It's a business trip. Showing off clothes for Schiaparelli.'

'Well I never. I must arrange to be there at the same time.'

12

Bill Lomberg felt the C47 Dakota come alive in his hands, and pulled into a climb out over Cap St Jacques before banking to port and heading for Lai Chau up in the north-west corner of Tonkin. If he could survive a few more of these missions for the MACG, the French army's counterespionage service, he might pocket enough to start his own airline. Back in southern Africa, that would be the ultimate.

Incredible what was going on. That meeting a month ago with the Corsican Captain, Antoine Savani, was an eye opener. 'Meet me at the Caravelle for a drink, and we'll go on from there. I've an attractive proposition which could make you a lot of money. Don't worry about breaking the law. What we're doing is directed from the top of the French army. De Lattre de Tassigny, the new Commander-in-Chief, is fully behind it. Instead of trying to stage set-piece battles, we're now being more intelligent and hitting the Viets inside their own heartland.'

That's how it started. That first encounter with Captain Savani.

'We're doing something special down here on the Cap,' said Savani, 'we call it the Action School. You remember the maquis?'

'Don't I just,' said Bill. 'I spent some time with one in the Vosges in '44.'

'It's a training camp. For the pro-French tribal people willing to fight the Viets up in the northern Highlands'.

That jogged Bill's memory. 'There's a name spoken of, a major involved in organising that kind of resistance. Trinquier, I think his name is?'

'Exactly. We run it between us, call it Operation X. Roger Trinquier commands the guerrilla units in Tonkin and Laos. And it's working. It's grown big since de Lattre put his weight behind it. Over a hundred French officers are now involved.'

'So, how would I fit in?' asked Bill.

'Okay, I'm going to tell you. But before, I have to know you will never disclose the secret behind the secret. A fair number of army and others are aware of the Action School at Cap St Jacques. Almost no one knows how the operation is paid for.'

'I've heard that the government in Paris keeps the military down here on a very tight budget. People in France just don't like this war.'

'Dead right.'

'I'm watertight. Served my time at Tempsford, flying agents in and out of occupied France in the war.'

'I made my inquiries,' said Savani. 'You have impressive experience.' He paused, looking around him. 'Yes, our biggest problem with Operation X is money. Where to fill the gap between the budget set by the army, and the cost of paying the insiders who recruit and direct the different maquis. Not to mention what we pay the guerrilla troops.'

'I can imagine. So, what's the secret?'

The Corsican didn't reply at first. He seemed to be allowing the suspense to build up. Then he looked hard at Bill. 'We've captured part of the opium trade.'

'What, surely not? Opium use is supposed to be banned out here.'

'That's as may be. Fact is that the trade is increasing rapidly. For use here in Vietnam, and for export to Hong Kong and elsewhere.'

'How does Ho Chi Minh's lot fit into that?'

Savani explained that the Viets in the northern Highlands wanted a share of the opium action to help finance arms and equipment purchases. By denying it to them, they stopped Ho Chi Minh using the proceeds to buy *matériel* from the Chinese. Savani and Trinquier bought the raw opium from certain of the hill tribes who grew and harvested it, the Meo in particular. There were Meo in Laos who were very pro the Viets. But the Meo in the Tonkin Highlands turned to them in exchange for very generous financial reward.

'Sounds a hairy business. What do you do with the stuff?'

'We fly the raw opium from Lai Chau in the north-west, close to the China border, down to Cap St Jacques. There's a certain, shall I say, organisation in Saigon, with whom we work. They treat the raw opium for us, boil out the impurities. Then they help us market it. The margins are high, and the net proceeds help balance the MACG's counterespionage budget.'

'And the French authorities know about this?'

'We don't broadcast the opium angle. But the top French here are in the picture.'

There was a short silence. Then Bill spoke slowly. 'So, you want me to fly opium down from the north?'

'Yes, we need someone like you. On the inside, we're known as "Air Opium". The take-offs and landings up there can be challenging, and you have that skill.'

'What about the French air force pilots?'

'They are combat men, fighter bombers and the like. Some also fly transports to parachute in troops, and bring out casualties. But they're in squadrons and we don't want them swapping information with their team-mates. The same applies to the American volunteer pilots. They're good, but their allegiance is questionable.'

'Yes, I've met some of the Yanks, a good lot.'

'There are CIA guys here, nosing around. If they discover we're in the opium trade, all hell will break loose. The US Administration could cut off their supplies to us of arms and aircraft. They would assume that some of the opium, processed into morphine and heroin, would be reaching the streets of America.'

That's how it started.

⋯⊷◉⊶⋯

As the Dakota reached cruising altitude, his thoughts went to the cable the concierge handed to him as he left his hotel for the airfield. From Justine Müller who, he'd heard, was now a top Paris mannequin with Schiaparelli. What few people knew was that Justine was his partner during the war in Europe in an escape from Buchenwald.

The cable told him Justine wanted to communicate by tele-printer about a 'new project', giving him a telex number in Paris and asking him to dial her up in two days' time. He asked the concierge to acknowledge safe receipt, as he jumped into a cab to head for the airfield.

⋯⊷◉⊶⋯

Bill stood by in the aircrew centre at Tan Son Nhut airfield, as the teleprinter clattered to a stop. Tearing the printed paper off the roll, he read Justine's message. Would he meet her when she arrived in Saigon. She was looking forward to seeing him after so long. On the same flight there would be a star, a famous dancer and singer, coming to entertain the French forces.

He typed in a reply, confirming he looked forward to meeting the DC4 aircraft due in from Bahrain, the Air France flight DC499 from Paris in a week's time.

The phone went in Bill's rented bungalow the next day.

'Is that Squadron Leader Lomberg?' the soft but purposeful American voice drawled down the phone.

'Yes, or at least I was,' said Bill, a thumping pain in his head. 'I'm not in the RAF any longer.' It was still early, and the night before was spent with the hard-drinking overseas press at the Hotel Caravelle.

'My name is Lansdale, Colonel Edward Lansdale, United States Air Force, on US government duty here in Vietnam. I would like to meet you, Bill.'

'Okay,' said Bill. 'How urgent is it?'

'How about coffee this morning, say ten at La Pagode?'

'Okay, ten it is.'

La Pagode on rue Catinat lent itself to various interpretations, according to why you went there. Tea shop, Buddist temple, bar, and rendezvous for the night life. There was no mistaking Lansdale even though he wasn't wearing uniform. In a chair out on the pavement, laid-back but not missing anything. Long thin face, sleek black hair, reading the *Washington Post*. Bill, with some years of mixing with intelligence people behind him, thought immediately he was probably a spook.

'My main interest here is counterinsurgency,' said the Colonel, after they shook hands and ordered coffee with cognacs. 'I know something of your background, Bill. South African upbringing. English education. Helped the FFI in France in the war. Not to mention special Mosquito missions. Moon flights, that's what you called them at Tempsford, wasn't it?'

Bill said nothing.

Lansdale poured cognac into his coffee, and stirred it slowly. 'Then there was that raid on Amiens prison. You Mosquito guys were really the best by that stage in the war.'

Bill grinned, still keeping his mouth shut. Definitely a spook, he confirmed to himself.

'Look, Bill, I know you're up to something interesting around here. I know a lot more than the French would like to admit to. In particular, the activities of your friend Antoine Savani, the Corsican. He's a well-connected guy. Maybe too well connected, from what I hear. Do the *Bình Xuyên* mean anything to you?' Bill shook his head. 'Well, they run organised crime in this city, and the so-called river pirates.'

Bill knew what was coming.

'They monopolise the opium business in Saigon. It's said that the French secret service buys the raw opium from the tribes in the northern Highlands, close to Laos. Somehow, it finds its way down here. They refine it in their boiling plants, then either distribute it to the opium dens or export it to places like Hong Kong, even to France.'

'How come the French would allow that, let alone be part of it?' said Bill.

Lansdale explained that the Deuxième Bureau had two reasons for getting involved. First, they wanted to block Ho Chi Minh from getting his hands on the opium crop, and buying arms with the proceeds. Second, they used the funds generated from selling the stuff to the *Bình Xuyên* to supplement their budget so they could fund the Montagnards to make life uncomfortable for the Viets in the Highlands.

'Sounds neat,' said Bill. There was a pause, as he wondered how he should respond to Lansdale, bring his work for Savani into the conversation. He remembered Antoine's request for total secrecy.

Lansdale then said, 'Can I ask you, Bill, why are you here, and what do you think is going to happen to this place as a French colony?'

'I'm here to make some money, Ed. I only know about flying. I want to make enough to start my own air freight business, ideally back in South Africa, where I come from.'

'That's a good straightforward answer.'

Bill went on. 'As far as the French are concerned, I think they have an impossible job. Sure, you Americans help them a lot with the arms shipments, and aircraft. But the Viets are now much better equipped, thanks to China. And all the time, they are growing the size of their army in the north and guerrilla forces down here.'

'You don't have any special ties to France?'

'No. Except that I know a couple of French girls from wartime days,' he said, half laughingly. 'One of them is coming out here very soon.'

'Great,' said Lansdale. 'Don't get me wrong. I'm not here to recruit you to spy for America. But I would like to keep in touch, see a bit of you from time to time to swap stories. In fact, if you ever need advice or help, I would love to help. As for your French girlfriend, let me invite the two of you to join me for dinner.'

'That's grand of you, Ed. There'll be a once American singer and dancer with her, who changed her nationality to French. You might have heard of her.'

'Oh, and who's that?'

'Josephine Baker.'

13

Saigon, April 1951

As the Peugeot station wagon turned into rue Catinat, Justine looked in delight at the old colonial buildings and street cafés, and the tropical trees bordering the road. Exhausted as the Schiap team were, arriving from the airport after the last leg of their flight, she felt excited by the sight and smell of it all. Bicycles and mobylettes were everywhere. School children en masse as they pedalled to school, chattering to one another. French military personnel on leave, and in search of their coffee and rolls for breakfast. Above her head ran literally thousands of telephone wires, the terminals on the edge of buildings looking as though no engineer could ever find a fault. A young man without shoes ran alongside the open window of the car, calling out to her, 'Latest Graham Greene, *Quiet American*.'

At the Hotel Continental, the concierge handed her two messages, while an immaculately groomed Vietnamese hostess offered a deliciously cold *citron pressé*.

The first message was from Bill Lomberg. He would meet her for breakfast in the hotel restaurant the following morning. The second was from Ka's tutor friend from the Sorbonne, Glun. He was in Hanoi with his family, and gave a telephone number for her to reach him.

As soon as she was in her room, Justine called the hotel operator and asked to be put through to the Hanoi number. She was walking out of the shower booth when the phone buzzed in the typical way French phones did. Glun said he would pass through Saigon in two days' time, on his way back to Paris. The news from his family was promising, as he put it, not wanting anything incriminating to be overheard by telephone operators, or agents of the Sûreté. They fixed a time for him to come to the hotel.

Justine lay on her back on the bed, looking up at the large fan which revolved leisurely above her, and thought of Bill Lomberg. Mosquito netting was drawn back at the bed posts on all four corners, and across the floor the tall windows opened out onto a quiet courtyard.

She knew Bill better than any other man. Not surprisingly, having lived shoulder to shoulder with him after their breakout from Buchenwald in the summer of '44. And before all that, he was the boyfriend of her closest friend, Françoise de Rochefort. She always found Bill attractive, with his soft South African accent, and the broad shoulders of the rugby player she knew he was. It was clear from her lunch conversation with Françoise the month before, that the relationship was not flourishing any longer. How would she get on with him now, cut off as they were on the other side of the world?

They couldn't be in a more different environment than during the war in Europe. It was Bill and his Lysander aircraft that flew her and Françoise out of occupied France. Once or twice she saw him with Françoise after her training in Scotland. She hardly knew him until that day he walked into her life in the canteen at Buchenwald. They recognised each other as he saw her serving up the slop that was lunch. Their escape together led to her re-capture in Freiburg. They were not reunited until her rescue. That extraordinary time with a maquis in the Vosges, leading to all three of them finding their way to Switzerland and freedom.

From the breakfast table overlooking the bustling rue Catinat, Justine watched a mass of teenage girls cycling past in groups on their way to college, their straight backs in long white costumes, jet black hair flowing out behind.

'There you are.' His voice with just that slightest South African lilt to it, burst into her thoughts. 'You look fantastic,' he said as he strode up to her, and they embraced.

'Oh, Bill, hello,' was all she could say at first. She stood back and admired him. 'You've won back that weight you lost in the camps, you're looking great.'

'We both made it, didn't we. Remember that Christmas in Gstaad, with the others, the last one of the war.'

'I know, magic. We were so lucky to get out. I'll never forget that feeling of freedom,' said Justine. 'You know, I lunched with Françoise just before I came out here. She sends her love.' She sensed a slight awkwardness in Bill.

'Oh, darling Françoise, I've not been good to her,' he said. 'We keep in touch, but I went my own way.'

'I know. I keep an eye on her. She's in the Sûreté, attached to the French secret service.'

'Come on let's have some breakfast, and you can tell me what you've been up to.'

Justine reminded him she'd been at Schiaparelli early in the war, before being caught in the Rafle when she was rounded up and put into Drancy. Rescued by Françoise before deportation to the East. That was when Bill flew them to England. Then the reason for her being in Saigon, her project. Sourcing the opium direct from the growers. About Glun coming to Saigon the next day. The problem of transporting the raw opium down to Saigon.

Bill, listening intently, suddenly interrupted her. 'Justine, I may be able to help. I fly merchandise between north and south of the country. I'm just starting to fly into Lai Chau. Would that help?'

'On the face of it, that would certainly help. I don't want you to take risks with the powers that be.'

'Dear Justine, in this part of the world there are risks in everything one does. It's just a question of degree.'

'Okay, that's great. My contact with the growers is coming here tomorrow, we've a meeting fixed at this hotel. I think you should be with me if you can make it.'

'Fine. I can do that. I'm not flying until the next day. What time?'

'Lunchtime. He's on his way back to Paris. The name's Glun. He's a Vietnamese professor at the Sorbonne. Very young, clever. His family are Meos, a tribe on the borders with Laos and China.'

'Yes, I know the Meos. More friendly to the French than most people up there. It's the Meos who grow most of the opium.'

It suddenly occurred to Justine that Bill knew a lot about the subject, maybe he was in the game already. But she was not going to ask him, just yet. 'Exactly. Come here for lunch tomorrow with me and Glun. My work for Schiap is first thing in the morning, and in early evening.'

From her room the next morning, Justine saw Glun cross rue Catinat, heading for the hotel entrance. Downstairs in a flash, she intercepted him in the lobby. They chose a corner where they could speak safely. She liked Glun's style, straightforward and confident. His message on the phone the day before made it clear his family was positive towards their proposal to supply her pipeline with the raw opium. They were ready to negotiate with a particular plantation owner, and would confirm price as soon as they received the go ahead from Glun. Could funds be transferred by Justine to the family's account at a Hanoi bank?

She expressed profuse thanks, and her enthusiasm for working with Glun in this way. There should be no problem with the transfer of funds. After some sparring over what he would earn from his involvement, they agreed it would be based on a share in the final profit generated in France.

Justine gave Glun some background on Bill, saying he would be joining them for lunch. When his large frame appeared, coming towards them across the lobby, she leapt to her feet.

'You lunch in the best places,' said Bill as he kissed her on both cheeks. Justine introduced him to Glun, saying Bill was a long-time friend from the war in Europe. 'I suggest we eat right away, and talk business after,' she said.

Following a light meal, they moved for coffee to a table out of the way of others.

'Down to business,' said Justine, turning to Glun. 'As he's just described to us, Bill not only flies freight up and down to Hanoi, but also into airstrips in the Highlands including Lai Chau. I've taken him into our confidence and explained our plan to source opium up there and send it, via Saigon, to France. I believe he could be the solution to how we transport it down here.'

Justine noticed Glun focusing all his attention on Bill, this person she was proposing should become one of their inner circle. She guessed he might need some convincing, and was pleased all three of them were taking the chance to get to know one another.

Glun asked Justine, 'Have you found a way to transport the merchandise to France?'

'I think so,' she replied. 'There's the opportunity to ship it to Marseille, using spare capacity on vessels that have brought military supplies out from France.' So far, she reflected, she would keep Jean to herself.

It was agreed that Bill and Glun would have a further meeting that afternoon to discuss arrangements for communications, and the collection of shipments from the grower. After Justine finished her Schiap business, the three of them would meet again over dinner.

14

Saigon, rue Catinat, April 1951

How could it happen, she marvelled. The four of them coming together in this way. Bill's friend Lansdale insisting on being host. Lansdale's idea to meet at L'Amiral. Justine was thrilled, a night out like this was long overdue. Having Josephine as well was a bonus.

L'Amiral reminded Justine of Rick's night club in the wartime film *Casablanca*. Humphrey Bogart played by Lansdale, Ingrid Bergman by Josephine Baker. Her mind raced away in a fantasy induced by a Saigon night club so far from the hard reality of life in Europe as was Rick's in Casablanca at the time the film was made.

Lansdale broke her train of thought. 'Sorry we aren't at a brasserie in the open along Catinat, enjoying the world go by,' said Lansdale, as the barman arrived with the cocktails. 'That used to be the fashion. Until the Viets came down south and chucked the odd grenade in among the tables.'

'Ed knows a lot about this country. You were in Korea before, weren't you?' said Bill.

'I sure was. I'm supposed to be a counterinsurgency expert. Turning the tribes in the Highlands up north against the Ho Chi Minh guerrillas. Had some success, but the French secret service aren't that keen on me. They actually had Washington pull me out at one point. Right now, I guess they regard me as better to have on their side than not, but I have to watch my step.'

Josephine Baker, who seemed to be listening avidly to all this, broke in. 'It does sound exotic, and dangerous. Reminds me of the night clubs in Berlin in the twenties. Bolshevik spies, the early Nazi thugs, American jazz music, and no censors. Wild, it was.'

'You certainly survived and thrived,' said Justine. 'France's most popular cabaret artist, that's saying something. Like when you were at the Folies Bergère.'

'Why did you chuck your American nationality?' said Ed Lansdale, pointedly, but with a grin.

'Do you really want to know?' Josephine hesitated for a moment. 'Well, I was invited back to the States to do a tour. Starting in Florida, they gave me a great welcome. Then I discovered the top night clubs in Miami were segregated. No blacks in the audience. I refused to perform unless they lifted the rule. They wouldn't, almost anywhere. So I cut short my visit and returned to Paris.'

'And the French heard about it?' said Justine.

'Yes. They seemed to love me by then, and invited me to become French.'

It wasn't unexpected when the maître d' came over to their table, took Josephine's hand, and led her over to the dance band. Conversation around the room ceased. Everyone by now knew who this very tall, strikingly beautiful black singer was.

'Mesdames et Messieurs,' the maître d' announced to the audience. 'I present to you, direct from Paris, the most sensational cabaret artist in the world, Josephine Baker.' With much clapping from everyone, the band led Josephine into 'La Petite Tonkinoise', and then 'J'attendrai'.

Suddenly, a voice behind Justine said, 'Mademoiselle, I would love to dance with you, come out onto the floor for a couple of numbers.'

She turned her head around and there was Jean, Jean from Saint Germain des Prés, from the small bar behind Saint-Sulpice.

'Why Jean, what a surprise.'

'I thought I might find you here. I came in on yesterday's plane.'

Justine introduced him to the others. Then they danced, as the band and Josephine started the lilting melody 'Polka Dots and Moonbeams', Jean holding her close enough to speak into an ear without others overhearing. 'I've already made a date with my silk merchant friend. If you could come tomorrow morning to the Majestic, I will introduce you to him. I think he's going to play ball.'

'That's good news, Jean, though not awfully romantic,' Justine whispered back as she felt his hard body rub gently against hers.

Josephine ended her surprise session and, with a wave of the longest arm ever to grace a cabaret floor, she wended her way back to the table.

⋯⊷⊙⊶⋯

Off centre from the smart hotels along rue Catinat, the locals still regarded the Majestic as the best hotel in Saigon. The concierge said it could be walked in fifteen minutes and Justine was soon submerged in the bustle and smells of this extraordinary city. It seemed to reach out to her, the profusion of tropical plants and trees everywhere bringing the stranger closer to nature than ever at home.

The Saigon river came into view, and turning left she followed the line of vessels berthed end to end until before her was the Majestic. The doorman bowed and looked on appreciatively as she walked through the hotel entrance as she would through Place Vendôme. In the lounge running along the front of the building, she spotted Jean in a far corner. With him was with a lean middle-aged man, sunburnt, probably a *colon* Justine thought. They both rose as she approached, and Jean introduced her to Jules.

Politely asking how she was finding Saigon, as the waiter brought over a silver jug of coffee, Jules came straight to the point. 'Mademoiselle Müller, the matter we're going to discuss is highly sensitive. While strictly you will not be breaking French law in transporting opium to France, you will be cutting across powerful vested interests.' He stopped and looked hard at Justine. 'And that is putting it mildly.'

'Monsieur Jules, I understand perfectly,' she said, trying to reassure him she wasn't going into all this in ignorance of the consequences if something went wrong.

'Good,' he said. 'I'm prepared to help you because I've heard from Jean about people you're friendly with in the Sûreté as a result of your war experience.'

Justine nodded.

'My business is silk. We ship it direct from the factories, via Saigon to Marseille. If we can agree acceptable terms, I can arrange for your merchandise to be packed with mine. We maintain the tightest security.'

'That sounds feasible,' said Justine.

'I do have a special interest in helping you,' he added. 'I understand you represent the House of Schiaparelli. We produce some of the finest shantung silk and you might wish to help me market it in Paris haute couture.'

'That would be worth discussing further,' said Justine, unsure in herself how she would go about it but not wishing to put Jules off.

Jean opened a briefcase on the floor beside his chair. He pulled out some papers. 'I've had a protocol drawn up between the three of us. It doesn't refer specifically to opium. Just says that in view of spare shipping capacity on the return route Saigon to Marseille, space will be provided for ancillary merchandise to be transported "cif" Marseille.'

'Meaning, Mademoiselle Justine, that you will arrange for payment of the agreed cost, insurance and freight, when you take delivery at Marseille docks,' said Jules.

'That's wonderful, Monsieur Jules. I will advise you shortly when the first shipment is to be made,' said Justine. 'My contact in Saigon is Bill Lomberg. He flies Dakotas up and down the country, including to the Tonkin Highlands. He's a close associate and knows what I am doing.'

Jean interjected, 'We should buy the currency necessary in Paris, at the international market rate. Our supplier will benefit from the Banque de l'Indochine's subsidised rate if he sells the piastres for dollars or francs.'

'That should help hold down the price we're charged,' said Justine. She looked at her watch. 'I'll have to get back to the Continental now, to prepare for a dress show there this evening. Come if you can and see the latest Schiap creations.'

They both said they would be there.

'Afterwards, I can introduce you to Bill Lomberg,' she said to Jules. 'We can talk about the project together, and hopefully sign the protocol.'

Justine could see things falling into place, but knew she must be on guard. It was wise to keep close to Jean, her protector. He'd made clear that they were treading on dangerous ground, the territory of the *Bình Xuyên*.

15

21 Place Vendôme, April 1951

Still no news from Justine. The message to Ka at work came from Glun, just back from his trip to Hanoi. Could she dine with him at a Vietnamese restaurant in the Latin Quarter? They agreed to meet late, so she could finish her work on a costume needed for a client fitting the next day.

Glun was enthusiastic about their project. His family reacted positively to the proposal to source the opium directly from the Meos growers, and introduced him to the contact with the plantation. He'd given the good news to Justine in Saigon, and was in touch with her friend Bill who was to fly the raw opium down to Saigon as part of his regular freight business. Glun wanted to discuss his share of the profits, but Ka calmed him down, explaining that Justine must be part of that conversation.

It was late when they finally parted, and she decided to walk home rather than the short ride on the Metro. A warm spring evening in Paris was something special, even to a Vietnamese. Now almost dark, she turned into one of the side streets, a short cut to where she lived. An odd sensation crept into her. Was she really alone, or was someone watching her, following her? She tried to think clearly, must not to let her nerves over-take her senses. If there was a follower, he must be tricked into giving himself away. If he wasn't after her, and she evaded him, he would walk on past. How could she make him lose sight of her long enough for her to check? Ka's heart began to pound.

Somewhere on her side of the road there was a building set back where the pavement was dark, so she could drop out of view without him realising it. Yes, it was coming up now, just past the only shop in the street. She increased her pace somewhat and entered the pool of darkness. No one walked past. So, she was being followed. Her nervousness became unbearable. Her apartment building was now in view on the other side of the street. In a flash she was across and mounting the stairs to the third floor. No noise behind her.

Her hand went for the key in her bag, then turned it in the lock just as a shadow appeared across her path. Someone was already up there, behind her.

The arm came round her shoulders, a hand over her mouth. The voice hissed in her ear. 'Don't make a sound. Open the door and go in.' A second man came up the stairs and joined them inside. One was Asian, she assumed Vietnamese. The other was big and swarthy, maybe a Corsican, she thought. Between them, they tied Ka to a chair with some cord they had with them, and began to question her.

'Your name is Ka. We know a lot about you,' said the Corsican-looking man. 'You have some explaining to do.'

Ka was shivering with fear. 'I just have no idea what you're on about. Anyway, who are you? Presumably not police, or you would have identified yourselves.'

'Very clever. The boss would not be amused. He has some questions for you, and has asked us to obtain the answers.'

'I don't speak to strangers,' said Ka. 'If your boss wants to question me, take me to him.'

'He's a busy man. He also wants to be sure you will cooperate. If you don't answer the questions here in your apartment, you will come with us and we will see how we can encourage you.'

'What do you want to know?'

'You have been supplying opium to certain clients in Paris. Where have you been getting it from? Are you working with a business partner? Tell us the full story, and you won't get hurt.'

'Until I know who you are, I can't talk about such things, even if they were true. Identify yourselves.'

'We're wasting our time,' said the Corsican to the Vietnamese.

With that, they gave her five minutes to pack a bag and then took her downstairs. They made for a Traction Avant on the corner of the narrow street. Pushing her into the back seat of the Citroën, the Corsican climbed in beside her. The Asian's driving was abrupt as he alternately gunned the throttle, then stamped on the brakes.

Ka tried to remain cool. She mustn't panic. These thugs were working for Bao, doing his dirty business. Somehow he received word she was in league with an alternative supplier. He didn't know who that was, and has employed these two to find out for him. He was a weak man underneath, couldn't do it himself. They would interrogate her. It could be unpleasant, and she must be brave. There was no way she would disclose Justine's involvement.

Where were they taking her? Probably to rue de Bac. Awful things happened there, she was sure. In her case, they wouldn't be wanting to kill her. She was more valuable to them alive, at least until they learnt of Justine's identity. So she must say nothing, take no risk that they could work out that Justine and her pipeline were going to compete.

16

Paris, Office of Peace and Liberty movement, April 1951

Justine arrived just as René Pleven was about to speak, and sat in the back row. Feeling the exhaustion of the endless noisy flights back via the Middle East, it was the day of her early morning arrival at Le Bourget. Not due at Schiap until next day, she was thinking of Ka. She mustn't miss this meeting, and would meet her right afterwards outside work. She must tell her all about the trip. In the meantime, politics were in the forefront of her mind.

It was Pleven's meeting, open only to those like her who supported the Movement and its mission to combat the power of the Communists in France. He headed his own political party, the Democratic and Socialist Union of the Resistance with which the Peace and Liberty movement cooperated in a common mission to defeat the French Communist party.

The audience stood up and clapped as Pleven walked to the podium and started his address. 'As you all know, the Communists claim they led the Resistance. That it was they who were decisive in liberating France, with the help of the Allies. Their policy was to shoot Germans in the back at every opportunity. It was they who caused so many civilians to die unnecessarily in reprisals taken by the Nazis in response. The Communist resistants took their instructions and support from Stalin and Moscow. The other Resistance, of which some of you were part, looked to the General and to London for leadership and support. You probably know that I joined General de Gaulle in London in the early days of the Free French.'

Pleven paused, his studious face and round steel-rimmed glasses appearing to take in everyone individually in the audience. 'Today I want to tell you about a vision, one in which the Communist party can have no part. This vision is the future of not just France, but of Germany and other European nations. It is based on economic cooperation, on coming together where there are commercial activities of common interest. This is the vision of Maurice Schumann. Its first manifestation is his proposal for France and Germany to coordinate their coal and steel interests, creating an industrial community more organised and effective than at present. To make these great industries capable of satisfying the massive demand for coal and steel as Europe recovers from the ravages of the war. Growing out of that, Mr Schumann foresees a step by step advance, over time, towards political as well as commercial convergence across Europe.'

Justine couldn't disagree with that, which clearly René Pleven believed in passionately. Her concern was that such grand plans would be pursued in disregard to the immediate and desperate needs of the French people. Basic food supplies and housing required urgent attention. The taxation system as it applied to the underprivileged must be revised.

'Do you have questions?' she heard him say.

Immediately she was on her feet, tall, elegant and imposing. Her auburn hair was tied back behind her neck. All eyes looked back towards her. Perhaps the odd person recognised her from a fashion magazine.

'Monsieur Pleven, thank you. My name is Justine Müller. I understand and support what you are saying. My pressing concern, however, is the status of the ordinary French person.

As of now, hunger persists and children lack warm clothing. There are appalling living conditions in the cities. If something isn't done rapidly, these people will turn to the Communists, if they haven't done so already. The French Communist party will be perceived as the solution to their misery. We must have a political party which the destitute, an important part of the population, can look to as an alternative to Communism.'

Pleven looked across kindly towards the wonderfully tall and elegant questioner. 'Mademoiselle Müller, I understand your cry for a solution to today's conditions. I hope to become President of the Council of Ministers in the coming year. As prime minister, one of my first aims will be to deliver on what you are calling for.'

The meeting over, Justine saw René Pleven coming towards her.

'I don't think we've met before, Mademoiselle. But I do know of you. I believe you expressed your passion for addressing the hopelessness of so many people, during a Schiaparelli Collection last year. We read about it in *Le Monde*. My wife drew it to my attention. I think a friend of hers was present when you ended the show in the wedding dress.'

Justine was amazed. Such an important political figure. Someone who people were saying could be the next prime minister. 'Thank you, sir. I had to speak as I did just now. I feel so strongly that something has to be done, and that I must play my part in it.'

'Well, Mademoiselle, you live in a country where once more, you are able to do and say what you believe in. Under a fascist government such as we were forced to endure in the war, that was impossible. I wish you every success. I respect your ambition to pursue this goal while still working. The fashion world must be a hard life.'

'Yes, it is, sir. And we starve like others, except we do it on purpose.'

With that, René Pleven gave a short laugh, shook hands, and moved back towards the stage.

Pleven's last comment stayed there in Justine's mind as she made for a bus outside. It wouldn't leave her. How in fact could she combine the demanding role of mannequin extraordinaire, as Jean put it, with the life of a political agitator? When Schiaparelli was her only source of income, there was only one rational choice to make. Now that there was the prospect of enough money to live off and hopefully more, the option of leaving Schiap opened up. The first importation of the medicine was about to happen. Better not rush her decision. Wait until the pipeline was proven. Wait for the cash to flow.

⋯⋯⟡⟡⋯⋯

Justine made straight for Place Vendôme. She wanted to tell Ka all about Saigon.

'Ka didn't come in today, Mademoiselle Müller,' said the woman in the box at the staff entrance. 'She didn't come in today and she didn't let us know.' There was a tone of officious disapproval in the woman's voice.

Justine felt a stab of doubt. Ka wasn't like that. Must go round to her apartment in case she was ill. Too ill to let them know? No time to lose. She took the bus across Concorde and over the river, onto the left bank and east along the Boulevard St Germain. At the Boul'Mich, she jumped off and half ran, half walked up the boulevard, then dived into the side streets on the left just before the Panthéon.

At the apartment building, she went in and ran up the staircase, becoming more and more concerned with each step. No answer when she knocked hard on the door. Then again, harder. Where was she? A man spoke behind her, must be the concierge. 'She isn't there. She left with two men late yesterday evening.'

'Did you see them, what they looked like?' asked Justine.

'Not properly, it was dark. One man was short but well built, and somehow looked Asian. The other was a big man. He gripped her arm.'

She's been taken, Justine said to herself. The poor darling, the bastards have taken her. Why? It must be to do with Bao. Somehow he's found something out. He thinks she's double-crossing him. A feeling of guilt spread through Justine. It was her fault. Where was Ka? What were they doing to her?

If it is Bao, then they'll be at the rue du Bac, thought Justine. Ka spoke about the convent next to Bao's place, the nuns singing could be heard, she said. Must go there, she decided, not knowing what she would do when she arrived. Before leaving, she found a knife in the kitchen, just in case.

⸱⸱⸱⸱⸱⸱⸱⸱⸱

It was almost dark, and Justine walked the fifteen minutes to the rue du Bac. That's where Ka said she met Bao. If he was behind Ka's disappearance, then that was likely to be where she was. Arriving at the convent, she heard the nuns singing from the inside, just as Ka described. The building next door to the convent, an old dilapidated block. There it was. Could she get in through the back? There must be access for collecting *les ordures*, where the garbage collectors went in. Justine found her way down to the first road across the street, turned right, and worked her way back up an alley until she reached the rear of the building. Assisted by the fading light, she would climb up over the wall and drop into the rear yard of the building.

Using a street lamp, by pressing herself against it as she climbed, Justine made the three metres or so upwards to the top, and let herself down the other side. In front of her was the rear door. She paused a moment to regain her breath and wipe her hands. She then felt for the door handle. Not locked and, once inside, she saw a staircase. If Ka was here, what floor was she on? Or maybe the basement.

Waiting to regain her composure, Justine leant against the inside wall. Something made her remain still and silent. Was it a sound? What was that? Now she could make out a door leading downwards. Opening that, she heard the sound again. A sort of cry, dull, muted. Could be her, below.

She took the steps down as a cat would descend a staircase, one foot slowly and lightly after the other. Feeling the knife in her raincoat pocket, all her senses were focused on what was to come next. Not unlike the double-bladed knife she was trained to use at Arisaig. What was it that man Fairbairn said? 'Go for the vulnerable points, the abdominal region is the principal target. Cut an opening in the clothing so you can reach that region. Before that, slash across face, hands, wrist and fore-arms. Or fling gravel, a stone, a hat, a handkerchief, etc, in the opponent's face. That will cause him to raise his hands.'

Another noise, a sloshing noise, then a whimper. How many of them were there? First, she must take a look. A sliding panel in that door over there, like in a prison. Very carefully, now, do it all in complete silence. The panel in the door slid open. There, what was that? A bucket of water. Oh God, the brute was holding Ka by her hair. Only a couple of metres away from the door. Holding her head down in a large bucket of water, half drowning her.

Justine's thoughts raced. She can't wait. Any delay and it could be the end for Ka. Must act now. Would the door open?

Yes. No sign of anyone else. The rule she was taught above all others at Arisaig. Kill the enemy, don't try and wound, remember you are at war. Otherwise it could be you who is killed.

Justine took some deep breaths, judging the time it would take her, checking there was nothing in the way. It happened all in one movement. The door burst open and she was in. The Corsican swung around, dropping Ka's head. Too late to defend himself. Justine was at him already. The blade slashed upwards from chin to forehead. His hands rose to his face. In a sweeping motion, the blade circled down and was thrust into the abdomen, just above the belt. Once in, the blade turned and worked in and around the soft tissue. A fountain of blood pumped out by the body's circulatory system.

He would be dead in a minute, but she wasn't going to wait. Justine wiped the knife in the bucket as her other arm swept up Ka and wrenched her out through the door. Getting Ka over the wall might have been a problem, but by then the adrenalin was pumping through Justine's body. Back in the alley in no time, Ka was wrapped in the raincoat and in her arms. The bistro nearby seemed the obvious place, she'd marked it down earlier.

The waiter looked surprised and started to make a remark that it wasn't a hospital, when he felt the notes in his hand. They were guided towards a washroom. The door locked, Justine set about bringing Ka back to life. In a few minutes she was talking, holding onto Justine as hard as she could. White as a sheet, clearly nothing left inside her, Ka managed to take in some food.

A taxi pulled up outside and Justine had the waiter hold it up. Directing the driver to head for Ka's apartment, they lay back in the cushions and said nothing to one another.

17

'Justine, you saved me. I was almost done for. That brutal man, he kept asking me the same question.'

'What question, Ka?' Justine was making an omelette in the hope Ka would eat sensibly.

'Who was I working with to supply opium to clients in Paris? Who was finding the opium, where it was coming from?'

'So you were covering up for me.'

'Yes, Justine. I would never give you away to bastards like that.'

'You suffered for me.' Justine took Ka in her arms. 'How long for?'

'He kept on. Time after time. You killed him, Justine. Straight away. Deadly. All that blood. How did you do it?'

'The same way as in war. He was the enemy. You don't try and wound someone who can fight again. You kill him.'

Ka was silent.

Justine continued. 'On the way to the rue du Bac, I knew what I was going to do, something irrecoverable. I knew if I did it, I wouldn't be the same person again. I thought of going to the police. It was the time, the urgency which made me decide to do it. Your life was threatened. I don't know what that makes me. Am I a murderer?'

'You were right,' said Ka. 'Thank God you did it. I wouldn't have lived. God was on your side when you needed him.'

'I should have come earlier, instead of going to a political meeting. How selfish could I be?'

There was silence for a bit. Justine fought back her emotion. It was as she'd just said. She'd done something that would change her life. She was now a killer.

Back home, Ka looked at herself in the mirror. 'Oh, dear Lord, look at the mess I'm in. What are we going to do, Justine? Will the police find us?' Then, suddenly remembering, 'The knife?'

'Okay, I have it here,' said Justine, pulling the knife out of her bag. 'I rinsed it in the bucket. I'll wash it properly now and put it back in your kitchen drawer.'

'Thank God for that.'

'Try not to worry, Ka. I can't see how the police can link the death of the Corsican to us.'

A silence. Then Ka said, 'I hope you're right. What about Bao? It happened in his building. He must have sent the men. He'll be after me. Clearly, he knows something.'

'I was thinking about that,' said Justine. 'Asking myself, who knows about our project? There's Glun.' She paused, 'And Madame X.'

Ka looked startled. 'If it's Madame X, she'll have exposed you as well as me.'

'Can't be her. Why would she?' Justine thought about Jean. Why should he tell Bao? She wasn't going to mention Jean to Ka. 'Here, let me help you clean yourself up.'

She helped Ka off with her clothes, turned on the shower. Took her own clothes off, stepping in with her. 'I'm going to soap you all over. Stand still, enjoy it, my poor darling.'

Afterwards, Ka made coffee and cut a baguette up the middle and toasted the two sides on the grill. They sat together in towels, on the sofa, eating their tartines.

'We should go on working at Schiap as though nothing has happened,' Justine said. 'Let me stay here for a few days. I'll follow you to work, and follow you back again, at a distance. To check you aren't being followed.'

'That's lovely of you. You're wonderful,' she said as she pulled Justine towards her.

'What is Bao going to do?' whispered Ka.

'What can he do? He won't go to the police. He'll get rid of the body.'

'What about the clients I'm supplying opium to?'

'You can turn some away. Say you can't get it any more, or ...' They both said it together. 'We can supply them with ours.'

Silence. Justine then said, 'The first shipment arrives in Marseille end of next week.' As she spoke, she was suddenly gripped by the shock of it all, the words hammering her mind. I've crossed a bridge. Importing opium, does that make me a criminal? Smoking it isn't against French law. Killing someone, that's certainly criminal. But when you are saving someone's life?

18

The train went on and on. First to Lyon, then on to Marseille. They sat together, all day. The bill of lading in Justine's bag. Just present it to the shipping company. Shantung silk for the House of Schiaparelli.

At the warehouse down in the port, there it was, all beautifully wrapped. They would separate out the raw opium afterwards. It must be broken down into small quantities. Glun's friends in Paris knew where to go, where the crude opium could be boiled to separate out the impurities.

The pipeline was starting to flow. For how long, wondered Justine. Long enough to make a stack of money. They were all in it together now. Could she trust Jean? She would give him a large reward for setting up the shipping arrangements in Saigon. If she became worried she was in trouble, she would fall back on Jean for protection. She must trust him.

On the journey back to Paris, the merchandise in a large suitcase they'd brought with them, she thought about her entry into politics. She must prioritise her objectives. Top of the list was power. The power to do what she knew must be done in France. It must be a party committed to divert state funds away from wars, to help the destitute. René Pleven was not right for her. He was anti-Communist, fine, but he was for holding on to the colonies in south-east Asia.

She knew she must meet Mendès France. His Radical Socialist Party wasn't her ultimate solution, but he alone among powerful people in Parliament had the courage to call for a stop to the war in Indochina. She knew Pierre Mendès France was born Jewish, like herself, and served as Finance Minister in her hero Léon Blum's Front Populaire government in the thirties. Having joined the French air force, he was imprisoned by the Vichy authorities but escaped to join the Free French in '41. He wanted France to give up its colonies and withdraw from the war in Vietnam. How could she reach him?

It came to her as the train entered Lyon station and she looked at the indicator board. A train to Strasbourg was about to depart. It suddenly came to her. Baron Philippe, whom she'd met on her arrival in London with Françoise. Both Rothschild and Mendès France were prominent in the Jewish community in France, they must know one another. Baron Philippe just gave her his card when at Schiap with his friend Pauline the other day. She knew he'd lost his wife during the war, taken by the Gestapo while he was in London. She'd died in Ravensbrück. He said he'd love to see Justine again.

Paris, Place du Tertre

Justine decided to look really smart for the occasion. Not to overdress, but why not take advantage of that very useful mannequin perk at Schiap, borrowing an outfit from the house. After all this was a grand occasion in her book. Dinner with a senior member of perhaps the world's greatest banking family, and with a potential prime minister of France. Surprisingly, the restaurant sounded simple, in Montmartre. The answer? An on-the-shoulder dress in dark blue shantung silk with a bow at the tight waist, and long flared skirt. With her auburn hair specially coiffed by the in-house hairdresser, she looked a million dollars.

There was no maître d' to meet her at the door, just a friendly waiter who took her cape and showed her to a corner table where the two great men sat. Both stood up as she approached, Baron Philippe coming forward and embracing her. He turned to introduce Pierre Mendès France, short in stature, with a lovely friendly smile on his rather moonlike face and dark features. They invited her to sit between them at the round table.

'Pierre can't be seen dining at Maxim's,' said Baron Philippe, jibing at Mendès France for his left-wing politics. 'So I decided we should try a simple kosher place.'

The owner hurried towards them and further introductions were made.

'It's wonderful you got in touch, Justine,' said Baron Philippe. 'Watching you enter this room was a feast in itself.'

'Well, entering a room the right way is all part of a manne-quin's trade, Monsieur le Baron. Thank you for inviting me here and,' she looked sideways at the other man, 'making it possible to meet you, Monsieur.'

'I'm so pleased your parents are back in Bordeaux,' Baron Philippe said to Justine, 'And in the wine business again.'

That really pleased her, that he remembered her parents' move to England as the Gestapo were closing in on them. The British secret service saw to that, after Justine's escape from Drancy. 'Yes, thanks to you,' she said. 'My parents were German Jews,' she said, turning to the political leader. 'And, Monsieur le Baron, you were wonderful when we met in the Vosges just before the end, flying into that maquis camp in your own aircraft.'

Mendès France broke into the exchange. 'Philippe told me about the terrible time you had, Mademoiselle. Ending in your escape from the Natzweiler-Struthof camp, near Strasbourg.'

The waiter arrived. Justine noticed Baron Philippe go straight to the wine list, no doubt to ensure that Château Mouton was there.

Mendès France turned back to Justine after they'd chosen from the menu. 'Mademoiselle Justine, Philippe tells me you want to enter politics.'

'Yes, sir.' She paused, thinking how best to put it. 'My mission in life now is to help make France a fairer country. Five years after the war ended, many people remain on the edge of destitution. We must house them properly, educate their children, if this country is to have a future.'

'How right you are. And we can do it without becoming Communists.' He sat back while the waiter placed a plate of foie gras in the middle of the table, and a basket of small brioches. 'Did you know the Jews brought foie gras to the north of France? It was because goose fat was more acceptable to their dietary rules.'

Justine saw Baron Philippe look hard at the Sauterne bottle as the wine waiter poured it for him to taste, and seemed satisfied at the Château Rieussec label.

'I am an admirer of Léon Blum,' Justine threw in.

'Ah,' said Mendès France, 'so am I. He had a bad time, locked up by Laval and his thugs. I was in his Front Populaire government, until our support of the Republicans in the Spanish Civil War caused us to be voted out of power.'

Baron Philippe interjected. 'This Fourth Republic is as bad as the Third was. Seems to work against continuity in government. All this dealing in coalitions. De Gaulle's hand was forced after the war ended because of the strength of the Communist vote. He actually brought them into coalition. The president should be given more power to appoint governments, and keep them in place for the term.'

Silence for a bit while they enjoyed their food. Then Mendès France asked Justine, 'What do you think about Indochina?'

'A disaster, so many dying. I don't see how we can win, whatever you believe about holding on to the colonies. The cost is enormous, and is starving France of funds. Funds which could work magic in this country.'

'You could join my Radical Party,' Mendès France said suddenly. 'You'd need to stand for the National Assembly, become a deputy. We must have more women with ambition in the Assembly.'

'At present, I belong to the Peace and Liberty movement,' said Justine. 'We have to push back against the Communists.'

'Indeed. Yet to form a government, my Radical Socialists party might have to admit the Communists into coalition. What do you think about that?'

Justine thought for a moment. 'If it's the only way to gain power, then it would be a means to an end.'

'I don't like the sound of that,' said Baron Philippe.

'I didn't think you would,' said Mendès France. 'My advice to Justine is to stand for the Assembly on a Radical Party ticket. Then we will see, once you're elected.'

She felt enthused by Mendès France's words.

He added, 'Becoming a deputy requires some money, for campaigning. The Radical Party has limited resources. Do you have any personal wealth, Justine?'

'I have some,' she replied. 'Mannequins are paid almost nothing, and I don't have a rich boyfriend or patron.'

Baron Philippe looked as though he was going to choke. 'If you were right wing, I might be able to help,' he said jokingly.

'No chance,' said Justine. 'Anyway, since I get paid next to nothing at Schiap, there's little to lose if I quit. I do have some income from elsewhere,' she muttered, rather obliquely.

'Good,' remarked Pierre Mendès France. 'I like your enthusiasm for my kind of socialism. I would give it a go, as long as you realise that campaigning is hard toil, and often ends in disappointment. I'll put you in touch with the person who runs candidate selection. All being well, you could be chosen to represent the Radicals in the next Assembly elections. But don't burn your boats in the fashion world until you have to. It can be very disillusioning to work hard for election and then fail by a few votes and find yourself without a job.'

Justine understood the danger inherent in standing for election to the Assembly, and then failing to make it. One couldn't do one's regular job whilst at the same time campaigning seriously. And that was the only way to stand any chance of success. Her mind was made up. She must prepare herself carefully for the interview. If successful, she hoped she would have at least six months to get to know her prospective constituency before an election to the Assembly was called. She must approach Schiap now for leave of absence when the time came. She just hoped they would understand and allow her the time off. She would approach Giselle who was the most understanding, and as *premiére main* had the power to make her own rules.

Paris, Pigalle

Justine found the theatre. After the lunch with Mendès France, she remembered one piece of his advice she could act on now. 'Start building up a team of supporters and helpers. You can hit the ground running when you are selected as a candidate and know what constituency you will be fighting, what arrondissement to concentrate on.'

The main doors were locked and barricaded, so Justine went round to the rear and found the stage entrance. An old man was inside the guichet smoking, and she asked whether Josephine Baker was there. Learning that she was in rehearsal, she asked for a message to be given to her.

It took nearly an hour but then Josephine came flying out and embraced Justine. 'So sorry you've been made to wait. This place is a tragedy. It was built in the twenties by Baron Philippe de Rothschild as the most modern theatre in the world, and it's just been closed. Sign of the times, there's no money anywhere right now,' said Josephine. 'Some of us still use it for rehearsals. How did you know you'd find me here?'

'I just lunched with Baron Philippe,' said Justine to an astonished Josephine. 'I met him in London during the war. He invited me out to meet Pierre Mendès France. I have political ambitions, but that's off the record, my dear.'

'Of course, Justine. I'm intrigued, though.'

'Well, strangely, that's why I wanted to talk to you. I've been thinking about it since we met in Saigon. Where can we go for a bit of privacy?'

'Straight back inside the Théâtre, I would say. It's like a tomb.'

Once inside they headed for the auditorium and sat down in a loge. 'All to ourselves,' said Josephine. 'What is it you need help with?'

'It's to do with my entry into politics,' said Justine. She went on to explain first her motives for this change in career, and then the canvassing work a candidate must perform after being selected and the helpers she would need for door-to-door surveys, leaflet dropping and fund raising.

'I think the same way as you do,' was Josephine's response. 'Someone has to take a lead and shake up the Assembly. I'm with you all the way. They treat me like a star, but I love the ordinary people. Like you, I grieve for those who have nothing.'

'Oh, Josephine, that's wonderful of you. I've been invited to apply to be a candidate for the Radical Socialist Party. If I'm accepted, I'm going to start work straight away. That will mean taking a few months off modelling, so I can become known in my constituency. Then, when the next general election is announced, I will have built up my team and can start campaigning effectively from day one.'

'That sounds exciting, Justine. What can I do to help?'

'I'll find a small office as a base for myself and helpers. If you could drop in now and then, it would help morale. You can have a real impact when official campaigning starts. If you agree, my idea is that at large campaign events, you would introduce me to the public. They all know who you are, and love you. Having you up front on my side would have a great impact.'

'Oh, yes. Count me in. I'm all for that. We'll do it together, Justine, and we'll win.'

19

Leo Beckendorf looked up from his research in the Academy's library, and then jumped to his feet and saluted. Commandant Trinquier was known to most of the cadets at St Cyr, from lectures on his exploits in China during the Second World War to airborne operations in Indochina.

'Aspirant Beckendorf,' Trinquier said as he lowered himself into a chair at a small round table nearby. 'Could I take a moment of your time.'

'Certainly, sir,' replied Leo, joining the other at the table.

'Aspirant Beckendorf, I have studied your background and the affinity you have for intelligence. You know Indochina well, and must recognise the importance of our listening posts in Tonkin in particular. The signals intelligence being generated now is much improved. It is evident also that the Viets are now listening to our signals.'

'Yes, sir, I have noticed the improvement on both sides.'

'General de Lattre wants the army to change the way it engages with the enemy. He is forcing us to accept that new techniques must be introduced. I've been working on these.'

'Can't be easy to convince your senior colleagues to change their ways,' said Leo.

Trinquier nodded. 'I've convinced them, at least for the moment. My plan is to create an airborne commando group with the mission of attacking the Viets using guerrilla methods similar to what they themselves employ. It's to be called *Groupement de Commandos Mixtes Aéroportés*, or GCMA.'

Leo was listening hard. His man was on the right track. 'That sounds interesting, sir. I'm convinced we need to change from trying to draw General Giap into set piece battles that just result in our units arriving too late to engage with the enemy before they melt away into the jungle,' said Leo.

'Precisely.' Trinquier paused. 'You have nearly finished the special shortened course here, and will be returning to your unit in the Legion paras. I hear that in addition to combat duties, you be will be specialising in signals intelligence in conjunction with the Deuxième Bureau.'

'That's right, sir. '

'Lieutenant Beckendorf, and I say Lieutenant because you're on the point of receiving your commission, I'd like you to work also with me in the GCMA, my airborne commando group.' He paused, and Leo waited. 'I'd like to talk you through what I'm intending. Would you be free to dine with me, tonight perhaps?'

'Yes, certainly, sir,' said Leo, intrigued by what Trinquier was proposing.

'There's an excellent family restaurant in Rennes, where they know how to cook fish as good as you'd find anywhere. We'll be able to speak freely about the way forward in Indochina, and hopefully you'll be able to give me your views. Thanks to General de Lattre, there's a step change coming in how the French army hits back against Ho Chi Minh.'

⊶⊷

Leo knew he was in for something exceptional as he looked around the restaurant of the Taverne de la Marine. The two of them were in civilian clothes, but from their haircuts, if nothing else, few would have doubted where they were from. The Patron welcomed Roger Trinquier as Mon Commandant, proposing a kir royal while they chose from the handwritten menus.

'As you can imagine, Lieutenant, being close to the Atlantic coast, we can enjoy fish one can only dream of in Saigon,' Trinquier said as he perused the menu. 'I chose the turbot last time, and you couldn't do better.'

'Thank you, sir,' said Leo. I always try to take advice from an expert. And on matters concerning food, as a German listening to a Frenchman, that goes without saying.'

'I heard from my colleagues that you're about to become a Frenchman,' Trinquier suddenly said.

'That's correct. Both my parents died in an air raid just before the war ended, and I was their only child. The sole occupation I am trained for is soldiering, not much use in Germany right now. With the offer of a commission in the French army, it makes sense to change nationalities.'

'Bravo, that's all I can say,' said Trinquier, raising his glass.

They decided to start with a warm paté de foie with brioche, the Patron filling their glasses with Château Rieussec Sauterne.

The arrival of the turbot was an event. Grilled fillets, vivid white under the crisp skin, served on celeriac with a sauce of crevettes. And a Chablis from a top domaine.

At Trinquier's suggestion, Leo talked about his time in the French Foreign Legion, giving his impressions on how a mix of nationalities can be welded into a true band of brothers. How, probably more than in any other military formation, the legionnaires lived, fought and died for their regiment rather than for the French Republic to which the Legion bore allegiance. Only the officers were French, chosen from the top quartile of successful cadets completing St Cyr.

As they finished the soufflé au Grand Marnier which followed, Leo saw the Patron approaching the table with a bottle of old Calvados and two balloon glasses. These he placed on the table, along with a box of Havana cigars. Now for the academic part of the evening, thought Leo.

'Forgive me for asking, Lieutenant, do you have a wife or any important relationship in your life? Not because you would be asked to volunteer for suicide missions like on the RC4, but one never knows.'

Leo put down the glass of Calvados he was about to taste. That was not what he expected to be asked.

'Well, I'm not married. But there is someone important who just re-entered my life.'

'That sounds interesting. You don't have to tell me the detail.'

Leo didn't see why he shouldn't recount the saga. 'She was a Luftwaffe nurse. We met on an airfield in the Libyan desert. Her name's Theresa. She volunteered for front line duty during the first battle on the Alamein line. I was a Fallschirmjäger, of course. We ended up at Cassino, but were then split up.'

'How did you meet up again?'

Leo paused. After all, it was an extraordinary story. 'She was in Paris right after the war, and saw an advertisement saying the French Foreign Legion was looking for nurses to go to Indochina.'

'Did she know you were signing up with the Legion?' said Trinquier, asking the awkward question.

Silence. What could Leo say? 'Oh, I like to think so.' And they both laughed.

Leo continued. 'We ran into one another again in Saigon. She wasn't amused when I told her I was about to go back to France for the course here. Threatened to volunteer to become a *convoyeuse*. You know, flying into war zones to bring out the wounded. I told her not to.'

'Bloody dodgy,' said Trinquier.

'Exactly. But I wouldn't be surprised if she went straight off and did just that. She's a very determined girl.'

'Anyway,' said Trinquier, bringing the conversation down to earth. 'I want to explain my thinking. Let's start with the maquis.'

'Maquis as in France in World War Two?' said Leo, surprised.

'Yes. I'm proposing two strategies. First, to win the tribes in the Tonkin Highlands over to us, rather than have them helping the Viets. Second, to train them in sabotage, and to cooperate with regular units on say escape routes. And, importantly, to provide intelligence.'

'How on earth do you achieve all that, sir?'

'Some tribes are traditionally anti the Viets. Others we have to induce by cash, sometimes gold.'

'How do you make contact with the friendly tribesmen?' Leo tried not to appear sceptical.

Trinquier continued. 'I've done some test flights over groups of Montagnards in a light plane, aiming for a friendly reaction. Like if they show the French flag, I land and have a chat with the chief. If they shoot at me, I make a note of the coordinates, and fly on.'

'I see,' said Leo. 'And how would you train them to become guerrilla fighters?'

'We'd fly them down to Saigon and the Commando training camp at Cap Saint-Jacques.'

There was silence, before Leo said, 'I've heard something about the opium traffic involving the Montagnards.'

'You have your own sources of information, Lieutenant. Yes, the opium traffic must be swung over to us. This year the Viets purchased the opium crop and sold it in Bangkok. Substantial profits were made and used to buy Chinese and Russian arms. That must not happen next year.'

The conversation lulled as they drew on their cigars. Leo felt the Calvados having its effect. Thank God the driver and jeep were coming back for them.

'So, Lieutenant, there's a lot more to discuss. Are you interested? I think you'll see that intelligence is going to be an essential part of my plan. Would you like to meet again when you get back to Hanoi?'

Leo liked what he heard. 'Yes, I'm certainly interested. When do you return to Indochina?'

'In Saigon the end of next week,' said Trinquier. I will head straight for the north, and contact you when you're back. My plan has just been approved by General de Lattre de Tassigny.'

20

So, six months more waiting. After all, she waited six years and then sailed round the world to find him again. Theresa lay in the hammock as it swung gently on the lawn behind the staff rest quarters. She must accept it, so much better than not knowing where Leo was. Gone to St Cyr, all that distance away. At last she knew their relationship could be renewed in spite of six years of separation. A miracle after all, his affections could so easily have moved on.

'Hello, Theresa, you are in a dreamland.' It was Denise, only just recovered from the shock of her friend's sudden romance with the German parachutist. 'Must be devastating for you to lose him to France after so little time together.'

The beast, thought Theresa, she has that infuriating talent of saying just what her friend didn't want to hear, and at the worst time. Why should Theresa tell her she'd been with Leo in Libya and Italy during the war. After all, she was now a French national. Krüger might be a German name, so what. Her French carried no accent you would notice.

'I'll live through it, just hope he isn't seduced by some local slut.'

'More likely to be the wife of an officer on the staff of the college,' said Denise, with a laugh.

'Denise, lay off. I'd concentrate on that Legion Lieutenant, the one a few years younger than you. You could tie him in knots.'

The bell went for their mess dinner. Justine's mind moved on to the months ahead. Now they were up in the north, she was really keen to be put on flying duties.

'Please come in and join us, Nurse Krüger.' Theresa shook hands with the French air force colonel. And also with the army medical officer seated beside him.

'You have volunteered for the casualty evacuation flights, Mademoiselle. We just want to ask you a few questions.'

'Certainly, sir,' Theresa responded.

The air force colonel glanced at his notes. 'Did you fly in ambulance aircraft at all in your duties with the Luftwaffe during the last war?'

'No, not flying. I did serve at front line dressing stations in summer 1942 on the Libya/Egypt border, when we were short of male nurses on the Alamein line. It was rare for the wounded to be flown out, sir.'

'As you know, we're looking for experienced battlefield nurses to fly in the Dakotas which transfer the wounded from forward airstrips to the base hospitals, Mademoiselle Krüger.' It was now the medical officer speaking. 'It's hazardous work, we already know how capable you are, but must be assured you know what risks you would be taking.'

Theresa's memory flashed back to that day in Benghazi when she was being questioned after volunteering for transfer to forward dressing stations on the Alamein front. Act normally, don't draw attention to yourself, that was the advice after she'd secretly changed her identity, back in Munich. Before, she was Jewish and a nurse called Elisabeth. Then she took on the identity of the dying nun, to become Theresa Krüger.

They were watching her closely. Theresa drew herself up, saying what just came to her. 'I know it'll be risky. But it will take me into where the action is. It's frustrating to try and help your patients when you've no idea what the front line is like.' Even though I enjoy speaking German to the ex-Fallschirmjäger in the Legion parachute battalions, she was about to say but thought the better of it.

'Very good, then.' The colonel was smiling. 'You are appointed *convoyeuse de l'air*. Congratulations.'

The C47 Dakota, jack of all trades, was rapidly becoming her new home. Passengers, freight, airborne drops, now medical evacuation plane, medivac as the Americans called it.

The medical officer moved around the interior now transformed into its new purpose. Stretchers lashed to the bulkhead. Blood transfusion equipment. Racks for the morphine, penicillin and other drugs, and bandages. At the far end, a table and lights for emergency treatment while in flight.

'Get ready to feel sick as hell,' she remembered the MO saying early in the flight. 'The weather up here in the Tonkin Highlands throws the Dakota around. One just has to live with it. Hopefully, the pills we've given you will help. If you're sitting strapped in, stare out of the window at the line of the horizon, that helps.'

Justine was on her fourth flight, this one for real. The landing was to be close by Hoa Binh. The MO's voice called out, 'Hang on tight, keep strapped in, we're in the battle zone. The pilot will take her down like an elevator, to cut the time the enemy flak has to knock us out.'

She looked down and saw the Black River winding its way down from the north-west Highlands towards the south.

There were bursts of flak on either side of the aircraft. Then the wheels hit the ground and they were rolling over the hard packed surface towards a shed alongside a small control tower. There were the ambulances already lining up, stretchers being slid out by the orderlies.

This was it, she felt the excitement coursing through her. Leo didn't want her to take it on. Too bad, from where he was he couldn't stop her. These were his pals, his men shot up. They must be got back to hospital, to give them a chance.

'Everyone out,' the MO called out. 'Give those legionnaires over there a hand to load up the wounded.'

A voice called out to her, 'You speak German, don't you, Fräulein.' It was a legionnaire NCO. How did he know? Anyway, she must get over to him and the wounded legionnaire he was standing alongside. 'Hit in the chest, coughing blood,' the NCO said as she arrived beside him. 'He's a Fallschirmjäger.'

Theresa grabbed the other end of the stretcher and the two of them rushed the wounded paratrooper towards the Dakota. Only as helping hands leant out the side door in the fuselage, did she realise the ground under her feet was shaking from enemy mortar bombs landing around them.

'Two minutes to take off,' an American voice shouted from a face leaning out of the cockpit.

Theresa went back to help two walking wounded lurching towards the plane, one with head bandaged over an eye, the other wobbling forward on crutches. On board, and the fuselage door slammed shut, engines roaring as the Dakota turned into the wind and started to roll down the rough runway. The voice from the first stretcher case said to her in German, 'They told us at the briefing this trip to the Highlands wouldn't be a ski holiday. Someone still said Alles Gute! Hals- und Beinbruch! like us Germans say to one another when a friend is off on a ski holiday.' He paused for breath, then adding in a hoarse whisper, 'I've broken something deeper inside me, Fräulein.'

She squeezed his hand, and didn't let go.

21

Now a Frenchman and Lieutenant in the French army, Leo's first action on arrival back from St Cyr, was to try and reach Theresa. The address he was given by the Legion's personnel office was for nurses serving on the medivac flights operating out of Hanoi, confirming his worst fears. Against his strong advice, she'd gone off and become a *convoyeuse*.

The line wasn't good even though he was also in Hanoi. He decided to tread carefully. 'Theresa, it's me Leo. How are you managing?'

'Oh, Leo. I was giving up hope you would call. Where are you?' Loud static on the line. 'Where? Hanoi, thank heavens, so am I.'

'I know, the Legion's personnel people told me.' A pause. 'Look here, I have a week's leave to settle in, let's spend a few days together somewhere. Can you get the time off?'

The voice from the other end seemed to leap out of the phone. 'That would be wonderful. It may only be three or four days. I always wanted to see Halong Bay.'

'Yes, super idea. We could get an army truck down to Haiphong. Call me later, when you know. Oh and, Theresa, I love you.'

Silence a moment at the other end. Then, 'Leo, darling, I love you too.'

The truck wasn't as uncomfortable as he'd feared, particularly with Theresa close beside him. He avoided asking the obvious, why she'd become a *convoyeuse*, exactly what he'd told her not to do. He worked out that she must be the one to talk about it first. When she did, he tried to understand, though her descriptions of some of the flights into war zones confirmed his worst fears. He was fighting his inclination to say, 'I warned you.'

At least there was his commission for them to celebrate, although changing his nationality took some explaining. He couldn't think why, since she'd also changed hers.

'So, what next, French paratrooper?' she asked.

He said he'd have to be ready to take up his new intelligence duties very soon, and talked about his discussions at St Cyr with Colonel Trinquier whose GCMA Commando group reflected that the army was re-thinking its tactics against the Viets.

'Is that stuff secret?' Theresa asked.

'No, but best not to announce it in front of Vietnamese waiters,' he laughed. 'And never quote me.'

'I'm not an idiot, Leo,' she laughed back.

The magnetism between the two of them was out in the open. Leo knew a time would come, not far away, when he should talk to Theresa about the future. This wasn't the moment, but he loved her and wanted to share that future with her, whatever it turned out to be.

The next day a message came through from Roger Trinquier. Would he please join the Commandant up in the north for a short induction into the new GCMA Commando group. The proposal was that they would fly into the Highlands so Leo could learn something of the mission to create maquis among the Montagnards.

⊷⊜⊶

Trinquier looked up as Leo entered the briefing room at the military airfield close to Hanoi. 'Lieutenant, welcome back, so pleased you could join me for a couple of days. Meet Captain Nicolas Martin who is going to fly us. Nicolas is air force liaison officer attached to the GCMA.' Everyone shook hands.

'Let me summarise what we've discovered so far,' Trinquier said, as they stared down at the map table. 'The small areas in blue indicate groups of Montagnards responding favourably to our proposals. Where the green crosses appear alongside, these groups have sent men to the GCMA training camp down south at Cap St Jacques.'

'How do you transport the recruits from the villages?' asked Leo.

'By light aircraft to the nearest airfield open to C47 landings,' replied the air force officer. 'Then by Dakota to Saigon.'

Trinquier continued. 'The unmarked areas are largely unknown territory. Where the red flags appear, that's where we've identified a Viet military presence.' He paused, looking up at Leo. 'Lieutenant, the challenge will be to create concentrations of trained Montagnards in areas where our regular forces are likely to operate.'

'And what will be their role?' asked Leo.

'They'll provide support for our units during active engagement with the enemy,' said Trinquier, 'And create escape lines. For example, after an attack by a *groupe mobile* on a Viet concentration, when the time comes for the mobile column to withdraw. They will give covering fire and act as guides.'

Kitted out with light arms, field glasses and supplies, the three of them went out onto the airfield.

'Brand new, first of its kind in Indochina,' said Trinquier as they walked over to the observation aircraft. 'The MH 152 Broussard, can carry five passengers. Usually I fly in the two seater Morane but with you here, I have the excuse to grab the Broussard for a couple of days.'

Nicolas commented, 'In spite of being larger than the Morane, it can land in less than two hundred metres, and has a range of a thousand kilometres.'

⋯⊷⊙⊷⋯

As the plane droned over high hill country and what looked like impenetrable jungle, Trinquier shouted out to Leo. 'I heard last night that Bernard de Lattre has been killed.'

Leo said nothing, clearly shocked at this news of the young officer he liked and admired.

'He was leading his platoon of South Vietnamese troops in a defensive action in the Red River Delta where General Giap is attempting to cut off routes to Hanoi.'

'I met Bernard de Lattre,' said Leo. 'Bold and committed, he was. A credit to his father, Big John.'

'And what a father,' said Trinquier. 'He's transformed our effectiveness since he took over as Commander-in-Chief. The death of his son will devastate him. They lived for one another.'

The air force officer was taking the plane down towards a clearing, and villagers were already waving up at them. 'That's the sign we want,' said Trinquier as a couple of *tricolores* showed below.

'Hold on tight,' said Nicolas, 'This strip's a rough one.'

How right you are, thought Leo, as the plane lurched and shuddered, then bumped to a halt.

The Montagnard in charge showed them to a long single-storey building constructed in bamboo, with thatched roofing. Leo was introduced to everyone. After an exchange of news, the Montagnard turned to Trinquier. 'Monsieur Savani was here last week. He wanted help with his opium supplies. He's offering gold for next year's crop.'

'If he has gold to hand out, take it while the offer lasts,' said Trinquier. 'One way or the other, we must stop Ho and Giap increasing their arms purchases by taking control of the opium poppy growing'.

'He says Ho Chi Minh tries to pay in piastres which his people have printed in China.'

'I wouldn't put my savings into those,' said Trinquier.

Supplies were handed over, and a simple meal offered during which plans were discussed for the next batch of trainees to be sent to Saigon and Cap St Jacques.

Back in the air, Trinquier pointed out a number of other settlements and identified them on the map as friendly or otherwise. 'We try to concentrate on areas likely to be the focus of future military activity. Aside from the formation of maquis, it's important to know who will be friendly when our forces are passing through,' said Trinquier.

'I guess that's where I can help,' said Leo. I'll be sure to feed you with intelligence on our planned troop movements. A friendly reception from the locals will be a big boost for morale.'

22

Paris, 13th arrondissement, September 1951

Justine smiled across at Glun and Ka. 'So, the pipeline's flowing,' she said, pouring rouge from the wine bottle. 'No champagne until we're sure of a profit, and it's in the bank.' Laughter from them all.

'Well done, Glun,' said Ka.

'That's the good news,' said Glun. 'The bad is that while I was away, you were attacked here in Paris, Ka.'

'I've been thinking a lot about that,' said Ka. 'You know, Bao may just have wanted to warn me.'

'He nearly killed you,' said Justine.

'He doesn't take prisoners. He's a violent man.'

'Maybe we should persuade him you didn't double-cross him,' said Justine. 'Let me give it some thought.'

I must brief Jean, thought Justine, and pick his brains.

St Germain des Prés

There he was, always at the same table. You wouldn't have thought we were in Saigon the other day, Justine said to herself as she crossed the floor and dropped down beside him.

'Jean, thanks for getting here so early. I just wanted a chat before work.'

'You did well in Saigon, pulling the threads together. I heard the first two shipments arrived.'

'Yes, Glun was good to his word, and Bill did his stuff.' Turning to the waiter, she said, 'Café crème s'il vous plaît.' Her hand moved across to Jean's plate as she stole a small piece of his croissant. Looking at him with a serious face, she said, 'Something happened to Ka, just as I got back to Paris.'

'Is she okay?' he asked, not having met Ka but aware she was close to Justine and part of the team.

'Yes. Let me tell you about it.' Justine recounted the story, only omitting how she'd dealt with the Corsican.

'Remarkable, I won't ask what you did to the brute trying to drown her,' whispered Jean, almost to himself. He added, 'That raises the question as to this guy Bao's motive in putting these thugs on Ka.'

'Yes,' said Justine. 'She and I just met with Glun. We want to find out. They still don't know about you, but I thought you might have some ideas. We thought maybe we should trick Bao into believing that she wasn't double-crossing him?'

'I already made some inquiries with my friends in the Sûreté, after you told me about him and Ka at our last meeting here, before we left for Saigon.'

'Oh, that's some foresight, Jean,' she joked.

'Well, he's Vietnamese, as you know. Originally from Cochin China as it was called, around Saigon. From the river pirates community. That means his opium comes from the *Binh Xuyên*. I doubt if he would have risked killing Ka, no reason to. More likely he wanted to put the frighteners on her. Perhaps his thugs were more clumsy than he intended.'

Justine didn't respond immediately. Her mind was on the Corsican. She'd killed him in her anger. The easy way to rescue Ka, the person she loved. What did that make her? Finally, she muttered, 'I suppose that's reassuring.'

David Longridge

As if penetrating her mind, Jean said, 'Can I ask you something about yourself, Mademoiselle?'

She looked at him sharply. 'Depends what you want to know about. I never speak about the past.'

'It's the future I want to talk about,' he retorted. 'I heard that you have political ambitions.'

'Oh, that,' she said, almost relieved. 'Well, I do, although as a means to an end.'

'That's interesting.'

'I don't believe there's a party in France that puts the poor and destitute first. Disregarding the Communists, of course. The Radical Socialists, Pierre Mendès France that is, come closest to what I want to be part of.'

'I admire you for that,' said Jean. 'Most politicians are after power. Power to grab what they want.'

'I agree.' Justine liked Jean's direct style.

'You know, to survive as a politician, you need to be squeaky clean. France isn't a country where you can buy protection from the press. You need to avoid any risk of being blackmailed.'

Justine was a bit surprised. He might be right. But that wasn't where she was coming from. There was a Corsican skeleton in her cupboard. She remained quiet.

As if reading her thoughts, he added, 'I'm speaking as a purist. We have a professional relationship. I'm here to watch your back.'

'Thanks, Jean, I value that.'

'Talking business, if I may. How are you going to process the raw opium?'

Justine thought for a moment. She felt she could take Jean further into her confidence at this point. 'Glun has a friend who already boils the stuff, for who knows whom. He says it's no problem. There will be no audit trail back to me and the team.'

'Okay,' said Jean. 'But I never like operating blind. It's best always to check out exactly who is doing what at each stage.'

'I agree,' said Justine. 'I'll press Glun for more detail.' She paused for a moment, considering the other problem. 'What about Bao, and Ka? They haven't of course met since the attack on Ka.'

'I think Ka should go back to Bao. Tell him she's not working with anyone else. After all, she has to think of her family, her sick brother. She can't risk Bao having something done to them.'

'That makes sense,' said Justine. 'Trouble is she's obviously worried he'll do something else to her. She's tough underneath, these Vietnamese are, but ...'

Jean interrupted. 'We have to protect Ka. I think she should send him a note saying she wants to see him but won't go back to the rue du Bac. She can propose somewhere else. Somewhere we can protect Ka in case he tries something.'

'Yes. Let me talk to her along those lines. In the meantime, think about where that place is, where he would think he was on neutral ground but where we could watch him.'

Back in her apartment, Justine waited for Ka to come round, as they'd agreed at work. Her feelings for Ka were something she'd not experienced with anyone else. The urge to protect, to be with her without anyone else interfering, for them to be left alone together. She knew Ka admired her, at least physically. The way she touched her when a fitting was going on, it was professional, but it was something else as well. What did she, Ka, feel?

They never talked about it. Justine admired Ka, not only for her dedication to her work, and her skill as a seamstress. Her talent extended further. She was so good with the clients, that's why she attended the fittings, they adored her. Justine was entranced somehow by Ka. The frailty and grace of her Asian figure, the elegance of her movements, the touch of her fingers.

There she was. The lift arriving outside the door brought Justine back to reality. Then the soft tap on the door. In the room, they held one another briefly. Ka was holding something in her hand. The happiness permeated between the two of them.

Settled together on the sofa, Justine pouring out the infusion into two porcelain cups she found in the *marché aux puces* the previous day.

'Here,' said Ka, opening the bag in her hand and placing several macarons, all in different colours, on a plate.

'How delicious, you spoil me, what would they say at Schiap?' exclaimed Justine.

'Anything for some time with you,' whispered Ka.

There was silence for a moment as each helped themselves. Then Justine said, 'I've been thinking about Bao.'

'So have I,' said Ka. 'I bet I know what you're going to say.'

'What?'

'That I can't do nothing. That I have to see him. Things can't be left hanging. In case he puts the thugs back on me, or goes after my family.'

'Well, yes. I was going to say something like that. You see, Ka, I want to protect you. It's too dangerous for you to go back to the rue du Bac. There needs to be somewhere else, where you're safe.'

'But what do I say to him?'

'I suppose you tell him straight you've not double-crossed him. That you will continue selling opium to your clients.'

'I know, I have to think of my family in Hanoi, my brother.'

'I'll be watching, I'll be close. He won't be able to hurt you.'

'But where?' asked Ka.

Jean ordered the glass of rouge for Justine, and talked about the latest government changes until the drinks came. He lit a Gitane. 'I've been thinking about a place for a meeting with Bao,' he said. 'That's assuming Ka can go through with it?'

'I put it to her. She realises she has to do something. She's a brave girl.'

'Yes. Well, how about the crypt of the Église Saint-Sulpice? There, she'd be alone with him but with us close by, out of sight. The area's not normally open to the public. It's large, with arches and pillars from where we can watch Ka without being seen. I know the parish priest. He'll let us in and see we aren't interrupted.'

Justine thought for a moment. 'Isn't it likely he'll bring a minder? I mean, after whatever happened when Ka was rescued.'

Jean stared at Justine, with an inquisitive look on his face.

Justine wasn't going to tell him she'd killed the Corsican. No one was going to know that.

'Well,' he said, 'there'll be two of us, one trained by Colonel Passy, that's me, and one by the British Commandos, that's you.'

'Yes, but …'

Jean interrupted. 'I'll be carrying a Thompson, you can borrow my .38 Beretta. You'll have trained on that at Arisaig.'

'My God, we'll wake up the dead,' she said.

'That's why I'm suggesting the crypt,' Jean said, laughing. 'Come on, the church is next door, let's do a recce. Wasn't it Wellington who said time spent on reconnaissance is never wasted?'

23

Paris, Church of Saint-Sulpice, September 1951

Ka didn't know the church, and was relying on Justine's instructions, arriving at exactly 9 o'clock that evening. Staggered by the sheer scale of everything, she walked to the top end of the nave, genuflecting to the Blessed Sacrament, the red light burning in front of the tabernacle. Like being back at school in Hanoi with the nuns, part of the Christian community out there.

Where was the crypt? The priest friend of Jean was waiting to let her in. The *curé* unlocked the door with a warm smile, switching on the lighting as she found her way down the steps into a large cavern. Really cool in there, a relief from the heat of the street outside. Justine and her friend would already be there, hidden out of the way. No one in sight as she sat down on one of the chairs against the wall. Five minutes, and still no one. Suddenly, a man entered. It was Bao. It was then that she caught a glimpse of two other men standing against pillars, buried in the shadows. The Vietnamese came up to Ka and sat down beside her.

'Well,' said Bao.

'That Corsican, or whoever he was, tried to kill me. It was in your building, where they brought me.'

'Too bad,' said Bao. 'You've been messing around with a woman we believe supplies opium. No one double-crosses Bao.'

'I didn't double-cross you. It was a misunderstanding. I want to continue working with you, Bao. But I'm not coming back to the rue du Bac.'

'Who killed the one you call the Corsican, the one who rescued you?'

'I'm not going to discuss it. I was half dead at the time.'

Silence for a bit. Then Bao said, 'You're playing with fire, Ka. I have connections back to powerful people in Saigon. They know everything that's happening in the opium world down there.'

'I always assumed your opium supplies came from there,' said Ka. 'You know I need the money. I'm ready to go on supplying clients. My only condition is we must have somewhere different to meet, somewhere neutral, if you like.'

'Where?'

'For the coming summer months, let's meet on a bench in the Jardin du Luxembourg. Only a few minutes from here.'

'Okay.' He paused, then turned his head towards her. 'You owe me money, Ka.'

'Yes, I've brought it. I'll continue to do my best, Bao,' she said as she waited for Bao to give her the commission due after he'd counted it out.

'It seemed to us it went to plan, Ka,' said Justine. The three of them were in the bar round the corner from the church.

'Yes,' said Ka as Justine introduced her to Jean. 'I don't know whether Bao is still suspicious, but he's willing to go on working with me.'

'Bao had two heavies watching over him,' said Jean. 'You know, I'm wondering whether there's more to all this than just opium.'

'Why do you think that?' asked Justine.

'I just get that feeling,' said Jean. 'Bao's treatment of Ka was extreme. And the level of protection he brought with him this evening. What else could he be up to?'

It was Ka who spoke next. 'Bao deals with the *Bình Xuyên* in Saigon. Maybe it's heroin, for the American market. There's talk of that in the Vietnamese community here.'

'Possibly,' said Jean. 'Justine, you mentioned this Madame X, and napalm. That her father was bringing it in from the States.'

'Yes,' said Justine. I heard from somewhere that elements in the French army want to use it more extensively, to be dropped from the air when one of their units is surrounded. Fortunately, there's political pressure against it, even to have it banned internationally.

'News that napalm could engulf civilians in Vietnam would cause outrage in the press here, no doubt,' added Ka.

'So, any ideas how we dig into Bao's habits?' asked Justine.

Jean took a long draw on his Gitane. 'I'll see if I can find anything through my friends based at the *piscine*. They work for the military high command, like the Deuxième Bureau.'

24

Paris, rue du Bac

Not much in life frightened Bao. Dieu Tran was the outstanding exception. Powerfully built for a Vietnamese and, when in Paris, immaculately dressed, Tran handled the export business of the *Bình Xuyên*. His staple diet was opium for the French market. Just to think of him, Bao would shiver uncontrollably. Now, he was seated opposite Tran, and he knew this was going to be a difficult meeting. Tran's hands were on the large desk between them, as were various implements designed for dealing with the mail. Bao suspected, indeed knew, there were other uses. Bao watched the two members of Tran's entourage, standing on his left and right.

'Tell me what happened, Bao,' said Tran, in a soft but somehow menacing voice.

Bao knew that Tran ran his business like a ruthless Mandarin. He never knew when to expect him. Showing up in Paris without warning, he expected instant response to any problem. Tran's last instructions to Bao were to find out whether one of Bao's people was double-crossing the organisation.

Bao tried to steady himself. 'After receiving the information you uncovered in Saigon, Tran, I arranged for a Corsican whom I use for interrogation work, to get hold of the woman and ask her some questions. I said to use some persuasion, if necessary. They were interrupted during the interrogation.'

'Interrupted?'

'I don't know exactly what happened. When his Vietnamese assistant went back into the room, the Corsican was on the floor bleeding to death. There was no sign of the captive.'

'Do you know who did it? How it was done?'

'He'd been slashed with a knife, upwards into the face, then into the abdomen, knife wounds. By the time I reached the room after hearing a shout, he was dead.'

'Professional job,' hissed Tran. 'I don't like mistakes, Bao.'

Then silence. Bao knew any excuse would make it worse. This was the moment of danger. Tran could dispose of him just like that. Worse, he employed tortures no man could endure.

'I told you there was a client at Ka's work who might supply information. You haven't investigated that.'

Bao watched intently Tran's right hand. It was moving slowly out of sight, under the desk. The eyes of the two hit men either side were focused in the same direction. The hand came back up above the desk. It was holding an electrical apparatus including a hand-operated generator and electrodes.

Bao knew immediately what it was, *la Gégène*. So did the others.

'You know what this is, Bao?'

'Yes,' gasped Bao, now sweating with terror.

'One electrode will be inserted in your ear, and the other will clamp neatly to your genitals. My two friends here are expert in its operation. So, tell me, Bao. Do you know who used that knife, and took Ka away?'

'No, not yet.' Bao's voice was a hoarse whisper.

'Then I want you to find out. I will be back in Paris very soon, and if I haven't heard from you by then, my two friends and you will spend some time together.

Bao walked along the lower quay on the left bank of the Seine towards Pont Neuf and Notre Dame. A few traders were opening their cases of second-hand books, pictures and maps in the hope of some early business. His mind was elsewhere, locked into Dieu Tran's threat earlier that morning.

What should he do? Could Ka be tricked into leading him to another opium supplier? That assumed the information from Tran was correct. The source was apparently a *Bình Xuyên* agent somewhere in Indochina. Following Ka wouldn't be easy. When he'd organised that the first time, she nearly gave them the slip. She'd admitted that during the water treatment. Why did she deny all else? Either she was afraid of giving away someone, or there was another reason she wouldn't give a name, nor even admit there was someone else.

What about her work? At the couture house in Place Vendôme. What went on in there? Clients came and went. Tran said originally something about the wife of a government official. He'd mentioned the woman again today. How could he reach her? As a Vietnamese of no public standing he, Bao, wouldn't get through the door. He needed an intermediary.

Something clicked in his head. That fiscal inspector, the one he used for occasional tasks for which Bao paid in kind. Could he get access to the billing records at the couture house? They should show the client names, and provide a trail back to the staff who worked on the costumes being invoiced. Yes, he would try Monsieur Dubois from the Fisc. Tax inspectors were powerful, they could go almost anywhere. Last time Dubois worked for him, no cash passed. Monsieur Dubois was introduced to a charming and very young Vietnamese girl. Just an hour in that twilight period between end of work and greeting his wife before dinner.

25

21 Place Vendôme

Monsieur Dubois showed his ID card to the woman behind the glass panel. He always went in quietly, through the staff entrance, on unplanned visits to such places. All he needed was the name of the *comptable*. Once with the bookkeeper, nothing could stop him. The sales ledger, and copies of the invoices issued in the past three months, was what he was to inspect. His official reason to be there would be to check that the correct amount of sales tax collected was being accounted for to the Fisc. The names of the clients billed in the last trimester would be easy to note down. All he was asking for was the surnames, and somehow Monsieur Bao would do the rest. Bao must have a link to connect to whatever name he wanted.

That done, he was already excited by the thought of the young lithe body that would be waiting for him in rue de Sèze, after he delivered the staff and client names to Bao.

⋯⊷⊷⊶⊶⋯

Bao knew the husband was a senior government official. All of the names given to him by Dubois drew a blank, except one. It cross-checked to the index in front of him. There was no difficulty having Monsieur Dubois make a second visit to Place Vendôme, to identify the *vendeuse* and mannequin who looked after the woman in question. As an added bonus, Ka's name was also found to be associated with her.

Now it was in front of Bao in black and white. Somehow, he must meet this client, Ka's client. Have they been scheming a new arrangement, opium from another source? Who was the supplier, not just Ka but someone else. How could he discover that? Bao thought long and hard. Then it came to him. Send someone to the client, and see if he or she could join the circle. There must be a group of women all into it, creating the demand for much more opium.

He needed someone who would fit naturally in the circle. If she was successful in penetrating the group, he'd only be one step away from the rival supplier. An obvious choice was the wealthy Vietnamese aristocrat Bao already sent opium to. The one in the villa on Cap Ferrat, when not in her apartment on Avenue Hoche. It would take time, but not too long. Will that be enough to keep Dieu Tran happy? The gnawing fear of that apparatus, *la Gégène*, didn't go away.

~∙≕◉≔∙~

Bao was almost there. His aristocratic contact did just what he asked, in exchange for a bonus quantity of laudanum. She went boldly to the home of Madame X, and left her card with a note saying the two of them might have something in common and could they meet. Madame X seemed to be looking for excitement, and agreed to take tea with her at Fouquet's on the Champs-Elysées. Somehow they hit it off, conveniently discovering a common interest in opium, and both agreed on the importance of a discreet yet steady supply. How she did it, Bao didn't ask, but his contact extracted from Madame X that she was now receiving her opium from a mannequin with a top fashion house in Place Vendôme.

To Bao, that could only mean one person. Her name was on his notepad, following the inquiries made by his tax inspector friend, Monsieur Dubois. The mannequin shown as part of the team that dressed Madame X at 21 Place Vendôme.

Dieu Tran looked happy, all of a sudden. Bao was sitting in front of his desk, as before. This time, there were no hit men on either side of the gangster who managed the export business of the *Bình Xuyên*. 'You've done well, Bao. I have already transmitted your message to my colleagues in Saigon.'

'Do you wish me to make contact with this Justine Müller?'

'No, Bao. We will be responsible for her from now on.'

26

Bill knew he was useful to Savani. Having a tame Dakota pilot able and willing to risk flying into mountain airstrips was worth a bit. Not only risky because of difficult terrain and improvised landing strips, but because Bill had to run the gauntlet of Viet anti-aircraft fire. The other plus was that the South African was an independent operator, not taking orders from the French air force. And his involvement in the secret moon flights in WW2 showed he knew how not to swap stories with his mates.

Operation X was an eye-opener to Bill. On the face of it, everyone should be arrested by the Sûreté and carted away. Buying opium from the Montagnards and having the controllers of Saigon's organised crime, *Bình Xuyên*, process and distribute most of it, was enough. Added to that, the balance of the crop was currently disposed of in Bangkok, there being no trace where the proceeds went. A life sentence for the head of the operation? Not a bit of it. The organiser of Operation X was none other than the French army's military intelligence arm, the Deuxième Bureau. And the officer in overall control, none other than Captain Antoine Savani.

Bill felt he was developing a good understanding with Antoine. After all they'd already been in some tight corners. Nothing like rolling the C47 to a stop on a makeshift landing ground, and being surrounded by locals with ammunition belts around the necks, not sure which side they supported.

Sitting with Bill one evening in Hanoi, the Corsican steered the conversation towards the developing market for opioids, as he called the products derived from the opium poppy. Naturally on guard because of Justine's developing business and the help he gave her, Bill let Savani sink into his favourite subject.

'The truth is, Bill, the export demand is insatiable. What we don't sell to the *Bình Xuyên* for their opium dens in the south, we can cash in on the world market without trying. We pay in piastres at the Bank of Indochina's artificially high exchange rate, and then sell in say Bangkok for half again more in dollar terms.'

'Aren't the Americans trying to combat the trade into the States?' said Bill. 'There are articles appearing in *Time* and *Newsweek* all the time about the emergence of heroin on their streets?'

'Sure. Trouble is that the profits in it are making drug smuggling and distribution attractive to the mafias across America. When they get into the business, the sky's the limit.'

Antoine paused for a moment. Something was coming.

'Bill, let me tell you a rumour I've picked up.'

Here it was. 'Okay, go right ahead,' said Bill.

'Your friend in the Paris fashion industry made a splash when she visited Saigon earlier this year. And it seems she used the opportunity to set up a conduit for moving raw opium down from the Highlands and somehow to France.'

Bill was silent.

'Any small private arrangement Justine Müller makes with a single grower is not threatening to me and my Deuxième Bureau colleagues.' He looked hard at Bill. 'The danger is that our partners, the *Bình Xuyên*, are paranoiac about competition. Their leadership has a black-and-white attitude, either you're in with them, or you're the enemy.'

Bill thought hard. 'I can't comment on what Justine does, or is planning to do. But I do appreciate you sharing such information with me. I'm close to her. If she's in danger, then I'm dead worried. I'll get a message to her right away.' It was also clear to him that Antoine would have worked out who was transporting the raw opium down south for Justine, but that could remain unsaid.

Commandant Savani, master in the nuances of persuasion, opened Bill's eyes a little further. 'I hear that Justine Müller is a candidate to become a Radical Party deputy. That could make her vulnerable to local sentiment in Saigon, and in the *colon* community generally. After all, Mendès France who heads the Radicals, is openly calling for France to pull out of Indochina.'

'I see,' said Bill.

'And the other exposure it opens her up to,' and he paused as if for effect, 'is blackmail.'

—••◉••—

Back on his own that night, Bill tried to plot a way out of a worsening situation for Justine. She was a fighter. No way she would close down the pipeline. She needed the money for her political ambitions, she'd made that clear. Maybe she could get a message to the *Bình Xuyên* top brass, to the effect that she wouldn't grow the business, presented no threat to their Saigon monopoly, nor to their export trade in opioids. From now, she'd need protection when in Saigon. And that was only a week away according to the cable she just sent him.

What about in Paris, would they go after her there? No way all eventualities could be covered. There was this character Jean she'd had with her on her last visit. He was Paris based. Bill would talk to her about how she used him back in France. Time was of the essence. He must warn her immediately she arrived in Saigon.

27

Hotel Continental, Saigon

'I need to talk to you before you do anything else,' said Bill on the phone, just after Justine's sudden arrival back in Saigon.

'Okay, come round right away,' replied Justine. It's room 241.'

'With you in half an hour.'

Justine replaced the phone slowly. Bill sounded concerned about her. What was going on? She used the time to unpack. She never thought she'd be back in Saigon only three months after her first visit. She couldn't wait to see Bill again, her greatest companion if nothing more.

His knock made her jump, even though she was waiting for it. She pulled open the door and in he came, the familiar heavy build, khaki shirt and shorts. No insignia on him, though she knew his outfit was known to the insiders as Air Opium.

'Sorry to rush you, Justine,' he said, as he kissed her on both cheeks. 'How do you manage to look so good when you're just off a twenty-hour flight?'

'Oh. Bill. I just light up whenever I see you,' she said back to him with a laugh. 'Why the rush?'

Bill's face changed to serious mode. 'I just heard something and wanted to warn you.'

'Warn me, about what?'

Bill sat in the corner armchair, and poured them both some iced water. 'God, it's sweltering already. How could any sane person come here during the monsoon?'

'The first trip uncovered some serious new client business for Schiap,' said Justine, now sitting on the bed, her long legs wrapped under her, auburn hair in full flood over a shoulder. Three of us are back to measure and fit the new clients, and show off some of our new *modèles*.

'Glad to hear it,' said Bill, looking up at the large fan which was thrashing the heavy humid air. 'Anyway, I told you last time of the Frenchman I'd met, called Antoine Savani. He's the key link between the authorities in the south and the *Bình Xuyên*. He's also behind Air Opium. I haven't said anything to him of course about our arrangement to transport your private supply of raw opium from the Highlands.'

'Yes, I remember you telling me about him.'

'Well, Savani thinks he knows everything that goes on, even that you were coming back here.'

'Oh,' was all she said.

'He talked to me about you when we were up north the other day. He'd heard that the *Bình Xuyên* are on to you. Somehow, they have information from your employer's office in Paris, linking you to some woman with a powerful father,'

'Go on,' said Justine.

'The *Bình Xuyên* smell competition.' He paused. 'So far, I've brought three batches of merchandise down for you. It travels in with the main load for Savani. Wherever their information comes from, it seems they suspect you're building your pipeline up into something big, and they intend to put a stop to it.'

'Thanks, Bill. I appreciate the feed-back.' She thought for a moment. 'Jean's coming in at the weekend. Could I suggest the three of us put our heads together?'

'Good idea. I'll stand by to hear when and where. In the meantime, Justine, you must be really careful. Don't show up in public places unless I'm with you. I'm going to have a word with the hotel security manager. Have you got a gun?'

'No. Do you think that's necessary?

'Who knows. I heard they put the frighteners on someone you work with at Schiap. Must be the Ka you spoke of. I'd have thought they would welcome a face-to-face meeting before trying anything like that on you.' He paused. 'But they are very dangerous people, so look out.'

'I will, and you'll hear from me about the meeting with Jean as soon as I've seen him on Friday evening.'

'Good on you, Justine,' said Bill as he delved into a bag he'd brought with him. 'Here, hold on to to this.'

She weighed it in her hand, commenting 'Walther .38 calibre semi-automatic pistol, PPK version, lighter than standard, designed originally for German police use. Easier to conceal, although doubt it would fit under the *robe de mariée* at a Schiap dress show.'

'Justine, you're unbelievable.'

'Not really. They had one at Arisaig, the training base they sent us agents to in Scotland.'

―◦―

Jean looked across at Justine and Bill. A bottle of Scotch and soda water syphon stood on the table they sat around in his Saigon office. On the wall above was a photograph of General de Gaulle on a Normandy beach, with Colonel Passy alongside, and another in the group who could have been a younger Jean. 'So, I guess it was predictable something like this would happen sooner or later,' he commented after hearing the *Bình Xuyên* were taking an interest.

'Anyone have a plan on how we react?' Justine asked.

'Unless we can take them on head to head, and we'd need a French Foreign Legion regiment to do that, should we not reassure them we're only a small private operator, not aiming to take business off them?' said Bill.

'What do you think, Jean,' asked Justine.

'If we ask them to let us continue, albeit on a small scale, I would think they'll ask for a percentage.'

'That sounds like paying for their permission to carry on our business,' said Justine.

'Welcome to Saigon,' said Jean.

'We need to know,' she said sipping her Scotch and soda, 'who betrayed us.'

There was a moment's silence before Justine continued. 'I guess it might be a case of someone reading our signals, overhearing a conversation.'

'It's unfortunate, to say the least,' said Bill. 'We're unlikely to find out at this stage.'

Jean got up and started to pace around the room. 'Trouble is, the game's now changed. You will have to watch your backs all the time.'

'Well, we all have military training and wartime experience to a greater or lesser extent.'

'An interesting angle, on a lighter note,' said Jean, 'is that if the French withdraw from Indochina, Ho Chi Minh will wipe out *Bình Xuyên*.'

'Then, Justine, you'll have to source your opium from Burma, and I can't fly there.' Bill laughed as he re-filled everyone's glasses.

'Back to basics,' said Justine. 'Bill, are you able to get a message back to the *Bình Xuyên*, via Savani, that I'm not entering the big time, just want to make some money in the coming year, and will then pack up?'

'I'll try,' he replied.

Jean turned to Justine. 'Clearly you're most exposed when here in Saigon. I propose to shadow you whenever you're out of the hotel.'

'Thanks, Jean, I agree. I'll give you my itinerary for the next few days, and will phone you each time I intend to leave the hotel.'

'I have an ex-legionnaire Corporal working for me. His name is Morel. He left the Legion in a hurry after being suspected of shooting an officer in the back in a firefight with the Viets. The officer wasn't popular, but nothing was ever proved. I'll have him stand in for me whenever I'm tied up.'

'Oh, how charming of you,' said Justine with a laugh. Then to both of them, now with a straight face, 'Remember everyone, as of today we're on a war footing.'

⁃≕◉≔⁃

Justine was up early the next morning, ready to meet the clients they signed up on the first visit. Almost finished costumes were to be tried on and final adjustments made. She and the team from Schiap met the women individually in the salon reserved for them in the Continental.

Lunch came as a relief. These clients were demanding, particularly the Vietnamese aristocracy. They threw their weight around. The close friends of so-called Emperor Bao Dai. He spent most of his time in France, enjoying the soft life of the Côte d'Azur. On the other hand, the wealthy *colons* were generally friendly and overwhelmed by the beauty of the clothes. A lunch buffet was put on for everyone, and Justine looked forward to an afternoon of rest before the evening's dress show.

Returning to her room, she found a note under the door. Could she meet Jules for tea at the Majestic. She expected to see him for an update on how the pipeline was working alongside his ship-ments of silk to Marseille. Odd that Bill didn't mention it, but he would probably be there. Anyway, there were a couple of hours beforehand, and she settled down on her bed with a Hemingway from the hotel's small library, and flask of iced water.

A buzz from the hotel operator woke her half an hour before she was due to meet Jules, and she showered and put on a pale blue cotton dress, grabbed a broad-brimmed straw hat, and dashed down to the lobby. A velotaxi was waiting outside, and she slid in the back as the heat of the late afternoon enveloped her. The rear seat was surrounded by shades which made it difficult to see anywhere except directly ahead and past the cyclist driver.

After crossing rue Catinat, they stopped with a jolt at the next traffic crossing. The flap of the shade on the nearside opened and almost in the same movement a skinny Vietnamese man stepped in and sat down beside her. Before she could make even an exclamation, she felt the muzzle of a pistol in her groin. 'Don't even move a fraction, or make any noise,' he hissed in her ear. The cyclist pedalled on, now with more than twice the load. The Majestic was nowhere to be seen.

Justine's brain was working overtime. Was this the *Bình Xuyên*? Probably, remembering Bill's warning. Where were they heading? For interrogation? No more of that, not after the Ustashi and the camps. Would rather die shooting it out, than face that again. A French candidate for deputy kidnapped. That was serious stuff. They must mean it. Play ball with them, see if they're willing to see reason.

Not a sound came from the gunman beside her. Must assume he meant business. Where were they? Entering a courtyard behind an old colonial style villa. There might be a chance now, when he got out. Depends on who else was going to welcome her. Two more of them came into view. Couldn't take them all on. They weren't taking chances, holding both her arms in a vice-like grip.

─────※─────

'So, Mademoiselle Müller, you know how to annoy us, don't you.' They were in a sparsely furnished room. Just a couple of chairs and square table. Nothing on the walls, a large fan revolving below the ceiling. The man speaking was right out of context, a *colon* wearing a well cut sand-coloured tropical suit. Middle-aged, he could have been a senior civil servant. Even a cream silk tie with his pale blue shirt, and buckskin shoes. He must be the interrogator.

Justine didn't respond. Jean should know where she was if Morel, his retired Legion Corporal friend, followed her from the hotel. Better to see first who this smooth *colon* was.

'My apologies for abducting you from your hotel in such dramatic fashion. But the people I work for like operating in such fashion. Maybe they think they will upset the victim so he or she will be ready to cooperate. Somehow, I don't think you are that sort.'

'Why have I been brought here? It's an outrage what you've done.' Justine judged she should react forcefully. No body search, they must be treating her as a soft target.

'I will explain.' He stood up and started to pace around the room. 'My employers control the opium market in Saigon. They also have a thriving export business for the commodity. It has come to their notice that you have established a supply line of your own, from the producers in the north, and that somehow you are shipping the opium to France.'

No reason to answer his questions directly, at least for the moment. Justine wanted to know more about him and his friends. 'Regardless of my business affairs and motives, I don't see why an organisation of the scale you describe yours to be, could possibly be concerned with someone's private arrangements. Arrangements that present no threat to your business.'

'Ah, that's for us to judge.'

'What I do is my business. I'm a candidate for deputy in the French National Assembly. It's not my habit to break the laws of France.'

'My friends are not concerned with what does or does not break the law.'

'That doesn't surprise me.' This was the moment to go on the offensive. Find out what this lackey of the *Bình Xuyên* was after. 'Tell me precisely what you want from me.'

He stopped by her chair, leaning against the table, looking down at her. 'I admire your style, Mademoiselle. You are the type who comes out fighting. But just remember that whether you are a French deputy or not, the organisation I'm connected with is used to getting its way. It has powerful friends in high places. It will not tolerate people getting in its way. My instructions are to convince you of your stupidity, to reach an agreement that you desist from procuring opium here and distributing it in France.'

His cards were now on the table. Why should she accept defeat? Ruin the work she and Ka were already seeing the reward for. They already pulled a gun on me. Given half a chance she'd do the same on them. The feel of the Walther .38 under her shoulder was reassuring.

'I'm going to take you to our in-house lawyer down the road. He will show you a document we want you to sign.'

'What if I refuse?'

There was a heavy silence. He rose and paced the room again. 'Mademoiselle, Saigon is a dangerous place. Accidents happen all the time. Come and look at these photographs.' He opened a folder and slid out some large images. 'These are some of the unfortunates who crossed our path. Maybe they double-crossed us, maybe they were just practising ...' He paused for a moment before adding, 'unfair competition.'

Justine looked at the pictures, moving them about the table top, then recoiled in horror. In one, the body of a man was being torn to pieces by two large shark-like fish. In another, a naked woman was tied face up on a raised plank. Her body was contorted in an unimaginable fashion, an electrode connected to one of her nipples and the other to the uterus.

For the first time that morning, she felt fear envelop her body. She couldn't go through with it, couldn't face the terror these people were threatening. The first time, in Trieste with the Ustashi, it was different. She was desperate to protect her sister's escape to England, escape from deportation to the exter-mination camps. Now it was about her business, making money to pay for her political ambitions.

'I prefer the first solution,' he said. 'It doesn't make any noise underwater, in the swamp.'

Justine was silent for a moment. 'Take me to your lawyer,' she said, trying to hold her voice steady.

He stood aside, following Justine out through the door. The same thug was waiting for them, his hand in a jacket pocket, obvious enough for her to know the hand was on a weapon.

'How far is it?' she asked. 'I badly need some fresh air.'

'Only five hundred metres. We'll walk it,' he said. They went out onto the street, setting off with him alongside her, the thug coming up behind.

The street was busy, but nothing like early morning and evening when the whole world would seem to be there, on a bicycle. She felt a faint breeze on her face, as the warm humid atmosphere clung to her. Smells from everywhere, fish caught that morning, newly baked baguette. The pavements were dotted with market traders, the children all at school. An older man with pointed beard smiled at her from his vegetable stall. She felt a closeness to the local people as they went about their lives. Some obviously making a good living, others living from hand to mouth.

There would be one chance only, look for the opportunity. Halfway already, not much time left. That Citroën *panier à salade* parked along the curb, just in front. Coming up on it from the rear. This was it. Her nervousness was suddenly gone, in its place just a coldness. Judge carefully the line of sight, calculate the timeframes. Speed and surprise were key. Actions must flow from one to the next. Give no warning, appear resigned to meeting with the lawyer.

Reaching the front of the Citroën van, Justine dived sideways to the left so its high roofline protected her from the thug walking some five metres behind. Her right hand came away from under the shoulder. The Walther was out and the wrist levelled it onto the line of fire from almost ground level up to the target. Fire one, sharp crack. The bullet hit the interrogator in the base of his neck at point blank range, travelling up inside the head and exiting from his forehead in a spurt of blood.

Twisting around, now on her back, she looked for the thug following. He was right there, coming for her, pistol in hand as she lay in his line of fire. It flashed through her mind, she didn't have time to aim and fire before he shot at her. Couldn't get her shooting arm back. Tried to twist her body over to the safety of the van, to get in a shot at him. Not fast enough. Sudden terror, this was it. A loud crack and she knew it was the moment, the end. Her eyes fixed on the thug, she saw him suddenly plunge forward, a hand flung up behind his back.

Justine lay there in the road, in front of the *panier à salade*. Confusion in her mind, why was he down, why was she alive?

It all happened so rapidly, the time it took from Corporal Morel's shot to Morel sweeping her up with his other arm. He'd saved her. Running together, Morel waved down a Foreign Legion truck that was coming the other way. The driver in his white *kepi* clearly recognised Morel as an old mate, and slammed on his brakes. Morel almost threw her into the back, and down on the floor as the driver gunned the throttle and the truck raced away.

⁓⊱⊰⁓

Bill felt uncomfortable, fidgeting as he sat with Jules and Jean in the front lounge of the Hotel Majestic. She must have got the message. Probably an inconvenient time for her, but Jules insisted, saying he must talk about his shantung silk while Justine was in town. She was a reliable girl, from keeping to her bargains to being on time. Now she was an hour late.

Jean, also there, away in a corner, suddenly saw Corporal Morel come into the hotel, holding Justine by the arm. In a flash, he knew something had happened and went over to them. Bill and Jules followed him. 'To my room straight away,' said Jean.

Jean fixed Scotch and sodas for everyone, while Justine phoned the Schiap team at the Continental to tell them she'd be back later that evening.

'Tell us what happened,' said Bill, looking at Justine and Corporal Morel.

She recounted the events of the past two hours. Jules looked decidedly sick on hearing the more gruesome details, Justine noted. He didn't look like he'd betrayed her.

'Corporal Morel's the hero,' she ended by saying, and the guys all pumped his hand and doubled his whisky ration. 'So, what now?' Justine asked, waving her arm at them, evidently still in some state of excitement.

'You get the hell out of here, and back to Paris. On the first flight, before the Sûreté starts asking you questions,' said Jean forcibly. 'And you, Corporal, should be okay if you were wearing that scarf half over your face and the dark glasses.'

Corporal Morel nodded.

'Okay,' said Justine. 'But I'm not closing down the pipeline.'

'So, Bill,' said Justine as he accompanied her back to the Continental. 'Who betrayed me to those bastards?'

'I doubt anyone did. The *Bình Xuyên* know everything. My guess is they have access to the Air France passenger manifests, and check them off routinely against names of those they're after.' He paused, evidently thinking out the consequences of what just happened. 'It wouldn't surprise me if Antoine Savani sounded me out on what I know about the killings.'

28

Justine tried to smile, to look confident. Impossible to feel anything like that. Almost paralysed with expectation, fear of losing after weeks of campaigning since returning in a rush from Saigon. Seven days a week of door-to-door canvassing, speaking in open spaces and smoky auditoriums. Josephine Baker turned out be a gold mine of help and encouragement. She inspired the rest of the team.

What would happen? Her constituency was not easy for a Radical candidate. Currently the deputy was a Communist. A tough deprived area, voters coming in wearing clogs. Sometimes a child pulled along by the mother, nothing on the little one's feet. This was what it was all about. Something must be done, her mission. Would fate provide the opportunity? If elected as deputy, she would burst into the new role. Tear the National Assembly apart until she was listened to, until she won the support she needed for change.

The time? Polls closed in an hour. It was worse than in the first round of voting. Second place in votes gained a week ago, against the five other candidates, so she was able to pass to the last round. Now was different, head to head with the current deputy. It all depended on how many of the votes cast for the losing candidates would be transferred to her.

Nothing to do tomorrow, Saturday, except pray. She didn't deserve help from on high. Never went to the Catholic church of her upbringing, nor to the synagogue of her grandparents in Germany. Sunday would be her D Day, when she hit the beach running. Giselle, the *première main* at Schiap, knew. If she entered the Assembly, her ties with the great fashion house wouldn't be totally cut. There was always scope for some representation work, maybe even promoting the interests of haute couture in the French Parliament.

Before that, she must win. The wait was intolerable. No good drinking with the likes of Jean, on an empty stomach. She would go round to Ka, maybe together they would shop in the stalls on the left bank of the river, before lunching on grated carrot and rouge in the rue de Seine. Then perhaps on to the rue de Sèvres for shoes. There was now money in both their bags, thanks to the pipeline. But still the waiting.

Finally the moment came, the monitor walked to the podium and explained that the legal formalities to comply with the rules of the Fourth Republic were in order. Then he announced

'Monsieur Blondi, French Communist Party, thirty-one thousand, four hundred and thirty-two.

Mademoiselle Müller, Radical Socialist Party, thirty-four thousand, six hundred and fifteen.

Mademoiselle Müller is elected deputy for Paris 13th electoral arrondissement.'

The rude grating ring of the phone in her apartment woke Justine. All at once she knew she'd overslept after the celebrations.

She grabbed the receiver, 'Müller here,' she almost shouted.

The voice at the other end of the line was familiar, as the last vestiges of sleep dropped out of her mind. 'Mademoiselle Justine? Mendès France here. I want to congratulate you on becoming deputy for the Radical Socialist Party.'

'Oh, thank you, sir. It will be an honour to represent your party.'

'Do please call me Pierre when we're talking one to one.'

'Yes, of course. And please call me Justine.'

'Thank you. I also wanted to say, Justine,' and he paused, 'that we start work today.'

'I'm ready to do what I can, sir, I mean Pierre.'

Saigon, the same day

Bill was on his first whisky of the evening when the waiter wheeled the telephone trolley towards him. 'Monsieur Lomberg, there is a call for you from Paris.'

'Bill, are you there?'

'Yes,' he responded.

'Bill, I did it.'

He heard the serious voice of Justine. 'Did what?'

'I've been elected as a deputy in the National Assembly.'

'Fantastic. Very well done, Justine. I'm proud of you, you're going to make it a great success.'

'Let's drink a glass of champagne to one another, today, Bill.'

'Right away, I will.'

Justine's next call was to her friend at the lycée, her friend in war and in peace, Françoise.

29

Justine chose the Musée Rodin for their rendezvous and discussion. She loved his work, the daring figures intertwined, the sexuality of his sculptures. The voice on the phone sounded Asian, so did the name Cho, clearly young and female. Would Justine be willing to talk about herself and her ambitions? A freelance journalist, the voice said. That could cover a multitude of sins. Anyway, it would be good practice for her new political career.

Walking through the entrance, she spotted her journalist, reading a historical note on Rodin's early work. The young woman turned as she approached, good-looking in a tight green silk dress, sleek black hair on her shoulders. 'So, you must be Mademoiselle Cho,' Justine said.

'Yes, and I'm thrilled to meet you, Mademoiselle Müller. Do call me Kim.'

'I hope you don't mind coming here, Kim. It's still so beautifully warm, and I love to walk through the gardens and sculptures. I'm new to being interviewed by journalists. Do call me Justine, please.'

'Mademoiselle Justine, you're now a busy person. Congratulations on becoming a deputy, and thank you for agreeing to meet me.' Kim paused a moment. 'I work on my own, submit articles to the magazines. *Le Monde* also prints a piece from me now and then.'

'So you're a free agent, not bound by the policy and instructions of an employer?' said Justine, over her shoulder in a light friendly manner as she led the way out into the garden.

'Basically, yes. Means that you don't know where the next meal's coming from. It's all about freedom, being able to write what you believe should be read. Anyway, I've decided that you would be the perfect subject for a feature on an extraordinary person, about a personal success story.'

'I'm flattered, but why me?'

'In a nutshell, because your career runs from resistance fighter to mannequin to deputy. A few others might claim two of those achievements, but no one else could claim all three.'

'I'm a little nervous about featuring in the press.'

'You're now a deputy. People will write about you whether you like it or not. Anyway, you have a very interesting mission in your political life, as I understand.'

'And, what is that?'

'You have joined the Radical Party because you want to put the underprivileged of France back on their feet, give them equal opportunity to learn and lead decent lives.' She waited for a moment, seemingly deciding whether to refer to something. 'I read in *Le Monde* and some magazines about what you did at that Schiaparelli dress show. To show yourself like that was brave.'

'You're perceptive, Kim, and well informed.'

'I hope so. That's my job. As a deputy, you'll need as much publicity as you can get, of the right sort. That will generate power in political terms. I can help you, as well as myself.'

'I see. Go on.'

'I try to write about people who represent the spirit of the moment, the *zeitgeist* as the Germans say.'

'Oh, and why do you think I do that?'

'Because you've chosen the political party of Pierre Mendès France, rather than other socialist movements. In particular, you share his views on the future of Indochina, of my country.'

'Where are you from, Kim?'

'Actually, my parents are from Phnom Penh, Cambodia. My mother is a school teacher, my father works for the Cambodian royal family. I was educated here in France.'

'How interesting, Kim,' said Justine.

'I love to meet people and write, and to be a first-rate journalist is my one ambition.'

'You mentioned I shared the views of Pierre Mèndes France. Do you have anything particularly in mind?'

'Well, yes. I know that you, like him, see no future for France in Indochina. You see much of the wealth created in the economy here being wasted on arms and manpower in the war out there.'

'That all sounds fine, Kim. But doesn't that view run counter to public opinion, at least those who read the smart magazines?'

'Yes, and no. I agree many of those people, the readers, say France should remain in Indochina. That so much money and effort has been sunk into those countries, it would be crazy to throw it away. And that France is an example to the western world in holding back the march of Communism in south-east Asia. But underneath, what do they really think? My view is that we have to ask them the question.'

Justine wondered how this freelance journalist went about her interviewing, how she sourced her information. She was certainly attractive. A bold personality, and a body that would excite the imagination. 'I'm still unsure you have enough of a story, Kim. Maybe, a profile of myself, what I've achieved, would fill a page in a glossy magazine. But don't you need a real story to hang it on. To make the headline, catch the reader?'

Kim looked surprised. 'Well, yes, that's the ultimate. But that sort of story requires a lot of digging for, and imagination, you could say. You have to go looking for it.'

'I would have thought you are pretty good at that,' said Justine.

'Sometimes, not often. That's what I'm looking for, all the time. I keep my eyes and ears open, as they say.' Kim stopped for a moment, as though she'd remembered something. 'You know, Mademoiselle Justine, there is something I'm working on. Normally, I wouldn't breathe it to a soul.'

'Now you're talking. It's suddenly like I'm interviewing you. You can trust me. Do go on.'

Kim took a breath. 'Napalm,' she murmured. Then silence.

'Napalm?'

'You know what it is, of course.'

'Yes,' Justine said, cautiously.

Kim explained she'd heard there was a group of officers in Saigon who believed napalm bombing should be threatened, and if necessary carried out, on villages in the south where insurgents were believed to be sheltered. Napalm, bombing with liquid fire, would terrify them into giving up the whereabouts of the insurgents, so the French army could lay traps and go in and take them out.'

'My God,' said Justine. 'If that's true, it would be dynamite if it hit the press here.'

'Not sure whether it is true,' said Kim. 'But, if it looks like it is, and I can convince you sufficiently, you might be prepared to raise it in the Assembly.'

'Oh, Kim. I have to have real evidence before I could do anything like that.'

'I realise that, Mademoiselle Justine.' Kim stopped for a moment. 'Look, I know someone, the wife of a senior civil servant. She is my link into that world.'

'What world?'

'The world of napalm.'

Something started spinning in the back of Justine's mind. There was something there, she couldn't put her finger on it, but it spelt danger.

Kim continued. 'This woman's father used to manufacture armaments for Germany in the last war. He escaped the *épuration*, his friends in high places protected him from retribution.'

Suddenly it came to Justine. Madame X, client of Schiap, now her own customer for opium.

30

This time they were in a small bistro off the rue Royale, the New Year celebrations just ended. Kim was bubbling over with excitement as she opened out a proof copy of *Paris Match*, spreading it over the table. On the left page, the mannequin was wearing a magnificent three-quarter-length evening dress in blue shantung silk. On the right page, the heading read 'From Buchenwald to the Assembly via Place Vendôme.'

Justine was ecstatic. 'Oh, Kim, that's wonderful. I do look okay. Anyone would in that dress. You're a genius.'

'I've kept to the story you told me. No surprises, hopefully.'

Justine read the article, including reference to the dress show at Schiap when she showed off her back. Kim's writing was spot on, repeating Justine's message, her ambition.

'Now Justine, are you out of modelling yet, can you eat a proper meal?'

Justine laughed. 'Yes, and no. I'm still employed, but on a part-time basis. Really, I'm part of the marketing department. Helping to promote the new *modèles* for the coming season, and Schiap accessories.'

'So, you can have a steak with me, and share my frites. We can celebrate,' Kim said, as she called a waiter and ordered champagne. 'Today, you're my guest. The editor at *Match* was thrilled with this piece, and it will do me a lot of good. As well as you, I'm sure.'

Justine was wondering when Kim would come to her napalm project. It was over their espressos that the word dropped into the conversation. 'Could I talk with you about the idea I mentioned last time, the contact I have whose father is a sort of arms dealer? Originally flamethrowers for the German army, now napalm for our army.'

'Yes, I remember.'

'Well, apparently there's a discussion going on in the army as to how napalm could be used against the insurgent problem in the south of Vietnam. You know that there have been attacks on military outposts in Annam and Cochin China by Viet insurgents from the north. Also, atrocities killing civilians in the towns and in Saigon.'

'Certainly, it's something the security services find it hard to control, as I understand.' Justine heard a lot about the problem during her visits to Saigon.

Kim went on. 'The idea being discussed, so I hear from my contact, is that by napalming villages believed to be supporting the insurgents, villagers can be persuaded to assist the army to trap the Viets and eradicate them.'

'So, what does that mean in operational terms?' asked Justine, who could guess what was coming.

'They would choose a village that was suspected of harbouring insurgents, and bomb it with napalm. Envelop it in a sea of fire,' Kim said very slowly.

'My God,' said Justine.

There was a long silence, finally broken by Kim. 'This woman I know, her father procures the napalm from Dow Chemical in the States. It was used in the Korean war.'

Justine was sure this must be the person she and Ka referred to as Madame X. 'I tell you what, Kim. I have an old friend in the Sûreté. She's close to the army's Deuxième Bureau, and might be able to check the truth in the discussions you've heard about.' She paused for a moment. 'Be careful in the meantime, wait for me to get back to you.'

⟨⟩

Justine found herself on the bus, heading again for the 20th arrondissement and Françoise at the *piscine*. How should she play it if her Bordeaux friend confirmed the story? It would be a great opportunity for her, if she could expose in the Assembly a plan to use napalm in this way. But immediately it would make her new enemies. The military establishment would be up in arms. Worse than that, if an investigation was started, it could expose Madame X's father as supplier of the napalm and mention their opium habits. That could reach out and trap Justine as supplier of the drug.

⟨⟩

'Great to see you again, my darling,' called out Françoise as Justine came into the bar. Slipping off the stool where she'd no doubt been swapping news with the barman, Françoise embraced her long-time friend. 'Let's go to that table in the far corner.'

'Good idea, this place is always full of spooks,' said Justine.

'Now then, keep off that subject,' said Françoise. 'You've really been busy since we last met. I hear you made two trips to Saigon. And that wonderful call saying you were now a deputy. Can't wait to hear about it all, where shall we start? Maybe in Saigon.'

'Okay. Do you want the sanitised version, or the Hollywood version?'

'The Hollywood one, please.'

The waiter arrived at the table with their lunch, and two beers.

'All right, here goes,' said Justine. It took her most of the meal to take Françoise through everything. How the first trip led to the setting up of the opium pipeline from Glun's family connections with the Meo tribe, and Jean's introduction to Jules who agreed to pack the merchandise with bales of silk destined for Marseille.

When Justine moved onto the second visit, she held nothing back, not even the interrogation by the *Bin Xuyen* and shooting in a Saigon street.

'Oh my God,' exclaimed her friend. That's the stuff of *The Quiet American*. I might have guessed, knowing your background. Just read it, Graham Greene's new book. Must come back to that, but tell me what it's like to be a deputy.'

'Well, I was exhausted after the campaign. My team were wonderful, including Ka, my Vietnamese friend at Schiap, and the wonderful Josephine Baker. Thank you for coming over yourself to drop leaflets.'

'That was the least I could do. That was clever of you to bring in Josephine Baker at the big meetings.'

'Now, tell me about yourself, Henri and your parents.'

'I worry about Henri, not just because he's a twin brother. He's so often in danger in Tonkin. Adjutant of his regiment. You know, these Legion regiments spend most of their time in battle zones.'

Françoise touched on life at the *piscine,* economical with the detail.

Justine wanted to talk to her friend about her relationship with Kim, and ask her to check the story about the use of napalm being extended. Finally the moment came.

'She's an independent journalist, and has somehow come up with a killer story. But her information is second-hand. She can only print if there's a strong indication of truth, really it needs to be corroborated.'

'Okay, tell me the worst,' said Françoise.

'She has a contact close to the military. The story is that the army is discussing using napalm to terrify villagers into helping them expose Viet insurgents in the south.'

Françoise was silent for a moment. 'Do you know what napalm does to a person?'

'I have some idea.'

'It sticks to the skin and clothing, usually all over, and burns slowly until the person becomes a black skeleton. Pain that cannot be endured.'

Now it was Justine's turn to go silent.

'I tell you what,' said Françoise, 'I'll make a discreet inquiry or two, see if there's any truth in what your journalist friend has heard. I have to come over to your part of the Left Bank on Saturday. Let's meet for a sandwich at St Germain des Prés. Bring Jean if you like.'

The three of them sat inside the Café Flore, steady rain outside, a miserable winter weekend.

Françoise sipped her *pression*, then opened the conversation. 'There is something going on. In fact a real argument is raging on the subject, very much under wraps. The hawks in the army's Deuxième Bureau want to go ahead and launch the technique on carefully selected villages. And the doves, mainly in the army's High Command, are taking the moral high ground. They don't want to know anything about it. So it could happen by default.'

'Now might be the time to have the press and public speak out,' said Justine. 'And what if I get up in the Assembly and expose the situation?'

Jean held up his hands. 'Why you? Wait for the press to draw attention to the debate going on in the army. Should that happen, you can decide then whether to speak out on the use of napalm.'

'Your party, the Radicals, is not in government right now,' said Françoise. 'Mendès France might encourage you to speak out, but remember he's likely to have to join a coalition the next time the government falls. This one's been in for a few months, so it's likely to collapse soon,' she said with a cynical laugh.

It was too dangerous for her to be involved in exposing the story. Good sense told her that. She would have to decide what to tell Kim.

She and Kim were together again on the Monday.

'Kim, there is truth in what you've heard from your contact,' said Justine.' Talks on the matter are going on in the army, although how serious and at what level, I don't know. Clearly, it is secret at this stage, so I can't stand up in the Assembly and announce that using napalm on villages in southern Vietnam is being discussed. You'll have to decide whether to pursue the matter, as far as the press is concerned.'

31

Justine looked again at the letter. The print was in individual letters cut out in rough squares from an exercise book. The envelope it arrived in was delivered by hand to her apartment. It read 'Cease your importation of opium, or risk fatal damage to your reputation as a deputy.'

Blackmail, she thought. She must discuss the letter with Jean.

———

'Yes,' said Jean after glancing at the letter, 'It's reputational blackmail.' He handed it back to her. 'Have you told anyone else about this?'

'No. What do you think I should do?'

'Clearly it's from someone who knows about your opium business. Who are they?'

'In Paris, it's Ka and Glun. Bao might still suspect it. And Madame X. In Vietnam, it's Glun's family in Hanoi. Jules who arranges the dispatch of the raw opium in his silk shipments to Marseilles, and the *Bình Xuyên*.'

'Okay, so we should be able to rule out Ka and Glun because they're involved in the pipeline and share the profits with you. What about Bao?'

'Bao has changed, Ka says he's even friendly. Not sure why, unless he needs something,' said Justine.

'Which leaves us with Madame X,' said Jean. 'We have to decide what her motive could be. Alternatively, whether she herself is under some sort of pressure.'

'Madame X,' said Justine. 'It could be she's being coerced into blackmailing me by someone else.' She put her hand up to her head, concentrating. 'You know, Jean, suppose the *Bình Xuyên* are pressurising her for something, and it's causing her to go after me. They may not want to risk threatening a deputy directly so they're having Madame X do it for them.'

'Yes,' said Jean, 'except that ...' he stopped in mid-sentence. 'Wait a moment. This Cambodian woman, Kim Cho who is helping with your publicity, didn't you mention she knows Madame X? Maybe there's a link there.'

'You mean Kim may have learnt of my opium business from Madame X?'

'Yes. Not good news,' said Jean.

'Oh God,' said Justine. 'What can we do about that?'

'I think I need to meet this Kim, and get the measure of her.'

'Careful, Jean. She's a very attractive woman. Exudes sex. If she wanted to turn the tables on you, she'd have you in bed in a flash. Colonel Passy, let alone the pious General de Gaulle, would never approve of that.'

'I could rise to that comment,' he said, grinning, 'except the thing's so bloody serious now, we need to be professional about it. Your reputation's at stake, Justine.' He paused, thinking. 'I ought to tail her, see where she goes after hours, so to speak.'

'That's okay with me. Presumably I should do nothing about the blackmail note in the meantime.'

'Correct. There will be more of those. Now, where do I find Kim?'

'I'm due to meet her in a couple of days. Be at the Café Flore on Wednesday at 5pm. Look out for me, and you won't miss her. When our discussions finish, you'll see us get up. Pick up the trail from then on. Watch out, Jean.'

Justine saw Jean over in the far corner of the café, as she came in off the street and went over to join Kim.

Kim jumped to her feet, put down a copy of *Elle*, and gave her a great smile. 'Hello Mademoiselle Justine,' said Kim. 'I've ordered a hot chocolate. These cold winter evenings get me down.'

A waiter approached and Justine ordered the same. 'What's new, Kim?'

'Nothing sensational. I covered the funeral of General de Lattre, with a photographer. Very moving. So soon after he lost his son. He will be a big loss to everyone in Indochina.'

'Absolutely.'

They went through their usual monthly summary of press coverage. Justine talked a little about the Assembly. After about an hour, they rose to go. Kim put on a smart black coat. Their practice was to meet each month unless something important arose in the meantime.

Parting at Metro St Germain-des-Prés, Justine headed on foot to her apartment, and Kim went down the staircase to find her train. Looking suitably nondescript, Justine saw Jean following close behind her.

Justine juggled her thoughts as she strode along, passing the brightly lit shops. She looked forward to the light spring evenings less than two months away. Receiving that letter shook her up, no good pretending otherwise. Who was this mystery tormentor? It was comforting to know Jean was on the case. Strange how one could feel confident about life one day, and then be shaken up by an unexpected happening the next.

Jean strode out behind the athletic-looking Kim after their Metro journey ended in the 14th arrondissement, until she disappeared into what he presumed was her apartment. He prepared for a wait. Was she going to stay in and have an early night, or would it be a night on the town? Jean was ready to lay his money on the latter, as he took a table at the bar conveniently overlooking Kim's home.

32

Paris, Latin Quarter, March 1952

Ka felt lonely. When did she become like this? Must have been around the time Justine won her seat in the Assembly. The electioneering was a lot of fun. She could only help at weekends because of work, but they covered so many apartments and homes. Started with surveys of what each voter thought on everything from health care to education, housing to the war in Indochina. From the surveys, they also learnt who would like to help at the next election, building up Justine's team of helpers.

Great excitement when the election date was declared. Leaflets to be delivered at every address in Justine's constituency. A bit like the blind leading the blind, neither had done this before. Ka remembered how shy she was to begin with, pressing the bell and wondering nervously who would respond. After a day or two of meeting the voting public, it became so much easier. People weren't unfriendly. Some wanted to argue on the doorstep, so you had to learn how to break off and move on.

Help did come from the Radical Party headquarters, with the supply of leaflets and posters. Large pictures of Justine posted up everywhere. As the date approached, so the effort increased.

Then suddenly he was there, shoulder to shoulder with Justine and her team, Pierre Mendès France. The friendly, almost surprised, face and heavy black eyebrows. The Radical Party supporters adored him. The rest of the public were intrigued to meet someone who might soon become prime minister. Ka looked back to that day as the highlight of their campaigning.

The public meetings were nerve-racking. Justine's idea for Josephine Baker to introduce the Radical Party candidate was a masterstroke. The tall black singer, so well known, stopped everyone in their tracks. When she introduced Justine as candidate, the audience was silent, ready to listen.

'There may be trouble tomorrow,' Ka remembered Justine saying to the team as they huddled together to plan for a weekend rally. 'All the candidates are on stage together at the municipal hall. We'll be asked questions from the floor. Josephine, you should keep away this time.'

'I guess you're right,' said the singer. 'Just look after yourself. Those Communist thugs are capable of anything.'

It didn't start well. The other candidates were all local men, and Justine went first. Lots of shouting and heckling. Being a rough arrondissement, emotions ran strongly, everyone with a point of view to put over. Justine responded firmly.

Ka stood at the back of the hall, watching for trouble. Suddenly, one man shouted 'Fascist, listen to the people. The people won the war, not the politicians. You work with the wealthy, how can you represent us?'

Justine tried to explain, as others shouted out.

Suddenly, Ka saw one man hit another, just in front of her. They were talking together earlier. It was staged, she thought. Deliberate, to disrupt the meeting. Must do something before the trouble spreads. Slipping outside, she grabbed the policemen she'd seen earlier and warned him.

'Wait here,' he said, and she saw him cross the street to a *panier à salade* across the street, four other *flics* piling out of the Citroën van.

Back in the hall with them, Ka saw several other men were fighting in the aisles. The shriek of a police whistle made everyone look to the back as the *flics* moved in and started to grab a trouble maker.

On stage, Justine saw a tough-looking woman heading in her direction, carrying a bucket of something. 'Watch out,' she shouted to the candidate seated next to her, grabbing his arm. The woman lifted the bucket to head height and attempted to cover them in what looked like red paint. One policeman coming forward through the crowd, shouted 'Stop.' The woman hesitated, and the contents of the bucket tipped back on top of her.

Looking back on that month of campaigning, Ka felt she and Justine were one. Every weekday, Ka would rush back from work to help. At the weekends, they were together all the time, both striving to achieve the same end.

Voting day arrived, or rather the first voting day. The second vote a week later would be between the two candidates who won more than fifteen per cent of the votes cast in the first vote. One of those was Justine. More campaigning followed in the period between the two votes. It was crucial that she didn't lose due to voters for losing candidates the first time casting their votes this time for the other candidate.

Ka was sorry for Justine that second Sunday. Everyone was on edge, as they waited at the *mairie d'arrondissement*, the local town hall for that wonderful result.

Yet, after the great day and the celebration they went to with Josephine at one of her night clubs, Ka felt a gap open up between her and Justine. They saw one another at work of course, but she spent much less time with Justine in the evenings and at the weekend. It was as though Justine was moving in another world. All her time seemed to be taken up in politics, and there was no place for Ka.

She loved Justine and wanted her for herself. The woman called Kim was a worry. Cambodian, it appeared, and from an educated family. She met her just the once, but that was enough. Smartly dressed to show off her body, more voluptuous than a Vietnamese woman. She was sure that Kim would be irresistible to men, and maybe to women as well. Clever, and not to be trusted, thought Ka. Not much she could do about it, but she must watch her and the relationship between her and Justine.

Then there was Bao. She was seeing him more often now. Somehow he was changing. He no longer bullied her. He seemed to have his own problems, and wanted to talk about them. He asked her about Madame X, knowing somehow that she was one of Ka's clients at Schiap. Why this fascination about Madame X, even about her husband and her father? What was his motive? Could he be attempting to blackmail the woman?

The pipeline seemed to be working smoothly. Glun didn't share much information with her on how he and his family were sourcing the raw opium. Being a Meo, that was the key to his access to the right people. How long would it last? Ka understood from Justine that the Viets wanted to control the opium production in the Highlands of Tonkin. Would they attempt a deal with the Meos? The French authorities would prevent that, surely. Maybe Justine's friend at the *piscine*, was where the information came from.

She must protect Justine. Now a deputy, it was even more important that Bao didn't learn of the pipeline. Ka would do anything for Justine. She adored the moments when she worked on her clothes at Schiap, and could imagine her glorious body underneath them. How could she bring her closer again, be an essential part of her life? That Kim girl, she was trying to control Justine by becoming an essential link between the deputy and how the public perceived her. Kim was taking over Justine's persona. She must be stopped. Kim could harm Justine by becoming indispensable in her life.

33

Paris, Latin Quarter, March 1952

The phone went in Justine's apartment, just as she was enjoying a fig and some yoghurt for breakfast. It was Jean. Would she join him in the usual bar, close by Saint-Sulpice. Yes, right away, she agreed. The latest letter was beside her. The same cut out letters, saying 'Stop your opium business. Otherwise, you can expect a story in the press, drawing the public's attention to it.'

Jean called for coffee, as she settled in beside him and showed him the new letter.

'Your friend Kim is quite a girl,' he said straight away. 'Do you want a summary, or the long version?'

'Let's have it all,' she said.

Jean described that evening after following her home. Kim re-emerged from her apartment an hour later, and walked into the Metro with him shadowing her in the next carriage through the connecting doors. They came out at Étoile and he followed her towards rue du Faubourg Saint-Honoré, stopping in the rue d'Artois at number 27.

The driving rhythm of Bud Powell and Kenny Clarke on piano and drums came from inside, as Jean made a discreet entry a few minutes after Kim. This was home from home to Jean as he shook hands with the maître d', ordered a Scotch Perrier, and made sure there was plenty of space between him and Kim. The Blue Note, shrine of modern jazz in Paris. With her was a large Asian man, powerfully built for a Vietnamese if that's what he was.

Without her winter coat, Kim made a dramatic impact in a stunning dress in green shantung silk. Her lustrous black hair was brushed down one side of the head and held in a clasp behind the neck. Each time she moved, her breasts struggled to stay inside the dress. Jean tried to concentrate on the music, as Bud Powell began a slow 'Polka Dots and Moonbeams' in chords that resonated with emotion.

Who was this Chinese-looking man? They seemed to be enjoying the music, saying little to one another. After a time, Jean removed himself unobtrusively from his table, and headed for a small office behind the reception desk. Its occupant, Felix, was an old friend on the Paris jazz scene, and Jean asked about the Chinese. Felix's response was 'Dieu Tran, from Saigon. Dangerous.'

'Dieu Tran?' said Justine.

'I checked with the *piscine* the next day. He's senior in the *Bình Xuyên*, comes to Paris often.'

'Do you think she hires herself out to him. Or is she on the inside?' said Justine.

'Hard to say. You don't go to the Blue Note to make love, you go there to make music. My hunch is that there's some business arrangement between them.'

Justine was silent, thinking out the consequences. 'That's further confirmation the *Bình Xuyên* are still on to me, even though blackmail is a softer approach than what they tried on me in Saigon.'

'Yes.' Jean paused for a moment. 'I've been asking myself, why the Blue Note? It suddenly came to me. These American jazz men live in Paris because they can't any longer get the heroin they want in New York. Most of the best are on it,

Charlie Parker is dying of it. There's been a massive clamp-down on narcotics on the East Coast of the United States. Here in Paris, it seems they can have what they want. I suspect the jazz club is an important outlet for the trafficker in that part of the city.'

'You said heroin?'

'Yes.' Jean explained that in the past four years, there'd been an explosion of heroin abuse in the States. Much of the drug that entered New York came via Marseille. The Americans were urging other countries like France to clamp down as well. He bet that the *Bình Xuyên*'s concern was that Justine would move into the heroin business, much more lucrative than opium. Possession and dealing in heroin were now illegal under French law.

Justine went tense. 'Jean,' she said passionately, 'I've never intended entering the heroin world. I would never do it, for very good moral and ethical reasons.'

'I believe you, Justine. The problem is that the *Bình Xuyên* has no such scruples, nor would it credit any competitor with having them.'

'If me moving into heroin is the opposition's concern, then they should be told I have no such intention, that I'm no threat to them. Any idea how we could do that?'

'If Kim already knows what you're doing, thanks to Madame X telling her, you could come out into the open with her. Tell Kim the extent of your present business, and that heroin will never be your thing, on the basis that she's become a good friend and you wanted to share the information privately with her.'

'That would be a big step,' said Justine. 'There's risk in that route. Kim's well placed to do me harm if she wanted to because she writes for the press. If I told her openly, she could trash me in the media without risk of being accused of libel.'

Jean was thinking. 'You could close down the pipeline right away and then tell her, but I expect everyone would like another year or two in the business to build up funds.'

They kicked the issue around for a bit. Justine couldn't make up her mind what to do in response to the letters. Going to the police was out of the question. Perhaps she should talk to Françoise? Her thoughts drifted to Kim. Why was she involved with the *Bình Xuyên*? Surely a Cambodian girl of good education and into a successful career, would realise that getting mixed up with the Saigon underworld was bad news. Justine was not as convinced as Jean that Kim was part of the *Bình Xuyên*. If she was, then it wasn't voluntary.

How should she handle Kim from now on? They enjoyed a strong working relationship. Kim really did help Justine in terms of her public image. You could say Kim needed her as well. A close relationship with a deputy on the way up in the Radical Party was something any freelance journalist would value. Kim couldn't be the blackmailer.

It looked like Madame X was being forced into it by the *Bình Xuyên*. Probably being blackmailed herself. They were using her to persuade Justine to close down her pipeline. They feared she would move into heroin, and capture part of that market.

Kim's role was unclear. She was a friend of Dieu Tran, maybe no more than that. He might be using the Blue Note as an outlet, she might be close to him because he was a powerful link with the Saigon underground, and a valuable source of information. Justine would just have to be doubly careful in what information she passed to Kim, and to avoid being trapped into anything that could compromise her as a deputy.

Jean was confident that the *Bình Xuyên* wouldn't harm her while she was in France. She would have to think about when to bring the pipeline to an end. It was time she took Ka into her confidence and explained the blackmail. After all, Ka ran the relationship with Madame X, through their contact at Schiap. Maybe Ka could find out more about the woman's involvement.

34

Leo found it hard to push aside his doubts. If the French army couldn't find a new way to neutralise the Viet threat in the north in the coming year, they would lose it to Ho Chi Minh. It was already touch and go keeping the main highways open in daytime. At night, they were bandit territory. Outside Hanoi and Haiphong, Viet influence over the population was widespread. Even with sustained support from America in equipment and aircraft, and France's commitment of their best fighting troops, they would go on losing Frenchmen in large numbers.

It was easier for him to confront the bitter truth than it was for the generals who were contending with the *colons* and the politicians as well. Leo was convinced that a fundamental review of military tactics was overdue. De Lattre achieved a great deal when he enjoyed supreme command of the military and the administration, but the inexorable resilience and growth in size of General Giap's army were undeniable.

Leo's intelligence work and liaison with Trinquier's network of Montagnards did provide some insight into latest military thinking. The call to attend a small conference at army headquarters in Hanoi indicated something special might be happening. As always when there was something new round the corner, excitement grabbed Leo. He remained a soldier at heart, and he found a new challenge irresistible.

General de Linares put Leo at ease the moment proceedings began. A strong Catholic, wonderful wife and thirteen children, de Linares represented the traditional heart of the French officer corps.

After introducing Leo to those present, the General said, 'Lieutenant Beckendorf, you and I came close to one another at the end of '44. I remember how tough it was when we tried to drive you lot out of the pocket at Colmar. Glad we're now on the same side.' The Commander of French forces in North Vietnam brought laughter to the room.

Turning to the small group present, the General suddenly looked serious. 'This discussion will be off the record. We're going to talk about new tactics, a way to take the fight to the Viets. Lieutenant Beckendorf is with us because of his depth of experience in intelligence as well as airborne operations. In due course, Lieutenant, I'd like to hear your views on what we are considering.'

Leo was curious as to what was coming. Clearly, there were new things happening other than Roger Trinquier's plan.

The General turned to the dark-haired, powerful-looking senior officer at his side. 'Colonel Gilles here is proposing an operation which is viable, in my view, provided intelligence confirms some suppositions. In particular, on the attitude of the local population. He paused as he looked at each of them in turn. He then nodded towards Gilles.

The Colonel walked over to the wall map of northern Vietnam. 'We proved at Hoa Binh the effectiveness of combining parachute troops with mobile columns. The late General de Lattre backed us and supported the tactics we wanted to employ. The result proved their effectiveness.

'That's a fair statement, Colonel,' said General de Linares. 'Tell the meeting what you're now proposing, please.'

'Certainly, General.' Gilles looked every bit the part as Commander of parachute forces. Tall and powerfully built, black hair slicked back, heavy eyebrows to match, and only one eye. He explained that the objective was to cut off any major advance by Giap's forces across the Highlands towards Laos. The solution he was proposing, was to overcome the impenetrable terrain by establishing a strong military presence at Na San. He pointed out Na San on the map, about two hundred kilometres north-west of Hanoi.

Gilles continued, that from the proposed air/land base, they could operate their mobile columns and take advantage of the maquis being established by Commandant Trinquier's Groupement de Commandos Mixtes Aéroportés, or GCMA. A *base aéroterrestre*, air/land base, in the vicinity of Na San was what he was proposing. Its defence would be organised on the hedgehog principle, crucial if they were to avoid being overrun and left without an exit.

Leo listened patiently. Gilles was undoubtedly an innovative officer, and proven as a fine leader of his men, but Leo had doubts about his proposal.

General de Linares interrupted. 'I want to be sure, Colonel, that everyone understands what you mean by hedgehog defence.'

'Of course, General,' said Gilles, explaining it was where the defence was structured in depth, with multiple strongpoints heavily fortified against attack from all directions. The enemy could penetrate between the hedgehogs, but each defensive point could fight on even when surrounded. This had the effect of keeping enemy forces tied down on a large scale. That in turn provided the defenders with the opportunity to counterattack using their own reserves, and cut off the supply lines of the attackers.

General de Linares broke in, using as an example of the hedgehog principle employed on a large scale the way the

British 8th Army constructed its line at Gazala in the Western Desert. A series of heavily fortified boxes, with names like Knightsbridge. Rommel's armour circumvented the line down below the southernmost box at Bir Hakeim. From that heavily armed enclave, General Koenig's Free French Brigade sent out mobile columns to cut off the Afrika Korps supply lines.

'Absolutely, General,' said Jean Gilles, adding, 'What we want is for Giap's forces to come out and attack us up front. A strong central post at Na San, surrounded by a large network of hedgehogs, would bring him into the open. Instead of responding all the time to in–out guerrilla attacks, we would have the chance to inflict heavy losses on him.'

'Thank you, Colonel,' said the General. De Linares turned towards Leo. 'Now, Lieutenant,' Please explain your thinking from the intelligence standpoint.'

Presenting to senior officers was nothing new to Leo after his intelligence experience in the European war. I'm not going to be intimidated by this lot, he thought, as he stood up and went over to join de Linares. At least I'm now in the uniform of a French officer.

'General, thank you. You'll be aware that we work mainly on radio intercepts which we cross-reference to what we hear from the army's Deuxième Bureau.' Leo turned to the wall map and pointed out the Tonkin Highlands. 'It's here that there's significant movement of Vietminh forces to the west, in the direction of Laos. Until now, Giap has concentrated his forces in the Red River Delta, threatening to close in on Hanoi. Already the route from Hanoi to Haiphong is too dangerous at night.'

The audience nodded, they knew all that.

'The question is,' said Leo, 'could the emphasis on the Red River Delta be a feint?' He paused for the idea to sink in. 'If Giap could occupy the western Highlands and capture the opium trade, that would greatly enhance Ho Chi Minh's finances, and therefore the volume of his arms purchases from China.'

'Very well, Lieutenant,' said de Linares. 'You could well be right. Does your intelligence analysis create any obstacle to Colonel Gilles's proposal to create a *base aéroterrestre* at Na San?'

Leo felt everyone's eyes swing back on him. He sensed the challenge. De Linares was testing him, this former enemy of years back. Careful now. Only say what you can support with fact. They won't take kindly to opinions.

Leo reported that intelligence told them Giap had two of his infantry divisions in that western region. The 'Lorraine' diversion didn't cause him to move those substantial forces back east. Colonel Gilles's proposal should cause this force to mount a frontal attack on the new base, particularly if Giap underestimated what he was up against. The trick therefore would be to delay reinforcement until the Viets were all but committed to attack in their present strength. Then to strike before they reinforced.

Gilles interjected. 'I agree. In fact, we would delay flying in the artillery as long as we could. What would we be up against, what Viet forces would be close enough to Na San, Lieutenant?'

'From latest intercepts, Colonel, it would be elements of Giap's 308th Division.'

'So,' commented Jean Gilles, 'at least two additional battalions of paratroops as well as artillery would be dropped at the last minute. That should give us adequate forces both to repulse the attack, and provide the reserves to break out and inflict major losses on the enemy.'

General de Linares interjected. 'Lieutenant Beckendorf, you have considerable wartime combat experience involving airborne operations. What are the risks, as you see them?'

Leo waited before replying, sensing again that he shouldn't waffle. 'Sir, my fear is that, strong as the *base aéroterrestre* argument is, its effectiveness relies upon support from the air, and a sympathetic local population for the moment when we decide to withdraw. That applies also to offensive sorties using *groupes mobiles*.

'My information is that the inhabitants of the surrounding area are against Ho Chi Minh, although not necessarily pro-French. In the Highlands approaching Laos, the Montagnards are not pro-French either, even though they dislike the Vietminh. The effectiveness of the Na San base proposed by Colonel Gilles would increase if we offered the Montagnards a strong incentive.'

'Oh, and what's the background to that?' asked the General.

'Goes back to the opium trade,' replied Leo. 'The Viets grabbed the opium crop last year, sold it in Thailand and, with the cash generated, bought arms from China. The flow of intelligence from the Montagnards to the Deuxième Bureau dried up when our opium purchases ceased.'

Jean Gilles looked restless. 'Do we have to get into that, Lieutenant? Certainly there needs to be a strong maquis around the area of the *base aéroterrestre*. But surely we need to concentrate our budget on maximising military strength, rather than paying truckloads of piastres to the Montagnards.'

General de Linares stepped into the exchange. 'You're right, Colonel. The fact remains that we need to fund the strategy to build up the maquis among the Montagnards. We'll only achieve that by giving them cash or by buying their opium crop from which, dare I say it, more cash can be realised. Our secret service has that as an agreed objective. They call it Operation X.'

'Opium is a key factor, sir, at least in my view,' said Leo. 'Our military intelligence personnel have made considerable efforts to discourage the Meo tribe, who grow the opium poppies, from working with Ho Chi Minh's people. They're ready to deal with us. The operation has been carefully prepared.'

'Yes,' said de Linares, 'the Bureau is ready to go live with Operation X. Leave that to me.'

35

Leo pulled his parachute shroud lines in, rolled up the canopy, and looked around him. The C47 Dakota crews clearly excelled themselves that day. His headquarters unit were all together, as tight a grouping on landing as he ever saw. Containers with heavier weaponry were coming down nearby. So the plan was unfolding. Last-minute drops, leaving the enemy no time to put right his underestimation of the French strength. The hedgehog defence, meaning a large number of defending posts connected by trenches and wire, to draw the Viets into massed frontal attack.

He would watch closely every stage of the enemy's deployment. Giap was still learning. The trick was to let him believe he was stronger than the French. As always, he was without air power although his anti-aircraft defences were improving. Leo knew this was the big test for the *base aéroterrestre* concept. Jean Gilles's brainchild, now to be proved gloriously or rejected in pain. Creating a forward, isolated land base, manned and supplied from the air. In his role as intelligence officer, Leo was working alongside Colonel Gilles, commander of the Na San operation. His job was to interpret the enemy's response at each stage of the battle, estimating the enemy's strength and their losses. Observing the efficacy of the *base aéroterrestre* at every stage, including any decision on final withdrawal.

Leo admired Gilles's preparatory steps. The work put into interlocking trenches between the hedgehogs was impressive. The plan was to hit back hard, and then follow up with *groupes mobiles* to exploit the advantage, unmolested by a local civilian population not anti-French.

Radio messages came into HQ confirming the first Viet attacks in late evening on two of the hedgehog defensive points, and both were pushed back. The following week, the Viets probed the French defences, testing their strength. It was again late evening, when the first major Viet attack was launched at brigade strength on two hedgehog points, each side of the HQ. Both were overwhelmed. The next day Jean Gilles ordered a counterattack. After severe fighting, both points were recovered.

General Giap launched his all-out attack that morning, and the battle raged most of the day, through the night, until the next day. The relentless assaults in waves of infantry, were cut down by the machine guns and mortars of the hedge-hogs. From above, French fighter bombers poured into them not only explosives but what the Viets truly feared, napalm. Unable to sustain the horrendous losses, Giap pulled back and all suddenly went silent.

The Viets could no longer withstand the severe casualty rate. They withdrew, hampered by Gilles's mobile patrols. Jean Gilles, with Leo at his side, could radio the High Command that it was all over. Leo knew what the consequences would be. While the Viets would re-group, even hold back for a time after the horrendous losses they incurred, for the French it was vindication of the *base aéroterrestre* air/land base concept. Impressive, even to the experienced and somewhat sceptical Leo. His naturally cautious German mind still told him that one win didn't guarantee another the next time.

He analysed General Giap's actions and identified his mistakes in a report to Gilles and de Linares, which drew on his intelligence sources. They estimated that the Viets suffered three thousand dead, and many wounded prisoners. They didn't expect him to repeat the same errors next time.

36

Ka and Justine were treating themselves to a very French meal at La Petite Chaise, a small family-owned restaurant on the left bank. After ordering their escargots, Ka said, 'You asked me to find out more about Madame X.'

'Yes, my darling. Madame X is a missing link in this chain that seems to be enveloping me. I told you about the blackmail letters. I just got a third.'

'That's frightening. What I've found out might partly explain what's going on. I was able to see Madame X at her home. I promised to show her some accessories which might go with the garments she recently added to her wardrobe. It's a lovely apartment in the Septième, overlooking the river.'

'Quai d'Orsay, I guess.'

'That's right. Anyway, we started talking about Vietnam. She seemed interested to hear about my upbringing in Hanoi. We got onto the war, and I said how bad an effect the fighting was having on the ordinary people in the Red River Delta. She asked if we had any friends affected by the French army and air force using napalm. She added that her father was involved in the supply of napalm and had received threatening letters.'

'Interesting,' said Justine, and they stopped talking while the waiter served them with their main course of rognons de veau.

Ka continued. 'She said that left-wing elements in France were onto the impact of napalm attacks on the civilian population.

Added to that was the problem that the army seldom knows whether a village is helping the Viets or not.'

'I know. The truth probably is that around Hanoi and in the Red River Delta, all villages are sympathetic to Ho Chi Minh.' Justine knew this was fundamental to the army's problems.

'She also asked me if I knew about the *Bình Xuyên*. I said I did, because most Vietnamese here knew they ran organised crime in Saigon. I got the feeling she thinks it's them who were sending the threatening letters, that they were looking to take money off her father.'

Ka was deep in thought, while they both enjoyed the delicious veal kidneys in mustard sauce. Using a piece of baguette to mop up the plate, she said slowly, 'The other message coming through was that her husband, a senior civil servant, was saying that her opium habit was becoming a problem for him.'

'Okay, but what's the link to blackmailing me?'

'Nothing involving Madame X. I'm sure it's the *Bình Xuyên*. The word in the Paris Vietnamese community is that they are moving into the heroin trade. They've watched the heroin supply from Turkey via Marseille to the United States grow massively. They want to share in the enormous profits to be made. The solution is for them to export Vietnamese opium to the heroin processors in Marseille. Maybe to start making it in Saigon.

'They know you've been successful with your own pipeline. They see you as a real danger, unable to resist moving into heroin in due course. They want you out of the business. They're probably using Bao or one of his thugs to produce and deliver the letters to you.'

'Ka, you're making sense. That's got to be the answer.

37

'It's a year since that first success we had.' Kim raised her glass to Justine. They were back in the bistro where opening the proof copy of *Paris Match* was the start of their business cooperation.

'You certainly did well,' Justine responded. 'That article launched me well and truly, just after joining the Assembly. Sorry I couldn't help you on the napalm front. Nothing came of it, as far as I know.'

'No, at least nothing yet. As I've heard, napalm is now used widely in battle conditions. Its use has saved fighting units in trouble. When the Viets see the Dakotas and Boxcars coming out of the sky with those silver eggs glinting in the sun, they get up and run.'

'Sounds ghastly,' said Justine.

Suddenly Kim said, 'You have to admit, the army's victory at Na San is an enormous boost for those who want the war to go on.'

Justine didn't respond.

'Anyway,' said Kim, 'I've made an important move.'

'Oh, what's that?'

'I've shifted my research into politics. You know the present government looks increasingly wobbly.'

'You can say that again,' laughed Justine. 'It's the seventeenth government in nineteen years, and it won't last much longer.'

'I think there's a story, and the subject of the story is your leader.'

'You mean Mendès France?'

'I think he has a fair chance of winning a majority in the Assembly this year, becoming prime minister.'

'That's what I think too,' said Justine. 'So, what can we do to help him?'

Kim was silent for a moment. 'Do you know there's a new French news magazine about to be launched, similar to *Time*?'

'I've heard rumours,' said Justine, guardedly.

'*L'Express*, that's what it's to be called. And, from what I hear, Pierre Mendès France is somehow involved and might even be on the front cover of the first edition.'

'You're very well informed.'

'As I always say, that's my business. Now, listen Justine. We need to come up with ammunition to boost his standing, grow popular support for him. That way, the Assembly will shift its vote towards him.'

'We need a story,' said Justine, looking questionably at Kim.

'What distinguishes PMF, as the media refer to him, is that he's the only party leader, aside from the Communists, who is adamantly for France withdrawing from Indochina.'

'You're right.'

Justine could see Kim was in one of her thoughtful moods. 'I'd like to interest a newspaper in writing a series of articles on PMF, maybe *L'Express*. Could be headed, "What makes Pierre Mendes France different?".'

'I like that.'

'You know, Justine, I think there's still some mileage in the napalm story. But this time, let's broaden it. Make it more general, rather than my original idea of a secret project in the army. In the past year, napalm is being used more widely, every time a unit is in trouble, some say. The angle I'd like to highlight is that there is often collateral damage. Human damage that is.'

'What do you mean, Kim?'

'That when these napalm fire bombs are dropped in a battle zone, civilians are sometimes involved, engulfed in fire. They're seen running from the fields, even the villages, as the petroleum jelly stuck to their bodies slowly burns them alive.'

'Horrible,' said Justine.

Kim looked hard at her. 'Justine, I need your help to get to PMF so he knows my thinking. If he agrees, he might even help me by letting me quote him.'

Here we are again, the impact of napalm on the civilian population. Kim could be right. Why not put it to PMF? Why didn't she want to? The risk that Madame X might be exposed because of her father being the importer of the army's napalm supplies from the States?

After a long silence, Justine said, 'I don't like it, Kim. You go ahead if you like, but I don't want any part in it.'

Justine knew that Pierre Mendès France would soon be having another shot at winning over the Assembly, to vote him in as prime minister. She must not expose herself to anything that could adversely affect his chances.

38

Paris, Latin Quarter, January 1953

They were together in Justine's apartment, and she started to tell Ka what she knew about Kim. 'She's an extraordinary woman. I mentioned to you how she started by profiling me in the article in *Paris Match*.'

'Cambodian, isn't she?' said Ka.

'That's right.'

'I'm suspicious of her,' said Ka.

'What? Why?' Justine was surprised, upset at Ka's reaction.

'She's getting too close to you.'

'Too close, in what way?'

'She's on to you every month. It's as though you were her spy in the Radical Party, her way into Mendès France.'

Justine was aghast at Ka's attitude. 'Where do you get this impression from, Ka? Has someone been talking to you?'

Ka waited for a moment. 'It's Madame X. She came into Schiap earlier this week. When we were behind the screen, she gave me the usual payment which of course I took to the safe deposit after work. She started asking about you, and mentioned Kim Cho's name, wanted to know about your relationship with her. She doesn't like Kim Cho.'

'Did she say why?'

'She gave me the impression Kim Cho might be blackmailing her. Madame X was very open, I couldn't work out why she was telling all these things. She seemed to want someone to talk to.

She said Kim knew about her father's business.' There was a long silence. Justine needed some space, to think. She went into the kitchen to make tea and some tartines.

Ka rose when Justine returned and put the tray down. They reached out for one another. Ka's slender figure pressed itself against the person she was so fond of. 'I love you, Justine. I don't want anything to happen to you. You must be careful of this Kim. I think she's trouble. Apparently she's very attractive, uses her body to obtain information.'

'Did you get that from Madame X as well?'

Ka didn't reply.

39

'So, Leo, over a year as an officer in the French army. Something to celebrate.' Henri lolled back, Scotch and soda in one hand, the other over the back of the chair, grinning at his old school mate. 'Let's drink also to the Na San operation. You and Jean Gilles have shown what's possible. Must have surprised Ho Chi Minh. I'm told the Viet dead and wounded are around four thousand. Staggering.'

'Yes,' said Leo. 'That's what can be achieved if you tempt Giap to attack in full strength. Let him think we were a lot weaker on the ground. He thought he could wipe us out. So he attacked, and we flew in the paras in force. When he couldn't take the losses any longer, he quit. Afterwards, we pulled back along pre-arranged escape lines.'

'I guess that's where your friend Trinquier came in.'

'That's right. The Montagnard maquis attacked the Viet supply lines during the battle, and afterwards provided cover when we withdrew some of our units.'

There was a pause as they re-filled their glasses, and a smart Vietnamese mess waiter took orders for dinner.

'The danger,' continued Leo, 'is that the *base aéroter-restre* plan having worked so effectively at Na San, the High Command will use it again on an even bigger scale to attempt a total knock-out of Giap's forces.'

'If the same principles are applied,' said Henri, 'why shouldn't it be successful again?'

Leo held his head in his hands, in thought, before arguing that two battles were never the same. There were always factors which could lead to a different outcome, which weren't fore-seen. If things went wrong, for instance if Giap moved in larger forces and more artillery than expected, and supplies couldn't be flown in, it could lead to annihilation or surrender. And the Viet army was growing in size all the time. In a year or two it could be fifty per cent larger, with lots more artillery.

Base aéroterrestre was what it said, a base cut off except from the air. France's combat air strength, even with American aircraft, was weak. No helicopters. There were signs the Viets were building up their anti-aircraft capability. In the north of the country, weather was an unknown factor. Add that together and repeating Na San on a bigger scale was questionable.

'I see what you mean,' said Henri. 'But the help we're receiving from America in arms and aircraft is building up all the time.'

Leo shook his head. 'Even with piles of new American equipment, we won't beat them. We'll never catch them, we can't win.'

'Oh, you're a pessimist,' said Henri with a shallow laugh.

Leo didn't respond, still in sombre mood. 'There are other things wrong out here. He paused, and Henri remained silent. Remember that last day at St Gregory's, just before we left in June '38?'

'You mean the session with Rooky, in his House Master's study.'

'Yes, with Bill also. Rooky talked about the suspension of morality in time of war.'

'How right he was,' said Henri.

'Trouble is, from what I learn from my intelligence friends, the colonial Sûreté here were doing things you and I wouldn't dream of well before this war broke out.' Leo managed a grim smile. 'And I'm the first to admit us Germans have nothing to be proud of.'

'You're now French, Leo. You're exonerated.' They both laughed. 'What are you referring to, specifically?' asked Henri.

'Torture,' said Leo. There was a pause before he added, 'What the Sûreté here are doing to Viet prisoners and suspected insurgents.'

'You say torture?'

Leo said the Sûreté were using electric shock treatment to make captives talk back in the thirties and they were still at it. That he was taken to an air force building in Hanoi recently, and shown a room where the equipment was laid out ready for use, magneto, rheostat control handle, electrodes for connecting to various parts of the body. It was still operational, installed by the Sûreté long before the current war started.

Henri didn't look surprised. 'I know beatings are the norm, but electric shock treatment, that's something else. I have heard of it.'

'On the walls were photographs, corpses of Vietnamese in various stages of agony and death, *pour encourager les autres* as Voltaire would have said. To encourage captives to speak out before being subjected to torture and probable death.'

'Horrendous,' said Henri.

'Apparently, it's now the practice for the Sûreté to take corpses of those who have died under interrogation onto the Paul Doumer Bridge at night and dump them into the Red River.'

There was silence for some time. Then Henri said, 'Where's this conversation heading?'

'The point I'm making is that if we, and I say we since I'm now a Frenchman, continue to treat the native population with such brutality, we have no chance of building successful civilian resistance against the Viet insurgents.'

'Going back to school and Rooky,' said Henri, 'I would stand in the way of torture, if it came my way. It's not going to happen on my watch.'

They went through to the dining area, out on the veranda. Over the meal, conversation strayed to their female friends. 'So pleased you and Theresa are together,' said Henri. 'I never knew her before she arrived in Saigon, but was very impressed when I gave her the initial briefing.'

'Thanks,' said Leo, cautiously. 'Now I'm her French boyfriend.' And they laughed.

Henri thought of his own position. Still unmarried. A couple of failed relationships. One in Cairo during the war, another after the war. And the question that came back to him every so often, shouldn't he do something else with his life? He was not typical of his fellow officers, in the audacious and brave style of an officer in the French Foreign Legion. He was more typical of the rushed 1939 intake from St Cyr, as war threatened. It was a family tradition, and he felt that on the whole that he'd done what was expected of him. But was he really cut out to spend his whole career as an army officer?

Changing the subject, Henri suddenly said, 'You know, it's Bill who concerns me.'

'Oh, why?'

'He knows Captain Savani.'

'The Corsican who runs Operation X, with the help of Roger Trinquier.'

'That's right. Bill flies a Dakota for Savani, "Air Opium" they call it. He collects the raw opium from the growers among the Montagnards, and brings it down to Cap St Jacques. I get this from my friends there.'

'Sounds lucrative,' said Leo. 'Looks like Bill will amass some capital for the air transport business he wants to start in South Africa.'

'Yes. However,' Henri said cautiously, 'I'm told that Bill may be up to something on the side.'

'On the side, what do you mean by that?'

Henri hesitated at this point. He didn't know the full story, he must be careful what he said, even to Leo.

'He has a female friend in Paris, she's now a deputy, powerfully connected. There's a business connection between them, maybe more. I just got tipped off they may be in trouble.'

Silence for a moment, then Leo said, 'I see Bill now and again up here, when he's on one of his trips. Should I do anything, make any inquiries?'

'No, just watch and wait,' said Henri. 'Let me know if you pick anything up through your Deuxième Bureau contacts.'

40

'Here we are again, same place, a month later,' exclaimed Kim, in a mood Justine couldn't fathom. The Cambodian girl seemed morose, not showing her usual spirits.

The waiter put down *pression* and *croque monsieur* in front of each.

'How's the article in *L'Express* going, about Vietnamese civilians suffering from the use of napalm?' asked Justine.

'Well, thank you. Should be out in two weeks' time. Now we need to agree on a story for the follow-up article.'

'I guess we do, what's on your mind this time?'

Kim waited a moment, taking a bite of the delicious ham and cheese on fried bread. 'You once mentioned to me the Bank of Indochina's overvaluation of the piaster.'

'Oh, did I?' Justine was immediately on guard. That was something she'd regretted afterwards.

Kim continued. 'Not so much the long-standing practice of inflating the local exchange rate. That makes sense to help businesses in Indochina, and expats working there.'

'So, what's the real story?' asked Justine.

Kim said she was looking to expose a racket where profits being made by currency operators buying dollars in Paris with French francs, and then selling them in Saigon for piastres.

'Oh, and what then?' asked Justine.

'The piastres are then converted back into francs at the Bank of Indochina's overvalued rate. The currency operator makes a hundred per cent profit. They double their money in what is a circular operation that has no substance. There's no underlying sale of merchandise generating the currency trades.'

'I see,' said Justine, relieved it was the artificial trading rather than bona fide business that Kim would be exposing. 'You are on to a good story there, I would think. Let's pass it by PMF and see if he'll lend support to it.'

Justine recognised that if the article received widespread attention, it would increase pressure on the French government to devalue the piaster to put a stop to the device. That wouldn't be popular with the locals.

Kim looked pleased with herself. 'What's more, there's a spin-off to develop from this one.'

'Oh, and what's that, Kim?'

'The word is that those who have been profiting from these currency trades include individuals of some standing in Paris.'

Justine sensed that something potentially dangerous was coming from Kim's fertile mind. 'Any names?' asked Justine, quietly.

'Well, there's that woman's father I mentioned to you way back, the arms dealer who started with flamethrowers for Germany, then graduated to napalm for the French army.'

'Yes, I recall you telling me about him.' Justine heard the alarm bell go off in her head. That's the father of Madame X.

There was a long silence. Justine didn't want to prolong the conversation, and it seemed to her that Kim wanted to say something but couldn't bring herself to do so.

Finally, Kim said slowly, almost in a whisper, 'Justine.'

'Yes, Kim.'

'I have a problem. It's not about business. It's just that I need to speak to someone I trust.'

Justine was surprised, also curious. 'I'm sorry to hear that, Kim. Do you really think I could help?'

'I think so. Just talking to you would help me. Could we go somewhere we can talk privately?'

Justine sensed there was something coming she would prefer not to know. On the other hand, if Kim was going to open up to her in some way, she shouldn't miss the opportunity to ask her a question or two, and perhaps resolve the issues surrounding Madame X.

'All right. We could go round to my apartment now, if you like. It can't be for long as I've an appointment I must keep this evening.'

⊹⊱⊰⊹

'Come in and see how a mannequin turned deputy lives, she said laughingly to Kim as she unlocked the door. I never moved when my life changed from fashion to politics, so forgive how cramped it is.'

'Well, it's just you, isn't it?'

'Yes, as always,' said Justine. 'Now, give me your coat. Would you like coffee, tea or rouge?'

'A glass of rouge would do fine.'

Justine took a couple of glasses from the kitchen and poured out the wine for them both. They sat side by side on the old French canapé. 'Kim, tell me what's troubling you.'

'I feel we've got to know one another well in the past year or two. I don't have that number of real friends,' said Kim, speaking softly as though feeling her way along a dark corridor.

'I've certainly enjoyed our regular get-togethers,' said Justine, noticing the other's nervousness.

'I want to start by telling you something none of my other business friends know, nor anyone else for that matter.'

'And what's that?'

Kim stopped for a moment. Then drawing herself up she turned to face Justine. 'I'm a heroin addict.'

Justine saw the moisture in Kim's eyes, she could almost feel the pain showing on the other's face. Her hand reached out to touch Kim's arm and Kim moved a little towards her. They didn't embrace, but Justine felt more than surprise and sympathy, something else between them.

'It only happened a few months ago. This man I met, it was in a jazz club. We both like modern jazz. He's a rich businessman, from Saigon. Tough and ruthless, I guess, but to me he's charming and understanding. You may have noticed, Justine, I'm a sexy person and need men. That doesn't mean I behave like a call girl. But I do give in to attractive men easily.'

'Nothing wrong with that, in my book,' said Justine. 'You'd be surprised what the characters who inhabit my world are like.'

'I can imagine,' said Kim, smiling just a little.

'I don't know anything about heroin, except what I've read occasionally in the papers. I know there's a heroin problem in the States.'

'That's right,' said Kim. 'From what I understand, Marseille is a turntable for the trade. Opium latex comes into the port, mainly from Turkey and Vietnam, and is processed into morphine and heroin before being shipped to New York'

'Were you into anything before being introduced to heroin?'

'I smoked opium with friends, but that's all,' said Kim. 'In Cambodia, that's not unusual. This boyfriend I told you about, he suggested I tried a tablet to increase the excitement of the sex we were having together. I took it regularly and it increased my energy at work as well as in leisure. I think he must have increased the dosage because, after a few weeks, I couldn't face a day without it.'

'That was heroin, Kim?' Justine remembered what Jean told her about following Kim to the jazz club and seeing her with the Chinese-looking guy.

'Yes, heroin. I have to have it, Justine, and it has tied me to him. He's in Vietnam a good part of the time, but has someone in Paris who supplies it to me. As long as I'm available for him when he comes to Paris, I don't have to pay.'

'My God, what a story. You poor thing. I'm not sure there's any advice I can give you.' Justine's brain was racing away from her. Kim's man, the one she was with when Jean saw them at the Blue Note, was big in the Bình Xuyên. Dieu Tran was his name, according to Jean.

Kim was sobbing quietly, her beautiful grey eyes showing the grief and suffering. 'Justine, I've been a fool. I've read about heroin. There are new books about it. The urge for it will increase. It will slowly kill me. It locks me into this man. He controls me, totally.'

'Is there not a treatment to take you off it, Kim?'

'I can't go to a hospital. They would lock me up and cut off the supply. I could end up taking my life. It's a new drug, there's little experience in treating the addicts. There may be a specialist treatment, but I don't know where to find it and doubt I could afford it. I just thought you were a broad-minded person who might be able to help me in an unprejudiced way.'

Justine filled up their glasses, thinking not only what advice she could give but also what questions she could put to Kim.

'Kim, I will do what I can. I have the odd friend or two who might have the right connections.' She paused. 'Can I ask you something that has been on my mind?'

'Justine, anything, I'll tell you anything if you can help me.'

'I don't want to take advantage of your condition. It's just that when we originally met you mentioned you knew a woman married to a senior civil servant. The woman whose father imported napalm from America, for the French army. Let's call her Madame X.'

Justine felt Kim go tense.

'Yes, Justine.' It was almost a whisper.

'Today, over lunch, you mentioned her again. You said her father might be involved in a currency racket, converting in and out of piastres where there's no underlying trade transaction.'

Kim hesitated before replying. 'I could tell you about your Madame X,' said Kim. 'But you have to treat the information as strictly private between the two of us. You see, it concerns this man I'm involved with.'

'I understand,' said Justine, surprised and now on guard herself.

Kim explained what she'd heard from her boyfriend. His organisation imported opium into France from Saigon. They tracked down Madame X because they'd heard she could lead them to a competitor entering the same trade. In addition, when they made the connection with Madame X and learnt of her father's napalm business, they realised there was scope for extortion. The press were writing stories about the effect of napalm bombing on civilian Vietnamese and anyone involved in procuring it wouldn't want to be exposed.

'I see,' said Justine. 'And I suppose your man asked you to put the shakes on Madame X by threatening to expose her father.'

'Something like that,' said Kim. 'And there's something else.'

'Oh, what's that?'

' I know who this competitor is.'

There was a tense silence, broken by Justine slowly nodding her head as the ramifications of what Kim just said penetrated her mind.

'Your man is Dieu Tran, isn't he?' said Justine.

'Yes, how did you ...' Kim's voice tailed off.

Justine switched track. 'Do you know a guy called Bao, I think he works for Dieu Tran?'

'Yes, a Vietnamese gangster, here in Paris,' said Kim. 'He behaves like one anyway. In truth, he's terrified of Dieu Tran.'

'So, the picture's getting clearer.' Justine moved closer. 'Kim, I'm going to explore what can be done for your addiction. In the meantime, I'd much appreciate if you could keep watching and listening to what Dieu Tran and Bao are up to, and let me know.' She paused. 'Put your arms around me, Kim. Have a good cry if you need to. I'm going to do all I can to help.'

41

Paris, St Germain des Prés, later the same day

'Thanks for coming, Jean. Something's happened. I could do with a whisky.'

'Good idea, particularly with this coming down.' He looked through the front window of the bar, towards Saint-Sulpice. It was snowing.

The waiter delivered two Scotch Perriers, as Jean lit a Gitane and sat back to listen.

Justine took him through the encounter with Kim that afternoon, holding nothing back.

'So, we know where we are, whether we like it or not,' he said. The *Bình Xuyên* already knew it was you, that's why they went for you in Saigon. I'm sure it's Bao who is blackmailing you, on the instructions of Dieu Tran. And we have confirmation that pressure is being applied on Madame X because of her father's napalm business.'

'Yes, that's it.'

'In theory, Justine, you're now at the mercy of Kim. She could threaten to rubbish your name in a carefully placed article in the press. In reality, she needs you, she's said so. She's looking for help with her heroin addiction. And, as a journalist, she values you as a political contact close to Mendès France.'

'Can you help on the heroin addiction, Jean, is there a cure?'

'It's a new problem. Cocaine has been with us a long time. The processing of opium into heroin, a drug many times more potent, is new as far as the public is concerned. It has only gone on sale in the streets and the clubs recently, and mainly in the States. I can make some inquiries.'

'Please could you, Jean.' I'll do the same, discreetly at work. Clearly it's important we help Kim, from all aspects.'

'You bet it is,' said Jean.

⁕

Quiet descended on the Left Bank as Justine walked home on the snow-covered streets. Even the cranking noises and groans from the old buses seemed muffled as they crept over the carpet of white, some drivers out in the open and bound up with scarves and woollen skull caps. The smell of roasted chestnuts wafted over from a trader's stall on the other side of the Boulevard St Germain. You couldn't escape the bundles lying over the steel gratings for the warm air coming up from the Metro rumbling below. The *clochards* were something you could never miss in Paris. The bodies of the tramps huddled against the cold always challenged Justine's conscience.

Kim, poor thing. Who can I turn to for advice? Maybe, Giselle. As *première main* of a top fashion house, she must have friends and contacts who have addictions of one sort or another, perhaps even heroin. I'll have her out to lunch.

⁕

'Do you remember, Giselle? You took me to lunch here on my first day at work chez Schiap.'

'I certainly do, Justine. We complained about food supplies in Paris, compared to Bordeaux. Both were occupied by the German army, but life was better outside the capital.'

'You should try Saigon. It was great of you to include me in the team. They live like kings down there.'

'Dangerous, though, from what I hear. You and the others really helped the business from that direction. I've heard one or two stories about you, Justine, but won't repeat them,' said Giselle mischievously. She always enjoyed showing she knew more than anyone else about what happened inside Schiap. 'We don't see a lot of you now that you're a deputy. Is life in politics okay?'

Justine explained how the Radical Party was growing its strength, and the excitement of being close to Pierre Mendès France. She knew now was the time to ask the question. 'Giselle, I have a friend who has done a lot for me in the press and magazine world. We've become fairly close, and I have a strong respect for her skills as a journalist who can exploit a story.'

'I read the first one in *Match*. It was quite something. Kim Cho's her name, I think.'

'That's right. Anyway, she's been led into a trap by some gangster boyfriend. To come to the point, she's a heroin addict.'

'Oh, Lord, that's not good,' said Giselle putting a hand over her face.

'The positive factor is she realises the danger, has read up on it, and wants to get out. I promised to see if I could help and wondered if you could give any advice?'

'She has to get away from Paris,' said Giselle. 'If she can raise the money, she should go to Switzerland. I have a contact who went to a clinic there, where they know what to do in such cases. There's no magical remedy. It's tough, but in the right hands she can break free from the thing.'

Justine knew the boss would have an answer. 'Giselle, that sounds like the solution, if the money can be found.'

'I'll let you have some more information. Leave it with me for a week or two. Now, Justine, let's talk about something less tragic. When's your new boss going to become prime minister?'

'Jean, sorry to bring you back so soon. Any ideas yet about how we can help Kim?' asked Justine, having left a message with the owner of the bar they always met in.

'You don't lose time, Justine. That was only a couple of days ago.' He thought for a moment. 'There are a few places dedicated to this sort of thing. She would have to stay there for some time.'

'That's the sort of answer I got. In fact my contact said Switzerland.'

'How on earth could she afford that?'

'I know, that's going to be the problem.'

'Then there's the man, Dieu Tran,' said Jean. 'Even if we get her out without him stopping us, what happens when she returns? He's likely to grab her, isn't he?'

Justine thought about it. I suppose Kim could write to him and say it's all over'.

'He doesn't play by those rules. He could just kill her, maybe overdose her.'

'What can we do about Dieu Tran? Can we stop him?'

'This isn't French Indochina, Justine. No way we can risk the Paris police force coming after us. Somehow we must get to him and explain you are closing down your operation, and that you never intended to deal in anything other than opium. If he doesn't accept that undertaking, we've got to warn the *Bình Xuyên* some other way that they've got to drop the case.

'Any idea how we do that?'

Jean was thinking, head in hands. 'I recall that when we were in Saigon, your friend Bill Lomberg mentioned he knew Captain Antoine Savani. He's key to the relationship of the local administration with the *Bình Xuyên*. If anyone can get them to lay off you, it's him.'

'That's right, Jean. I'll find out where Bill is and whether he can help with Savani. I'll use your teleprinter, if that's okay.'

'Sure.' Jean paused. 'And what about Kim?' he asked. 'Where's the money coming from if we find the right Swiss clinic?'

'Don't know yet,' said Justine.

The teleprinter clattered away, then silence. Justine tore off the paper and read the reply from Bill's base at Saigon Tan Son Nhut airfield. She turned to Jean. 'He's going to call me this evening. I'll see what he says about getting Savani's help.'

The call came in at Justine's apartment, close to midnight.

Justine was conscious of the dangers of an open line. She knew Bill was too. She asked how Antoine Savani was, whether Bill could give him a message from her that she wanted to speak with the Paris representative of 'the organisation'. That she was closing down her business. Bill knew what she meant and said he'd see what he could do.

The call ended. Justine felt relieved somehow. She climbed into bed thinking how fortunate she was having Bill in Saigon, and Jean in Paris. It gave her the firepower for a showdown she saw coming, with the *Bình Xuyên*.

42

'Guess what, darling,' said Theresa as she came out of the shower, a towel only around the tall slim body. 'You were talking about your old school friend Bill Lomberg the other day.'

Leo was on the bed, reading a French magazine he never saw before, *L'Express*. 'What about him?'

'Well, there's always a shortage of Dakota pilots for medivac duties. They need single men without family commitments.'

'You can say that again.'

'A decision was taken recently to accept non-French air force pilots. Yesterday, in the briefing room, Squadron Leader Bill Lomberg, ex-RAF, was introduced to us.'

Leo sat up. 'Amazing. That saves me having to search Vietnam for him.' He paused. 'Can you fix for us to meet?'

~≈≈◦≈◦~

Leo saw Bill come into the lobby of the hotel, jumped to his feet and went over to his old chum. They shook hands, laughing, then thumped one another on the back.

Over a jug of iced beer at a table in the bar, there was a lot to catch up on. Suddenly, Bill said, 'You might not know but Justine has been in Saigon a couple of times, some time ago. She's a remarkable person, went back to modelling after the war, now she's a deputy.'

'Extraordinary,' said Leo. 'Do you see much of her?'

'Not here, for the moment, but we're close and keep in touch all the time.'

'After that escape from Buchenwald, I'm not surprised,' said Leo.

Leo judged this was the moment to test Bill on what he was up to on an unofficial basis. 'I was with Henri the other day at the mess up here. He seemed to be worried about you, for some reason. Said you might have some business on the side.'

Bill reflected. He was sure he could still trust Leo, needed all the friends he could get. 'Yes, I've been carrying other people's merchandise down from the Highlands, as well as cargo I handle for the Deuxième Bureau. Improves my income quite a bit. You know I'm a South African. I have business ambitions when I can return down there.'

'I take my hat off to you. Just hope you keep out of trouble.'

'Frankly, Leo, I'm pulling out of all that dodgy business. I've told Antoine Savani. You might have heard of him.'

'Yes, I have,' said Leo. I work closely with his pal Roger Trinquier, building up the maquis in the Highlands.'

'Ah, so we both know what we're talking about. As I said, I'm getting out of all that.'

'And volunteering to fly C47 hospital and medivac flights, Theresa tells me.'

'Yes, I've thousands of hours' Dakota flying time,' said Bill. 'I can put them in and take them out of any landing strip you give me.'

43

Bill was unsure what Savani's reaction would be. How much control over the *Bình Xuyên* did he really have? Sitting, waiting for him, Bill thought over the telephone conversation between him and Justine the night before. He saw the Corsican approaching and stood up to shake hands.

'Hello Bill, good to see you. Really sorry we're losing you from Air Opium to medivac duties. You'll enjoy those brave nurses.'

'Antoine, you know how it is. You've paid me well. Now I have to think about the future.' He paused and thought for a moment. 'I have this close friend in the fashion world in Paris, Justine Müller. We've talked about her, and you know she has a business importing opium into France. She just spoke with me long distance. She's serious about closing down the business. Since she became a deputy, she can't afford to run foul of French law.'

'Yes, glad she's seen the light'

'Her problem is to reach the decision takers in the *Bình Xuyên*. She wants to speak personally to the right person on their next visit to Paris. Would you be able to fix it for her?'

'They're a very rough lot, Bill.'

'She knows that.'

'Yes, I heard a story about a shooting here in Saigon, which coincided with her last visit.' The serious look on Savani's face was now more of a grin.

'No comment,' said Bill.

Savani was serious again. 'I'll see if a meeting in Paris can be arranged. Justine will receive a message from them directly, if that can be done. Make sure Justine is covered when she's exposed to them. Anything could happen.'

44

'Bill's spoken with Antoine Savani,' said Justine. 'I'm to receive a message direct from the *Bình Xuyên* if a meeting in Paris is agreed to. Don't laugh, Jean, Savani told Bill I should be well protected.'

'He's dead right. I'll be there alongside you, but we'll need at least two others in the background. They'd be mad to attempt something in Paris, so would we for that matter. The Sûreté would be all over us. Where your friend Françoise works, you wouldn't half be popular with her.'

'What's the betting it'll be Dieu Tran,' said Justine. 'You know, if it is him, couldn't we extract cash towards covering Kim's costs at the clinic in Switzerland?'

'More like they'll want cash from you,' said Jean, with a wry smile.

'If we get the chance to propose the meeting place, where would you suggest?'

Jean meditated for a moment before saying, 'The crypt at Saint-Sulpice.'

'You're joking,' said Justine.

'I'm not. It's somewhere Ka already met them, with Bao. It's difficult to escape from. The priest is a good friend who will ensure we're not interrupted.'

Same place, next day

'Hi Jean, thanks for coming in again. There are two developments I must update you on.'

Their friendly bar owner placed two *demi pressions* on the table.

'I'm at your service, Justine.'

'First, I met with Kim. She's not in good shape. The beautiful and talented creature's slowly degenerating before your eyes. She's all for applying to the Swiss clinic for treatment, the one recommended to me. I'm sure she wants to go through with it.

'Secondly, I received a telephone call from the *Binh Xuyên*. Don't know who it was, perhaps Bao. They accepted the crypt at Saint-Sulpice, 3pm on Friday.'

'Ah, so we have four days to prepare. Right, Justine, let's get down to work.'

Jean pulled out a large notebook and put a drawing on the table next to it.

'Here's a drawing I made of the crypt, from a floor plan the priest gave me. He's in agreement, by the way.'

'Well done, Jean.'

He proceeded to act out the course of the meeting, as he would like to see it unfold. He explained he would have two 'assistants', although there was no way they would end up in a shoot-out. It was just to balance out the cover the other side would have. The crypt was a constrained space that could be blocked up, no way in and no way out if either side took control. Therefore neither side would be allowed to take control.

'Here's a copy of the floor plan, marked up to provide more information. Take it and memorise it.'

45

Paris, Left Bank, March 1953.

A cold day in early spring. Daffodils in the parks, no blossom on the trees yet. Justine walked into the Metro sitting across the centre aisle of the carriage from two girls in their teens, clutching skates. She felt inspired by the innocence on their faces, expectation of the fun they were going to have. The confidence they portrayed filled her with joy. This was the future of her country. It gave her the confidence to face today's meeting.

At the Saint-Sulpice Metro station, she smiled at the girls as she left the train, climbed the steps up to the street and headed in the direction of the massive church. Thinking the day before about the proposed encounter, she'd determined to put on a smart appearance. The long Schiaparelli winter coat was in a small black-and-white check, with deep black fur trimming at the neck, on the sleeves and at the hem.

Jean was waiting for her just outside the entrance on the north side of the edifice. 'You look just stunning,' he said as he kissed both cheeks and passed Justine a small shopping bag containing the Walther .38 and clips she was used to. There wouldn't be any shooting, but carrying a gun was essential to the tactics. Both sides would expect the other to be armed.

'Let's go,' he said. 'Thank God I warned you to dress up warmly. It's going to be freezing in that crypt.'

They knew exactly what they wanted, the traps to look out for, the risks. The preparation was thorough. The geography was memorised.

Who would turn up from the other side?

The priest was waiting for them at the entrance to the crypt. They took the staircase down to the large cavern, arches and pillars, lit by electric light. Although she'd seen it before when there with Jean to cover Ka, the extent of the crypt still surprised Justine. She looked around her. It was seriously cold.

The enemy were already there. 'The Chinese' as they used to call him, now they knew he was Dieu Tran. Tall and smart, in a suit and scarf. The smaller Vietnamese must be Bao, in a thin blue raincoat. No one shook hands. Justine felt empowered by the presence of Jean. He was her rock, ready for anything.

Dieu Tran waved towards a square table under the wall of the cavernous chamber. They followed him over and sat down on chairs they pulled over from nearby.

The big man spoke first. 'Mademoiselle Müller, I received a message you wanted to meet the Paris representative of my organisation. That is me.'

'Yes, thank you for responding to my request.' Justine waited a moment. 'I understand you and your colleagues in Saigon are concerned that I will grow my business to the point where it will pose a threat to your dominance of the market.' She paused, and the other side remained silent. 'I asked for this meeting so I could declare that it has never been my intention to develop the business to that extent. Further, and for reasons I won't go into, I have decided to close down this business activity completely.'

Dieu Tran replied, 'I hear what you are saying, Mademoiselle. Can I tell my colleagues that shipments have already ceased.'

'No, there is currently one batch in the pipeline and one or two more are likely. It depends on the time it takes from my sending the necessary instructions following this meeting to my supplier re-directing production elsewhere. All should have ceased by the end of May.'

'Very good. I will communicate your undertaking to Saigon. I think that is all, do you agree?'

Now was the moment for Justine to decide whether to raise the other matter, or not. She looked at Jean, his face was impassive. He was leaving it to her.

'Monsieur, there is one other matter I wish to raise.'

'Another matter?' Dieu Tran was evidently surprised.

Justine looked first at Bao, he was shivering uncontrollably, then into Dieu Tran's moonlike face. 'I have both a business relationship and a growing friendship with Mademoiselle Kim Cho.'

Dieu Tran looked more than surprised. Was there something else in his expression, a suggestion of anger? He said nothing.

'Kim Cho is suffering from heroin addiction. I want to help her. She knows that by going to a certain clinic in Switzerland, she can be helped to break away from this addiction. She is determined on this course of action.' Justine paused, then looked hard at Dieu Tran. 'I am determined that she shall go to the clinic.'

Dieu Tran again said nothing. Bao looked like he would settle for anything to get back upstairs out of the cold.

'Monsieur Tran,' said Justine slowly. 'I want your undertaking that you will not prevent Kim Cho from departing Paris for Switzerland. And that you will have nothing to do with her when she returns. I am making this a condition of our settlement.'

Tran spoke 'Is that all?'

'One final point,' said Justine. 'I expect you to pay the fees of the clinic in Switzerland.'

There was a long silence before Dieu Tran responded.

'You are in no position to dictate terms, Mademoiselle. I came here to discuss the discontinuation of your export of opium from Vietnam. Not an open-ended financial arrangement.'

Justine thought for a moment, ignoring that her feet were turning to ice. She must help Kim, must persuade him to contribute to her rehabilitation.

'In that case, Monsieur Tran, I propose that you pay Kim Cho now the amount of ten thousand United States dollars in cash. You can express the gift to her in any way you wish. The excess over that amount, in fees from the Swiss clinic and travel costs, I will cover personally. As soon as I have received confirmation from Kim Cho that she has received the money, I will give instructions to my supplier in Vietnam to cease shipments of opium to my account forthwith.'

There was a long silence from the other side.

'I require your undertaking, Mademoiselle, that the nature of this settlement will never be disclosed to the French authorities nor to any person other than those present here today.'

'You have my word, Monsieur,' said Justine. 'We both have witnesses,' she said, looking at Bao and then Jean.

With that, Dieu Tran turned away and left the crypt, followed by Bao almost running behind him.

Jean waited for them to disappear, and for two others he was expecting who finally materialised from behind pillars at the back. He then turned to Justine. 'Well, you did it. Congratulations. I had my doubts you would get away with the release of Kim, let alone that amount of cash.'

Outside the church, Justine said, 'I'll speak to Kim. Could I tell her you will accompany her to the clinic and hand her over?'

'It would be a pleasure, Justine. I wouldn't put it past those bastards to leave their mark on her somehow.'

The day after the meeting in the crypt of Saint-Sulpice, Justine was together with Kim. She recounted the events leading to the meeting with Dieu Tran and the settlement that was reached.

Kim couldn't believe it. 'You're amazing, Justine. I know Dieu Tran is in town, we're meeting tonight at the Blue Note. Let's see if he keeps to the bargain. I'll call you as soon as he gives me the cash.'

'Okay, I'll confirm with the clinic as soon as you tell me. They said they could take you right away. I've arranged for Jean to accompany you down there and make sure you're safely in the hands of the doctor and his team.'

46

Paris, Latin Quarter, March 1953

She must tell Ka and Glun of her decision to close down the pipeline. They might argue against it. Why take this step when it's running smoothly and lots of money is coming in? The two years of profits since that first shipment arrived in Marseille transformed the finances of the three of them, they all knew that.

Ka's dependency on Bao for protection of her family in Hanoi was long dispensed with. Ka told Justine she gave her parents all that they needed for the future care of her brother. Glun's career in the Paris academic world could continue for as long as he wished. As for Justine herself, there was now significant cash in reserve for her political ambitions while she lived off her meagre earnings as a deputy.

What was the best way to explain that the continuing stream of profits was going to end?

She invited Glun and Ka to dinner at an excellent Vietnamese restaurant in the Latin Quarter. They exchanged news, and talked about politics in France and the war in Indochina. Towards the end of a delicious meal, she said laughingly she was going to make a speech.

Justine started by summarising where the business now was and the external influences it was having to face. She pointed out that they all enjoyed reputations they needed to protect.

Ka was respected in the haute couture world for her work at Christian Dior and Schiaparelli. Glun was well established in the Paris academic world through his success as a professor at the Sorbonne. Justine was now a deputy in a party which might soon be leading the government.

The risks were growing all the time. The supply of narcotics for recreational use was under heavy attack in the United States, and being increasingly outlawed in Europe. With her growing influence in the political world, Justine couldn't risk becoming publicly associated with an illegal activity. She didn't mention it but there was a vote pending in the Assembly for a new prime minister. It could come any day. She couldn't risk adverse consequences for her affecting the chances of Pierre Mendès France. People knew she was a close colleague of his.

They listened in silence.

'I'm sorry to have to say all this, but we have to be aware of these facts. The time has come, in my view, to call it a day. We have benefited from a successful venture. I believe it is sensible to end it before we're forced to do so in a way that would damage us personally.' Justine waited for these facts to sink in, before adding, 'Danger is just around the corner in the world we're playing in.'

Ka almost looked relieved. Glun seemed surprised and disappointed.

'You realise there are consequences for my family and the Meo growers who supply us,' he said. 'If this has to happen, and I do understand your reasoning, Justine, we must give them adequate notice.'

'I propose the final shipment be completed by the end of May.'

Glun looked as though he might object, but was having second thoughts.

'Okay then,' said Justine. 'Glun, please give notice to your family on that basis. And please thank them from me for all they have done for us.'

As far as Bill was concerned, she'd written to him even before the meeting with Dieu Tran, using the simple code they'd agreed upon. In response to her saying she was considering shutting down the pipeline, he sent a teleprinter message back that he was already exploring a move into the Dakota medivac service.

⸺◈⸺

Upset and sadness followed a week later. The failure of Pierre Mendès France in his bid to lead the next government of France was a great disappointment. The voting for him in the Assembly was only 13 votes short. Another chance would come. There was much work ahead for his Radical Party, and for Justine if she was to help him succeed at the next opportunity.

47

Henri was surprised to be invited to General Navarre's conference. The death of Jean de Lattre de Tassigny from cancer was fresh in everyone's mind. To Henri, de Lattre would always be remembered for his success in pushing back the Viets in his period as Commander-in-Chief. He showed the army how to fight General Giap intelligently. A ruthless taskmaster, many succumbed to the 'shampoo' de Lattre inflicted on those he judged to be below par.

His successor, General Salan was an old Indochina hand, but was now handing over to Henri Navarre. Navarre was a choice that surprised Henri and his colleagues. Never having served in Indochina, his more recent background was the Resistance and the army's Deuxième Bureau.

On Indochinese soil for the first time, Navarre was holding small conferences in Hanoi and Saigon with senior and specially selected middle-ranking officers. Why was Henri chosen? Perhaps because his unit 13 DBLE as well as Navarre's unit formed part of de Lattre's advance up through France in August 1944, from the beaches of St Tropez to Strasbourg and beyond.

There was a hush, everyone standing up as the new Commander-in-Chief entered the room and walked to the podium. Not tall, but lean and elegant, Henri noticed his hair was now silver grey.

'The world does not understand the scale of our struggle against Communism,' was how General Navarre opened the session. 'In the past four years in Indochina, eleven thousand French nationals have died. Our commitment is enormous, French forces here including the army of southern Vietnam, are as big as the British 8th Army was in the Western Desert ten years ago. With reinforcements and more *matériel*, we can win this war.'

As important as what Navarre said was what he didn't say. Henri just heard that an opinion poll organised by *Le Monde* found that two-thirds of French voters believed France should withdraw unilaterally from Indochina. The politicians would surely be pressing Navarre to head in that direction, which would lead to peace talks with Ho Chi Minh.

As the session was breaking up, the young man on Henri's right introduced himself as Bernard Fall. In his late twenties and wearing civilian clothes, Henri was already curious as to who he was.

'How do you come to be here?' asked Henri.

'I'm over from the States, on a tour of Vietnam and researching for a doctorate. I aim to be a political scientist, although journalism will be part of that. In awkward places,' Bernard Fall added.

'If I may say so,' responded Henri, 'you seem to enjoy that gift of top journalists by being able to walk into anywhere.'

They both laughed, and decided to head for the bar, Henri telling Fall he was currently Adjutant of 13 DBLE.

'So the General intends to develop further the maquis in the northern Highlands,' said Fall. 'I joined a maquis in France in '43, so guerrilla fighting isn't new to me.'

'Interesting. You must have been very young for that,' said Henri.

'Sixteen, actually.' Fall grinned. 'I'd lost both my parents to the Nazis. We were a Jewish family from Vienna. Later I joined de Lattre's First Army. My native German took me into intelligence.'

'My unit, 13 DBLE, was also part of de Lattre's force,' said Henri. 'What happened to you after the war in Europe ended?'

'I was at the University of Paris, then won a Fulbright scholarship to Syracuse in the States, where I am when not in Vietnam. Having been a French officer, I manage to go more or less where I want, including the combat units.'

'Quite a story.' Henri realised that here was a really interesting person. 'What do you hear about Navarre from those in front line units?'

'They don't rate him. They say he isn't aggressive enough. I guess everyone compares him with de Lattre.' Fall paused for a moment. 'I've been concentrating on the situation in the Red River Delta. The French officers up there and around Hanoi claim they have control over most of the villages. Yet the friends I've made among the locals say that almost everyone silently supports the Viets.'

'Doesn't sound good,' said Henri, wondering how freely he could talk to this remarkable young man. 'I'm worried. I don't think we're going anywhere. General Giap is constantly building up his forces, and his military skills are catching up with ours.'

Bernard Fall nodded. Both agreed to maintain contact. Friendships as well as sources of information were to be treasured in that dangerous part of the world.

⸺◈⸺

Soon after this encounter, Henri received a temporary posting to join General Navarre's staff. There was to be a special planning exercise, expected to last two months. From the secrecy attaching to the assignment, it seemed that something big was under consideration.

Haiphong, July 1953

The planning assignment completed, there was some leave due to Henri. He tracked down Leo at the headquarters of airborne units, and Bill through his Deuxième Bureau friends. The three of them spent an enjoyable weekend together at the officers' club in Haiphong. Each was conscious that the other two knew things they were pledged not to disclose. Nevertheless, there was an air of foreboding overhanging this precious moment as the old school pals came together.

Hanoi, September 1953

Shortly after returning to his unit, Henri heard that 13th Demi-Brigade of the French Foreign Legion would be going on a major new operation codenamed Castor. As 13 DBLE's Adjutant, and promoted to Major, Henri would be going with them. Their destination was in a valley close to the border with Laos, a place called Dien Bien Phu.

48

'All good news, boss,' said Jean to Justine. 'Kim Cho arrived at the Gare de Lyon, safe and sound. She was full of enthusiasm for a new outlook on life, although still in journalism. Says she's been corresponding with Art Buchwald on the *Herald Tribune* and may be joining them.'

'That's much better for her at this point, being part of an organisation rather than freelance,' said Justine, thanking God again that Giselle recommended the right clinic and, not least, that Dieu Tran came up with the money.

'I took her directly to the new address. The location will be kept as quiet as possible, just in case Dieu Tran tries to get at her.'

'Well done, Jean. What are you going to drink?' The waiter was hovering. 'We never had that glass of champagne we promised one another.' She told the waiter to bring two coupes and leave the bottle in an ice bucket.

'Sorry to come to the business right away, Jean. There's something brewing. Having said that, the opium pipeline has its last batch in transit, so your original mission can now be closed, and thank you,' she said, raising her glass to him. 'Are you willing to stick with me pro tem?'

'I'd have terrible withdrawal symptoms if you didn't have something for me.'

'Wait until you hear what it is.' She waited a moment, looking him full in the face. 'Napalm B.'

'Napalm what?' he said.

'Napalm B. It's a new form of jellified petroleum made up of polystyrene, benzene and gasoline. Dow Chemical just developed it for the US army. Burns for up to ten minutes, instead of burning out in a few seconds. In contact with human skin, it sticks and ...' she stopped as he raised his hand.

'It may be an opportunity for my boss in politics to intervene,' said Justine.

'The prime minister in waiting,' he said. 'What's the story?'

Justine explained that a US warship would be transferring a cargo of Napalm B aerial bombs, destined for Vietnam, to a French vessel in Marseille docks. The source of the information was not Justine's friend Françoise at the *piscine* as Jean surmised, but Madame X with whom Ka now had a close relationship. Madame X overheard a telephone conversation when her father was arranging the shipping arrangements. She told Ka she was upset and wanted what she called 'this horror weapon' to be outlawed.

Justine reminded Jean that the *Bien Xuyen* were suspected of threatening Madame X because of her father's involvement in napalm. Madame X was now desperate to persuade her father to close down that part of his business. Ka wanted to know whether it would be practicable to have the shipment blocked in order to help her?

Justine added that she'd heard from another source that the United Nations were investigating Napalm B, with a view to including it in the list of banned weapons.

Jean thought for a moment. 'Trouble is, the French forces have been using napalm extensively for the past three years. Okay, this is a new, more effective version, but it's not really news.'

'No, but the public doesn't like it.'

'I can't see there's any physical action we could instigate to prevent the French vessel sailing from Marseille,' he said. 'If you were found guilty of disclosing military secrets, at best you would be locked up. At worst you could be executed for treason. Anyway, what's in it for you?'

'I could make a statement to the press on behalf of the Radical Socialist Party, that the cargo should be impounded and sent back to the States. That Napalm B was under consideration to be banned by the United Nations.'

'So, it's political mileage you're looking for.

'Yes. I'd have to clear it first with Mendès France.'

'You realise that the Sûreté would immediately launch an undercover operation to find out how the arrival of the US warship was leaked.'

Justine was silent for a moment. 'Yes, and that could incriminate Madame X, Ka and even me. What I was thinking of was mounting a big public demonstration in the port of Marseille, alongside the vessel that was going to carry the bombs to Saigon.'

'I'd go along with that if it wasn't for the risk of being caught up in an inquiry by the authorities.'

'So, we'd need to have another information source telling us the same thing but bona fide, so to speak.'

Justine could see Jean was into one of his thoughtful moods.

'I don't like it. On the other hand, if Madame X feels strongly enough about stopping napalm B, we have a possible solution staring us in the face.'

'How come?' asked Justine.

'Kim. She's been hot on the napalm trail for a long time now, from what you told me. When I met her off the train, she said she met Art Buchwald some time ago, and that was her link to joining the *Herald Tribune*. If an American newspaper were to drop the word that Napalm B was believed to be on its way from the United States to French forces in Indochina, that could be reason enough for you to organise a demonstration.'

'That makes sense,' said Justine. 'Jean, you're worth your weight in gold.'

'Better than piastres,' he said, both having a good laugh as they re-filled their coupes.

49

Hotel Metropole, Hanoi, December 1953

'I'm telling you again, my darling, get it into your head that the role of *convoyeuse* is too dangerous for you. Even when enemy fire isn't sweeping across the landing ground, there's still the flak. It's just a question of time.'

Theresa was curled up on the bed with a copy of *Paris Match*. She cast it aside, and stretched out, one of her long legs entwined in the mosquito netting. 'Leo, you know why I go on. There's a great camaraderie among the girls. We're all in it together. The wounded legionnaires we bring back depend on us. If we get them back fast enough, most survive. Medivac makes that possible. It's something you didn't have in the last war. It's transformed the survival rate.'

Leo poured them both Scotch and Perrier, and went over to sit by her.

He means it this time, Theresa thought. She took her drink, and put her other arm around his waist. 'There's a new girl with us. An air force nurse. Late twenties. From Paris. She volunteered to come out here. Geneviève's her name, and I get on well with her. She paused for a moment, then announced, 'There's something big coming up, isn't there, Leo? What does Castor mean?'

Leo turned towards her, kissing her shoulder. 'It's already started. You know I can't discuss things. I hear a lot, am told a lot because of my intelligence role. It's the old adage, only those who need to know should be told.'

Theresa changed tack. 'Geneviève says this one will be the decider. She seems to be well informed. Anyway, if it's already started, why can't we talk about it?'

'See how useless it is to try and keep the lid on things in this place,' Leo laughed wryly. 'The first paras dropped a month ago, to secure a valley close to the frontier with Laos. The airstrip is ready for use, there's a big build-up going on. Castor is the code name for the landing.'

'Is this to be Navarre's claim to history?' said Theresa, referring to the new Commander-in-Chief.

'How does your friend, Geneviève, get her information?'

'Seems to have powerful family connections. Don't get me wrong. She's discreet, doesn't blab her mouth off to everyone. It's just that we've become close. She knows my background, with the Luftwaffe and all that.'

Leo seemed resigned to Theresa's ability to dig things out of him. His mind was already focused on the operation code-named Castor. It owed its roots to the success at Na San. Navarre believed that victory there vindicated the *base aéroter-restre* strategy. Leo's worry was that a key to Na San's success was to deceive the enemy over the apparent weakness of the French defence. Then when General Giap was committed to an all-out frontal attack, the French would fly in artillery and additional airborne forces at the last moment. With Castor, the build-up was going to take time and be very public. Giap would be able to build up his strength as well. Given time, that could become considerable.

50

To Henri, Bernard Fall was an enigma. His early years in Vienna, then both parents murdered for being Jewish. Escape to France, and already fighting with a French maquis when he was sixteen. In de Lattre's army advancing on Germany when he was eighteen. University education in France and the United States, choosing Indochina for his doctorate. With his French passport and army background, made his way to the front in northern Vietnam, reporting on life in the front line.

Still just a boy, thought Henri as he watched Fall's jaunty stride towards him, camera over his shoulder.

'Hi Henri, how goes the Legion?' That American drawl with a French accent was infectious.

They both found speaking English as natural as French.

'Thanks for getting in touch, Bernard,' said Henri. 'Great to see you again. Join me in a beer?'

'You bet. We need somewhere private. There's a small conference room one floor up. Should be empty right now.'

They both took their drinks with them, as Fall led the way up the open staircase of the delightful French colonial villa used by the Club and the international press community.

'So, what's on your mind, Bernard?' Henri was curious.

'I want to be an embedded journalist with a unit in the Castor operation. I heard your 13 DBLE might be going in there, and wondered if you'd consider having me with you?'

'Well informed as always,' said Henri. 'I don't see why not. Must clear it with my CO.'

Bernard exclaimed enthusiastically. 'I can't thank you enough, Henri.'

Henri didn't share Fall's enthusiasm. 'I hope you'll feel like that in three months' time.'

51

Military Hospital, Haiphong, January 1954

'Nurses Krüger and de Galard, would you come with me, please.' It was as the morning assembly ended that the Duty MO called for Theresa and Geneviève to go with him to the conference room. Awaiting them there were the air force colonel and army medical officer who originally interviewed her for the job of *convoyeuse*.

'Thank you both for joining us,' said the Colonel. 'We have of course met before, but wanted to talk informally with you about a new operation already under way.' The waiter standing discreetly in the corner of the room came over and poured them coffee.

'Operation Castor involves a large force of mainly airborne troops,' the Colonel started to explain. 'The base of their operations is already under construction at Dien Bien Phu, in a valley close to the border with Laos. There will be at least one field hospital on base, but the intention is to fly out all seriously wounded. We need two of our experienced *convoyeuses* to help select the nurses to fly in and out of the airfield there, which has just been upgraded from what the Japanese left behind.

'Sounds interesting, sir,' said Theresa, much the more experienced of the two women. 'Certainly, I'll do everything I can to help.'

'Me too,' said Geneviève.

The Colonel explained that there had already been some minor fighting, and casualties. Within a couple of months, they expected at least one major battle to be fought at Dien Bien Phu or by mobile forces operating from there. In all medivac flights, the risks were very real. He didn't have to tell them that. They could be shot up by enemy gunfire on the ground, or in the air by flak. With Castor that risk ought not to be greater, but it would still be there. Furthermore, the base they would be flying in and out of was a long way from other French forces. It was therefore wholly dependent on supply from the air. He waited for this added risk factor to sink in, and asked if they understood the point.

'What you are saying, sir,' said Theresa, 'is that if the airfield is compromised, there will be no way out.'

'That's right. Should the airstrip become unusable, supplies can be dropped from the air but no one can be evacuated.' He paused. 'We don't envisage any such eventuality. That problem would only occur if your aircraft was destroyed on the ground at the time use of the airfield was lost.'

There was silence in the room. The Colonel added, 'Attempts would obviously be made to land a small aircraft and take you out with one or two seriously wounded personnel.'

Theresa caught Geneviève's eye and gave her a wink to encourage her. Perhaps they were both thinking the same thing.

The medical officer volunteered, 'Don't imagine you would be the only woman on the entire base. Remember, the Legion is there and so will be their BMC.'

Geneviève turned to Theresa with an inquiring look.

'*Bordel mobile de campagne*, my darling,' Theresa explained. 'Or in the other language we often speak, mobile brothel.' There was suppressed laughter in the room.

52

Dien Bien Phu, early March 1954

As the Dakota completed its landing at the north end of the runway, and turned back to where a flag-waving legionnaire directed, the side door in the fuselage was flung open. Through the swirling dust, Henri saw the unmistakeable figure of Bernard Fall, kit bag in one hand, bulky camera case in the other.

They shook hands. 'Welcome to Dien Bien Phu,' shouted Henri. 'Let's pile into the jeep and I'll show you to your quarters. Then we can have a look around.'

'Thanks,' said Bernard 'I can't wait to see everything. Very grateful to you for helping to set this up.'

Henri sat in the back of the jeep behind Fall, leaning forward to point out the defences of the Isabelle strongpoint which lay at the southernmost extremity of the base area. As they headed north towards the central camp, he explained how each strongpoint fitted into the topography.

Later that day, after a shower and change of clothes, the two of them were waiting outside the central command bunker. They could hear a loud discussion going on inside the conference room. When the staff officer asked them to follow him in, Colonel de Castries looked up, smiled and came across to welcome them. He was followed by the two top parachute commanders, Colonel Pierre Langlais and Major Marcel Bigeard, to whom Bernard was introduced.

'Make yourselves comfortable, everyone,' said de Castries. 'Mr Fall, we would all like to hear your views on the war out here.'

'First of all, I must thank you for permitting me to come here. I will respect your confidence at all times. I do write articles for publications in the US press, but that will not be happening while I'm here. I am of course French and a former French soldier. There should be no doubts, therefore, as to where my allegiances lie.'

'Thank you, Monsieur,' said de Castries. 'Of course, Giap's main attack hasn't happened yet, but we expect he will strike soon. Major de Rochefort is your supervisor during your visit. We will allow you latitude to visit the command posts as and when you wish. This is on the understanding that you will take direct instructions from Major de Rochefort. Is that acceptable?'

'Certainly, sir,' said Bernard Fall.

'We have a little time before the evening meal. Could we ask you for your views on one or two subjects, please?'

'Of course,' replied Bernard. 'Could I explain, however, that I am a political scientist. I am also familiar with current Washington thinking. What I am not is an expert on French Indochina, nor military strategy and tactics.'

Colonel Langlais asked first about the validity of a military solution to holding back the advance of Communism in South East Asia. Fall made clear he did support the principle that Communism could be defeated by military means. 'What worries me, however, is whether France has the manpower and equipment to do so. It's my view that the United States is not giving France sufficient help.'

Major Bigeard, Commander of 1 BCP, asked the next question. Do you believe that South Vietnam's army is capable of taking on General Giap's troops? Bernard replied, 'Yes, I do.

For example,' and he looked at Bigeard, 'the Vietnamese who form a large part of your 1st Battalion Colonial Paras are fine as long as we remember France and the United States help to train them.'

De Castries ended by asking, 'Do you think the Americans should be doing more to help France in its military commitment in Indochina?'

'Yes, I do,' said Bernard. 'I think direct action in terms of the US Air Force bombing the Viets is out of the question. That could well escalate China's involvement. On the other hand, more advanced aircraft and helicopters, including training of French pilots, should be offered by Washington.' He hesitated. 'As you know, there is always the counter-argument over there that by helping France they are making it possible for us to retain our colonial possessions.'

'Quite so,' said de Castries. 'Monsieur Fall, we appreciate your views. Now let's all have a drink and something to eat.' He nodded to Henri in the background to indicate he was invited as well.

Later that evening, the two of them were having a last whisky before turning in. 'You might want to read this, Henri,' said Bernard Fall. 'It's a rather out-of-date copy of the *Herald Tribune.*'

Henri glanced down at the newspaper, noticing the second headline on the front page, 'Washington supplying France with latest version of the napalm bomb.'

53

Bill watched from the cockpit the two *convoyeuses,* as they walked across the tarmac, both in the loose-fitting dungarees they wore in action. The tall slim one must be Theresa Krüger. She certainly fitted Leo's description, and he remembered being introduced to her in the briefing room a few months ago. The other was dark, younger, short in stature but appeared confident in the way she chatted to Theresa. He waved to them from the window as a truck arrived with medical supplies.

There was going to be a hot reception, Bill was sure of that. The rumour was that General Giap was about to launch his long expected all-out attack. The large red crosses on each side of the fuselage meant little in terms of escaping the enemy's fire.

News out of Dien Bien Phu was that the enemy's anti-aircraft capability was strengthening. The Viet gunnery might also destroy them on the ground from what he'd heard. A lot depended on the cover provided by the fighter bombers going with them, and their own artillery in the valley.

Must keep to the timetable, that was crucial. The two Pratt & Whitneys roared into life as they were cleared for take-off. At the end of the runway, he swung the machine into the wind and went to full throttle. Heading west-south-west, he checked that the Bearcat fighter bombers were in position either side of the Dakota.

The heart-shaped valley came into view on the horizon an hour later. Smoke rose high up towards them from an oil fire, and as they drew closer, Bill could pick out intermittent artillery flashes. It was dusk. He must concentrate on landing straight in, no second attempts by which time every Viet gun around the valley would be trained on him.

The altimeter fell to a thousand feet and continued down. There was the airfield, must adjust the line of approach slightly. Crack. The first flak burst just outside the fuselage. Inside were the two girls and the MO, and space for up to twenty stretcher cases. Must hold her steady for the last hundred feet. Small bounce, the two wheels now on the ground. Wait for the tail wheel to make contact as the nose comes up. Down and rolling towards the flag wavers showing where they wanted them. Now for a really fast turnaround.

Would be safer outside and under cover, in one of the drainage ditches, but there were other things to do. Side door open and stretcher bearers only a few metres away, the girls and MO were out on the tarmac, checking the case notes attached to each of the wounded. Where was the passenger, the officer who'd collapsed under stress? Must be him over there, being helped forward.

Suddenly, a massive explosion. They were hit. The whole plane jumped and landed back, resting on one wing. Fire in the rear fuselage. Must get out, the fuel tanks could explode. Check inside that no one remained on board. Clear, and no one's boarded yet. The ladder from the side door to the ground, still in place. Get down it, clear the area around the plane, make sure the nurses and wounded are out of the way. After that, run for cover.

Easier said than done. Bill spotted a drainage ditch nearby, sprinted over to it and flung himself in. Where were the two girls, and the doctor? A jeep came racing in his direction, and he waved it over. He was told the others were picked up and on the way to the centre camp. From what Bill could see of the high level of activity everywhere as they drove past some of the strongpoints, the balloon was about to go up at Dien Bien Phu.

54

Strongpoint Beatrice, Dien Bien Phu, 13 March 1954

Henri knew the threat was greatest when the air cover closed down, at night or in bad weather. Weeks preparing for the attack they were sure would come. Intelligence said General Giap was playing it clever, patient when his commanders pressed frantically for the go-ahead to attack and swamp the French. Giap wanted a decisive victory, wanted it before the peace conference in Geneva began. Victory would strengthen Ho Chi Minh's power to force the French towards a people's vote for independence. The victory which back in France would trigger public demand to end it all.

Why was everyone so confident when outnumbered five to one? Henri heard so often the mantra 'we chose this valley, chose to establish a *base aéroterrestre*; the principle proved itself at Na San; an air/land base from which to launch *groupes mobiles* to cut off the Viets on the route to Laos; our French and colonial forces are far better equipped; we have the artillery; no way the Viets can bring theirs hundreds of kilometres across terrible mountainous terrain.' So it went. Sounded good, so why not believe it? One good reason was that de Castries already ordered a stop to *groupes mobiles* after heavy losses in the previous two months. There would be no more mobile columns sent out to attack the enemy supply lines.

Henri's senses were tense as hell. Would the truth crash in on them suddenly, and ruthlessly?

His very own 3rd Battalion of 13 DBLE, commanded by Paul Pégot, was among the best in Indochina. Such strong morale. Yet few of the legionnaires had experienced truly heavy shelling. The unremitting shriek of sound and thunderous explosions almost every second were beyond the extreme most men could stand. In a tightly manned defensive post under such sustained barrage, those still conscious could no longer think.

By noon, no doubt it would be today. The enemy would be crawling forward in their trenches to within fifty metres of the French wire. They wouldn't strike until dusk. They never attacked until then.

Still only afternoon, Henri was out in the open, checking each bunker and trench with the junior officers and NCOs. Bernard Fall was with him, couldn't shake him off.

Suddenly, thunderous noise from across the valley. Worse than his worst fears. Viet artillery and heavy mortars were alive, two hours before expected. The first shells exploded as he dived into the nearest trench, close by a bunker. A barrage of mammoth intensity. He saw the bunker and gun pit close to him disappear under smoke and flying debris. Oh God, none of us expected such devastating enemy artillery. Must help the legionnaires underneath that devastation. Run in as deep a crouch as he could. No good telling Bernard Fall to stay put. That was him just behind, with camera.

Dust blocked out the sun, the stench of cordite and burning timber under the rain were overwhelming. Must tear away at the corrugated roofing and splintered wooden supports. What was that? A man's torso lay in there. Surely no one has survived. Obvious that the material for fortifying the bunker was clearly inadequate to withstand a direct hit.

Others came to help, and Henri crawled over to the open gun pit close by. Fall took pictures of the unfortunate crew who lay dead around their weapon. Proof of the precise artillery settings by the Viets, from weeks of meticulous reconnaissance.

A forward observation officer dropped down beside him after running back from his post beyond the wire. 'Major de Rochefort, sir.' He was breathless. 'It's remarkable. The Viets dug their guns into the front slopes of the hills. We just saw them hauling them out. That's why our air force bombers never saw them. The number firing is staggering,' he shouted.

'Their firepower's unbelievable,' Henri shouted back. 'Can't see how they brought heavy guns here through hundreds of kilometres of jungle, and hid them from us.'

Taking Bernard with him, they staggered towards the sector command bunker. An unbelievable sight, the bunker totally destroyed, everyone inside buried. Some were now trying to dig themselves out. Who was that? Oh God, surely not the Colonel. It couldn't be. Gaucher staggered towards them, both his arms torn off. A stretcher party was running over to help. Other medical orderlies arrived as more wounded clawed their way out of the bunker.

Henri saw Bernard put down his camera equipment and go in to help. 'Over here,' he was shouting to the orderlies as he knelt beside a radio operator where the blast of a shell blew pieces of wireless equipment into his chest. They gently lifted him onto a stretcher while a third orderly held a blood bottle and line above his head. The field ambulance was backing up and he joined those already on board for the short journey to the dressing station. Screaming from inside the bunker wreckage told them there was more to do.

Midnight approaching, the stark truth flooded through Henri. Beatrice was no more, fallen to the Viets. 13 DBLE's 3rd Battalion ceased to exist. The sector commander, Lieutenant Colonel Gaucher, was dead.

Morning the next day, fifteen hours since the horror and destruction began. The Viet guns were still firing. With Beatrice gone, Henri knew strongpoint Gabrielle would be the next target, positioned as it was between Beatrice and the central command area from which de Castries and his staff operated. Bernard distracted him, pointing out the familiar one-armed figure of Charles Piroth. The artillery commander was going from one gun pit to another, and to command posts on the way. A staff officer said to Henri, 'I was over there just now. Piroth is making apologies for the failure of his artillery to silence the massed enemy guns. Earlier, I witnessed Langlais give him hell, never heard anything like it.'

Henri could see Piroth was in a terrible state, staring at corpses in their poncho covers. Clearly, the morale of his surviving gunners was not good, and that was affecting him badly. A danger signal, Henri was fearful for him. He replied, 'The man can't go on like that. He's capitulated, leaving everything to his battery commanders.'

'Bill Lomberg?'

'Yes, that's me.' Bill took in the French air force officer rising from a trestle table in the tent. Deep underground in the central area, he and the two nurses were recovering from the trauma of twenty-four hours of bombardment. Although not yet the main target of the Viet shelling, the weight of it was still brutal, especially for those without experience of that intensity, like Geneviève. Theresa marvelled at how cool she remained throughout.

'My name is Moulin,' said the air force officer. 'I'm in charge of flight operations here. Sorry to tell you, your aircraft is a write-off. We've been hit very hard by the Viets since your arrival yesterday. They've taken a key strongpoint, Beatrice, and now Gabrielle is under attack. That's brought them closer to the airfield and we can't currently use it.'

'So, we're stuck here for the present,' said Bill.

'Correct. I'll show you to your tent, and set you up with your basic needs. You're welcome to eat with us in the officers' mess. Very simple arrangements, as you can imagine.'

'The two nurses and doctor here with me. They've asked if they could see the central field hospital. Is that possible, please?'

'Of course. Round them up now, and we'll all go over. Doctor Grauwin is the senior surgeon. He and the others have had their hands full, they must be exhausted by now.'

The group made its way along the network of communication trenches, heads down, in places plunging through the mud. As they approached the field hospital, the human carnage of the previous day's attack was there for all to see. Many brought in for surgery lay on stretchers outside the operating bunker under makeshift tarpaulins to give some protection from the rain. Incoming shells were falling in the area of the Gabrielle sector, but their own artillery was ear-splitting at times.

Theresa Müller and Geneviève de Galard stood close by with Bill. The two female faces under their helmets were generating much interest from all directions. A few minutes later a swarthy bald-headed man came out, stripped down to belt and trousers, hairy chest glistening with sweat. He adjusted his steel-rimmed glasses, and reached for a cigarette. Then looking up, he said, 'I'm Paul Grauwin. Is it you who are offering your services?' he said to Theresa and Geneviève.

'Yes, sir,' said Theresa. 'The two of us are battle-experienced nurses. I'm ready to help as best I can.'

'Me too, Doctor,' said Geneviève.

Doctor Grauwin looked them up and down. 'Really, I don't see how the two of you can join the existing team. They are all men, used to working together. They've been through hell in the past twenty-four hours, and will object to two women from outside being thrust upon them. I appreciate you both offering to help, but it wouldn't work.'

A silence, broken first by Theresa. 'I was in the front line at Alamein. We ran out of men,' she said. No reaction from the surgeon. Geneviève spoke up next, in an insistent but friendly tone, 'Why not give us a two day trial, Doctor Grauwin? That shouldn't upset anyone overmuch. You must be inundated with casualties right now.'

'We are, of course.' The surgeon hesitated. 'All right then, go with my MO here and fit yourself out. He will show you to your tents, and then report back to me so I can introduce you to the team.' With that, he stubbed out his cigarette and went back into the operating room.

Bill turned to Theresa and Geneviève. 'You did well, you two. I wish you luck. I'll let you know when they expect a plane to take us out.' He gave them a really warm smile. 'Come to me at once if you have a problem.'

55

Metropole Hotel, Hanoi

'Lieutenant Beckendorf,' said the concierge as Leo walked out of the stifling heat of the day and into cooler air of the hotel lobby. The large fans overhead swung lazily through their arcs. He handed Leo an envelope with the room key. It was from Roger Trinquier. Leo tore it open and scanned the printed message. 'Nurse Müller failed to return yesterday, her aircraft destroyed on the landing ground. She is safe and unhurt, and being looked after in the garrison. The same applies to the pilot, Squadron Leader Lomberg and one other *convoyeuse*.'

Leo made straight for the bar, ordered a Scotch and asked the barman to leave the bottle. His mind was working overtime. He knew about the Viet attack of two days ago, and the fall of Beatrice. He'd heard the airfield was out of action. How could they fly Theresa out? He squirted soda water on top of the whisky, and searched for some way he could ensure her safety. No way Dakotas can get in and out. Who could help? Maybe Trinquier could come up with something. He was in Hanoi, Leo was sure of that.

—❦—

'Lieutenant Beckendorf, come in.' Roger Trinquier was standing in his map room as Leo strode in. 'Bad show. Your friend Bill chose the right day for a medivac flight, they need evacuation flights badly. But the wrong day for him.'

'Is there anything we can do from here?' asked Leo.

'I've been thinking. The airfield there is effectively out of action now that the Viets have it in their sights after the fall of Beatrice. No aircraft are operating from there. No knowing when, if at all, flights can be re-started. Supplies will have to be dropped from the air.'

'Sounds like the writing's on the wall. The supplies they need to hold out indefinitely are much greater than can be delivered by air drops.'

'I know.' Trinquier paused, walking over to a more detailed map. He pointed out where he'd been using a remote airstrip to land his Morane reconnaissance aircraft on maquis operations, some fifty kilometres from Dien Bien Phu. Moving his finger on the map, he showed where there was a second strip at Dien Bien Phu, close by strongpoint Isabelle in the most southern part of the base. If they could fly in there to drop off a replacement battalion commander waiting to be sent in, they could bring out Theresa. The Morane could only take one passenger, but if he could get his hands on the MH 152, the Broussard he used to take Leo into the Highlands, there would be space to bring Theresa and Bill and the other nurse out.

'What are the chances?' said Leo.

'The air force won't like it. They won't want to risk a valuable machine like the Broussard, nor the pilot.' He paused. 'I'll try my friend Nicolas Martin. You know, the one who flew us into the Highlands. He has a lot of clout. We'll tell them there are urgent spare parts and medical supplies to get in, along with the replacement colonel. Maybe also replacement code books or something that can't risk falling into Viet hands. Why not speak with your Deuxième Bureau friends. They have their own way of bringing pressure to bear.'

56

Ka dashed back after working late, knocking on the door of Justine's apartment a little louder than usual. She was clutching a copy of *Le Monde*.

Justine opened the door and unlatched the chain.

After a quick embrace, Ka waved the newspaper. 'Have you seen this? The page one article on what's happening at this place, Dien Bien Phu?'

'I know there's trouble there, my darling, but I haven't read it yet.'

'The Viets have captured part of it, two strongpoints called Beatrice and Gabrielle, in a massive attack. *Le Monde* says the French have twelve thousand troops there, but it's now realised General Giap has three times that number, and the French garrison could be overwhelmed. Inside the paper, there's an article on the likely consequences if Ho Chi Minh wins the battle. It's horrifying.'

'I didn't know it was so big,' said Justine, concerned at the state Ka was in.

'It says the Viet have far more heavy guns than the French army thought. The airfield can't be used, the only way supplies and reinforcements can come is by air drops. The paper says defeat will have disastrous consequences for the French at the peace conference due to start in May.'

'I can see that.' Justine knew what was really upsetting Ka. A massive military defeat for France just before the major powers sat down in Geneva with France and Ho Chi Minh would mean France having to agree the handover of northern Vietnam to the Viets. 'You're worried about your parents and brother, aren't you, ma chère amie.'

Ka started to sob. 'The article says Ho Chi Minh will take over the north, perhaps as far south as Hue. They'll do terrible things to people who have worked with the French, like my parents.

'I've got to rescue them somehow. Get them away from Hanoi, to safety in the south.'

Justine thought. They needed to find out how serious the threat to Ka's family was. 'Ka, listen to me. I'm going to see my old girlfriend at the *piscine*. We need to know what the real threat is, not just what a journalist on the *Le Monde* staff is writing.'

'Oh, could you do that? I knew you would help me. I love you, Justine.'

Paris, 20th arrondissement

'I told you about my Vietnamese partner in the opium business, Françoise.'

'That's Ka?'

'Yes. That business is closed down, you know that. Jean and I met the *Bình Xuyên* and convinced them I was ceasing to compete.'

'That was a relief,' Françoise murmured.

'Ka and I are close.'

'I gathered that.'

'I would do anything for her,' Justine said. 'That moment has come. Ka realises her family in Hanoi will be in the firing line if the worst happens at Dien Bien Phu, and the French cave in at the Geneva conference. They'll pull out of northern Vietnam.'

'Which they will. That figures,' said Françoise.

'She wants to go out there and help them start a new life in the south.' Justine paused before asking the question. 'Before I try to organise something for Ka, I want to ask your advice. What's the thinking in the *piscine*?'

'What exactly do you mean by the thinking?'

'Is Dien Bien Phu going to be a military disaster, like the press say might well happen? If so, is Ho Chi Minh going to walk into Hanoi? And what would he do to those who have been working with the French?'

'That's three questions, Justine.' There was a long silence, Françoise glancing around her before saying, 'The answer to the first is that the garrison won't surrender, it will probably be overrun. As for Ho Chi Minh, he will ask for nationwide elections. China and Russia will be at the table, backing him. And most of the French population back home will be for getting out, giving up Indochina.'

'Elections for independence?'

'Yes.' Françoise paused, in thought. 'Elections would take time. In the meantime, he would be given control of the north.'

'And Ka's family, if they stay?'

'Not good. It would be bad for them.'

'What do you mean by that?'

'They would be taken to camps for years of indoctrination. That's the Communist way. Especially the educated Vietnamese like Ka's parents. Hasn't she a sick brother?'

'Yes,' murmured Justine.

'Many will perish in the camps. Those who come out, maybe after five years or more ...' She hesitated. 'They will come out different people.'

Justine felt fear spreading through her. 'And how likely is that, the Viets taking over the north?'

'Very,' said Françoise.

Justine knew, but didn't say, that Pierre Mendès France would be advocating that. He was close to becoming prime minister, and might well be leading the French delegation at Geneva.

Françoise reached out and held the arm of her oldest friend. 'Defeat at Dien Bien Phu is most likely. That's the inside view. The north would go to Ho Chi Minh. France would be out of Indochina within a year, the south becoming an independent state under Dinh Diem, with American backing.' She paused. 'That's what we think is the likely outcome.'

Another silence before Justine put her hand over Françoise's. 'Thank you, ma chérie. Now I know. I have to help Ka, and there's no time to waste.'

Paris, 21 Place Vendôme, March 1954

Justine sat in Giselle's small office just off the *atelier flou*. Most of the seamstresses were on their way home. It was dusk outside, and the dominant figure of Napoleon looked down on them from the pillar in the square outside.

She was telling Giselle about her concern for Ka and her family. The military news was bad, she didn't have to tell Giselle that. The papers were full of it, and of the political consequences.

'So, what can be done to help Ka?' said Giselle.

Shrewd as ever, thought Justine. She's probably guessing what's about to come.

'Giselle, the future in Vietnam is in the south. There's no reason why Saigon shouldn't continue to flourish. The wealthy, and that includes the Vietnamese close to the ruling families, will still want beautiful clothes. The Schiap visits there brought in good business. Those clients will want more, and the new rich, benefiting from American money, will want the same.'

'Yes, I follow that.'

'To service those clients, we need trained seamstresses on the spot, to back up the fittings and do alterations.'

'That makes sense,' said the *première main*.

'Sending Ka out to survey the scene, to report back to you on what is needed, would make sense. I know there's already been talk of opening an accessories boutique in Saigon.'

Giselle was thinking.

Justine saw her hesitation, adding, 'I realise people recognise there are risks out there. That it's not the right moment when there's uncertainty about the outcome of the Geneva conference. But I want to help Ka with her personal problem, her family. She has some money, and I will help her. If Schiap can sponsor her mission, so her arrival there is legitimate in the eyes of the authorities, my friends can get her to Hanoi, and back.'

'Okay, let's see what we can do between us,' said Giselle. 'It does make sense. We trust Ka, she's one of the best we have. I know she won't just disappear.'

Paris, Latin Quarter

'I have a plan,' said Justine, after Ka arrived at the apartment. They were settled on the sofa, a tray of tea and some macarons before them.

Ka's eyes sparkled, as though she could feel something exciting was about to happen.

'You have never been on an aeroplane, have you, Ka?'

'Good gracious no, I'm not sure I would like it,' she replied with her small musical laugh.

Justine told her about the conversation with Giselle, testing her, wanting to be sure she could take on something along the lines she had put to the *première main*.

Ka was surprised, then delighted with what was being suggested. 'How would I be able to reach my family?'

'I would ask Bill to fly you up. He's based in the north on medical evacuation flights, but I'm sure he still flies Dakotas down to Saigon. He could take you back with him.'

'Justine, you're fantastic. Yes, I want to get out there. I must help them.' Ka stopped for a moment. 'What about papers? The police out there will want to know what I'm up to?'

'You'll travel there as an employee of Schiaparelli. Giselle will give you a letter of assignment, referring to your mission to explore the opportunities for a support office for our clients in Indochina.'

'I'm a French citizen.'

'Yes, so you'll just need your *carte d'identité*. That's sufficient, you don't need a passport in a French colony.'

Ka suddenly thought about money. 'Who's going to pay?'

'The Air France ticket is the big cost. Giselle says Schiap will pay half if you pay the other half. I can help by paying some of your share, and you can repay me depending on what you have to spend on rescuing the family.'

'That's so kind. You're such a wonderful friend,' said Ka as she flung her arms around Justine.

Justine was thinking through Ka's trip. 'I'm going to ask the silk merchant who we were working with out there, to help you. You know his name, Monsieur Jules. Jean introduced him to me originally so I'll ask him to make the contact. We've helped him by introducing his shantung to the Paris couture houses, so he'll welcome another contact with that world. I'm sure Jules will help with accommodation.'

'When?' asked Ka.

'That's up to you. I would go at once if I were you. If Dien Bien Phu falls and the Geneva conference goes Ho Chi Minh's way, there could be a sudden rush to get out of Hanoi.' She paused. 'I've been to Saigon twice, of course. You'll love it. You know Hanoi already, after all you were brought up there.'

'Do you think Jean will be there? He goes in and out, doesn't he?'

'Yes, good idea. I'll find out when his next trip is and we'll fix your arrival date for when he's there. He can meet you at the airport and take care of you while you're fixing with Bill when to go Hanoi.'

'Oh, Justine, it will be dangerous.'

'Ka, you're thin and light, and beautiful. But underneath, I know there's steel thread – like in a Michelin tyre,' Justine said laughing. 'I don't recommend you carry a gun, but I can show you how to garrotte someone, if you like.'

'Justine, you're joking.'

'Only half-joking.' Justine looked around the room and her eyes latched onto the indoor washing line, coiled up and hanging just outside the kitchen. 'Bring over that line, Ka, and then stand in front of me, facing outwards. I promise to be gentle.'

Ka did as she was told. Justine circled the line in two loops, placing them over Ka's head, and down around the neck. She then pulled the two ends of the line gently until Ka could feel the tightening of the line on her throat.

'Now try and open the loops with your fingers, Ka.'

'Ouch,' said Ka. 'That hurts.'

'Yes, it will. The beauty of this double loop garrotte is that the more the victim struggles to open the loops, the more they tighten. They taught us that in Scotland in the war, at Arisaig. Now try it on me,' said Justine as she changed place with the other.

'It's very effective,' exclaimed Ka as she put the coils round Justine's neck.

'Piano wire is best,' said Justine, laughing.

57

Dien Bien Phu, 15 March 1954

Henri and Bernard Fall were together in the central redoubt that evening. The mood was black.

'Beatrice and Gabrielle strongpoints gone in forty-eight hours,' said Fall with some finality.

Henri remained silent.

'I hear that two senior officers on de Castries's staff have broken down.'

'Yes,' said Henri. 'Two lieutenant colonels are replacing them. The first I know well, Lt Colonel Maurice Lemeunier. He started in the *chasseurs alpins* but transferred to the Legion later and fought with me in 13 DBLE in the Western Desert. They plan to helicopter him in, probably tomorrow.'

'What about reinforcements?'

'With the airfield out of action, another colonial parachute battalion is standing by to drop. Trouble is, all available Dakotas are being used to parachute in shells, to re-build the reserves.'

Henri wasn't sure whether to pass on the classified news he'd been told that evening.

Bernard pre-empted him. 'I know no one's meant to know,' said Bernard, 'but I just heard about Piroth.'

Silence. Then Henri confirmed what de Castries was attempting to keep quiet. Charles Piroth, formerly the proud Commander of Artillery, told his closest friend how he had totally lost honour. Back in his bunker, he removed the pin from a grenade and forced it into his chest. His death could not be kept secret for long.

Strongpoint Isabelle, 25 March 1954

The flak burst above them as the five-seater Broussard reconnaissance plane came in as low as the pilot dared take it, touching down on the short auxillary airstrip. In the drainage ditch alongside, Bill crouched with Theresa. The replacement colonel was offloaded and then the supplies. Leo ran across to collect the new passengers. Seeing just the two, he shouted, 'Where's the other *convoyeuse*?'

'She wouldn't come,' replied Bill.

'I couldn't persuade her,' shouted Theresa. 'She wants to stay and help Doctor Grauwin at the hospital.'

'So be it,' said Leo. 'Right, on board immediately.'

Theresa felt Leo's hand on hers as the plane turned into wind, and was off the ground in no time.

They would both agree afterwards, a true miracle.

Haiphong Cat-Cat Bi airbase

Roger Trinquier was on the tarmac to meet the three of them on their return from what Leo was now calling the *Kessel*.

'Hi Roger,' said Leo. 'These two are the lucky ones. The other *convoyeuse* elected to stay behind. Turning to the others, 'I think you know Bill, but I must introduce you to Theresa.'

'Mademoiselle, I have heard a lot about you from Leo, all good things except the risks you take.'

'Yes, Major Trinquier, I did pick the wrong flight the other day,' said Theresa.

'Normally, I would suggest we go somewhere and open a bottle of champagne,' said Leo to all of them. 'Somehow, I don't feel like it.' Turning to Trinquier, he said, 'One of our old friends from school in England is at Dien Bien Phu.'

Bill said, 'That's Henri de Rochefort.'

'Tough,' said Trinquier. 'Let's go to the bar and have a beer. I'd like to know what it was like, your short stay in the …' he looked at Leo, '*Kessel*, I think German paratroopers would say.'

Leo and Theresa knew what he meant. Bill, from his knowledge of Afrikaans, had a pretty good idea. 'Kettle, or cauldron,' said Bill.

'It's bad,' continued Bill. 'Henri de Rochefort's 3rd Battalion of 13 DBLE was destroyed in the attack on Beatrice. Henri's okay. I didn't see him, but that's what I heard.'

'He was the first person I met when I arrived in Saigon three years ago,' said Theresa. 'The whole thing is horrible.'

They sat quietly, saying nothing and sipping their beers, each thinking of the path forward in the crisis that lay ahead.

Until Leo suddenly said, 'I'm taking on a new project.'

'What's that?' asked Trinquier.

'I've been asked to head a team that will handle applications coming in from volunteers who want to be parachuted into Dien Bien Phu. Apparently, there are so many that we don't have sufficient air transport capacity to fly them over.'

58

Theresa said, 'I just heard the latest on conditions at the main hospitals in Dien Bien Phu?'

Leo was with her in the cafeteria.

'I imagine they are pretty bad,' said Leo.

'There was a transmission from Dr Grauwin directly to the surgical team here. I was present. They're doing a hundred and fifty operations a week in the three underground hospitals. That's in spite of the dressing stations doing as much as they can to minimise transport to the hospitals. When those arriving at the two main hospitals can't be admitted right away, their stretchers are put outside on the mud and in danger of exploding shells.'

'That's bad. We're now in the monsoon season, rain every night.'

'Yes, and that means rats. The floors are covered with a mix of mud, human excrement, and hospital disposables.' She paused. Almost as an afterthought, she added, 'The girls from the Legion's *bordel mobile de campagne*, Vietnamese prostitutes, are now nurses.'

Theresa ate some of their meal without elaborating further. Then suddenly she said, 'Leo, you remember Geneviève de Galard who stayed behind when you came and flew me out?'

'I do, never met her except when she boarded the outbound flight with you.'

'She's turned out to be someone special, has an extraordinary effect on the badly wounded and post-operation cases.' Theresa paused, and Leo could see she was moved by what she was saying. 'They call out for her, by her first name. She's able to do the most awful tasks, things which normally degenerate a man's self-esteem. Yet, when she does it, with a smile and maybe some humour, the patients accept it as straightforward.'

'She's a qualified nurse, of course?'

'Yes, and at a high level. She takes charge of serious incoming wounded and applies the first treatment and tests herself. Everyone here is talking about it. She does a lot for the surgeons, like identifying cases of shock and not treating wounds that could generate new shock. Also blood transfusions and applying needles to infuse penicillin.'

Leo said nothing, somehow guessing what was going to come next.

'Leo, my darling, I should be there. I shouldn't have left. There's so much I could be doing.'

'Theresa, you shouldn't think that. Instructions were for you to be brought back.' He placed his hands over the back of hers. 'The contribution you've made and the risks you've taken as a *convoyeuse* are immense. You deserve a medal for that.'

Neither said much for a bit. Then Theresa almost pleaded, as she said to him, 'Darling, when is this all going to end?'

Leo didn't respond at first. He wasn't sure how much of his thinking he should disclose to her.

'Theresa, it's not good, as I see it. We're not replacing our losses in men and supplies. Everything has to be flown in. Giap, on the other hand, has supply lines of thousands of his followers across northern Tonkin, and more troops he can transfer from the east. Many are now trained in China.'

'What about the Americans?'

'True, they're doing great things for us in terms of *matériel*. But they won't commit their own troops. Ho Chi Minh has China to draw on for *matériel*. Since the Korean war ended, the gates have opened. Some of their artillery even comes from Russia. But not troops.'

Theresa was solemn. 'It's going to become desperate. Thousands could be taken prisoner, after thousands have died.' She paused. An idea seemed to come into her mind, 'I read an article in *Time*. The writer thought that a massive bombing offensive by the Americans would stop Giap in his tracks.'

'Possibly, my darling, but I don't see the Americans taking such an aggressive stance. Their relations with China and Russia are delicate, to say the least. To upset that balance would be to invite retaliation.'

'So what can France do? If they're wiped out at Dien Bien Phu, Ho Chi Minh will arrive in Geneva for the peace conference in a very strong position, won't he?'

'Yes. He will push for independence. Back in France, public pressure on the government to pull out of Indochina will be overwhelming.' Leo stopped for a moment, thinking. 'I told you I'm now in charge of requests from volunteers wanting to drop into Dien Bien Phu to help the fight.'

'How effective is that going to be?'

'Henri Sauvagnac, the new head of Airborne, plays by the book, he's not going to throw away lives. Having said that, I'm going to press for those who can prove the right background to be dropped in.'

'Yes,' said Theresa, in a resigned way. 'It's all become terribly emotional. The foreign press is full of the battle. Whatever happens, it's never going to be forgotten.' She hesitated. 'If your poor school friend Henri survives, he would be taken prisoner, wouldn't he? The camps they put them in sound awful. Brainwashing, and all that.'

'Don't talk about it.'

59

Saigon, Tan Son Nhut airfield, April 1954

The Air France Douglas DC4 bumped along the concrete on touchdown and the air stewardesses jumped up from their seats and told everyone to sit tight until the plane came to rest. For the umpteenth time after the gruelling flights and re-fuelling stops, Ka inspected their turnout. Impeccable, even at the end. Dark blue suits nipped at the waist with straight skirts just below the knee, pencil line seams up the back of their nylon stockings. She couldn't inspect the stitching on the inside of the clothes, that would have told her the true quality of the garment.

At last, Saigon. Must prepare for the police checks. She hoped the Schiap letter would do the trick. Where was her *carte d'identité*? Okay, everything was ready. Here came the steps, on the back of a truck. Mustn't leave anything behind. Suddenly a blast of heat as the doors were opened. Of course, Saigon was close to the Equator, fifteen hundred kilometres south of Hanoi.

She wished Justine was with her for the checks, but it turned out okay. No awkward questions at the immigration barrier. No suspicious stares even though she was a Vietnamese rather than European like most of the other passengers. There was her suitcase, after only a short wait. Now, where was Jean who was to be waiting for her after the customs check?

'Mademoiselle Ka, welcome to Saigon. How lovely to see you again.' Jean gave her a peck on each cheek and grabbed her case. 'How was the flight?'

'There were several. We re-fuelled three times. It was exhausting.'

'Poor you. I have my car outside, We'll go straight to where Jules and I agreed was right for you to stay in Saigon. They're a charming family, and the cost is modest.'

It was all Ka could do to stay awake as the car began to move.

'Good news,' said Jean. 'Bill is down here, coming to see you tomorrow morning.'

Ka was overjoyed. Justine was always talking about Bill. Meeting him would be next best thing to seeing her. She knew they were close after everything that happened to them during the war in Europe.

Jean explained the family Ka was staying with were from the north, having moved to Saigon ten years before the war with Japan. Somehow she was wide awake by the time he stopped outside an apartment house. A warm welcome awaited her. After a light meal with the family, Ka couldn't wait to get the feel of Saigon, and ventured out into the streets nearby. Very different from how she remembered Hanoi with its grand boulevards and villas in the French colonial tradition. Here it seemed to be a much more commercial, busy atmosphere, at least where she was.

Ka thought about tomorrow's meeting with Bill. What would he be like? According to Justine, his loves in life were rugby and flying. He was from South Africa, educated by the Benedictines in the west of England. She was also from a Catholic school, in Hanoi. That was important, something they had in common. She knew little about rugby in France, it seemed to be a murderously rough game played between towns in the Massif Central region, from Lyon to Toulouse.

After breakfast with the family the next morning, Bill was suddenly at the door.

'You must be Ka,' he said in rather shaky French, as his broad-shouldered frame eased its way into the apartment.

'Yes, Monsieur Bill,' she said as they shook hands.

Settled afterwards in a café down the street, they got straight to the point.

'So you want to visit your family in Hanoi, Ka?'

'That's right. My father has always worked for the French administration and the army, he's a builder. My mother still teaches at the convent where I went to school. I have a brother with palsy, a form of paralysis, and they look after him. If Ho Chi Minh took the north, they wouldn't have a hope. They would die in the indoctrination camps, if not before.'

'So, you want to get them out before it's too late?'

'Yes. Justine wondered if you could fly me up there.' Ka tried not to sound too anxious.

Bill was thinking. 'It would be unofficial. I'm under contract to the French army. I used to fly cargo, still do a bit of that. But my main job is casualty evacuation. If the wrong official caught you on board, there would be the devil to pay.'

'I'm here officially on business for my fashion employer in Paris. Couldn't I just be using my spare time to visit my mother and father in Hanoi? I could say my brother was ill, which is not incorrect.'

There was a long silence. Then Ka said, 'You know we were in the same business, Bill?'

Bill hesitated. 'Yes, I flew the merchandise down from the Meos in the north. We were in it together, Ka. And I guess we all made good money.' He paused. 'I want to help you in any way I can.'

Ka was thrilled with Bill's friendliness. 'I would like to get up there and make contact with my parents as soon as possible. I have a telephone number, maybe you have a phone I could use?'

Bill explained she could call from where he was staying. He would work out how to take her on board his Dakota. If that wasn't possible, it might have to be a long train journey with hold-ups on the way, or a three-day journey by ship. He would feel happier if she was with him.

Bill went to Antoine Savani himself for clearance to fly Ka up to Hanoi. He told an accurate if incomplete story about Ka's role in Schiaparelli, her connection with him and Justine, and the potential plight of her family in the north. In what he described as the tradition of Air Opium, Savani waved her through.

Now they were out on the tarmac of Tan Son Nhut airfield, walking towards the Dakota.

Ka said, to Bill's surprise, 'Looks like they are loading bombs.' She was pointing at what looked like large silver eggs stacked on a trolley, being loaded into the hold of the Dakota.

'Don't worry about those,' was all he said.

Ka remained curious. As they approached the steps to climb into the plane, she noted the crate the egg-shaped objects were being transferred from was marked 'Dow Chemical. Napalm B'. Something to do with Madame X's husband, thought Ka.

During the flight, Ka's thoughts were on her family, the excitement of seeing her mother and father for the first time for years. She wondered how she would find her brother. She knew the steroidal treatment made possible by the money she transferred was working, and she hoped to see a recovery from his partial paralysis.

Her mind drifted back to work and then to Madame X. It was only months ago that her client was so upset about her father's involvement with the new version of napalm and its shipment to Saigon. Now it was on board the plane she was in. Where was it destined for, and why?

Bill was up in the cockpit of course. There were just a few seats behind in the cabin, the rest of the interior partitioned off for cargo. They flew over the ocean, just off the eastern coastline of Annam. Eventually, Bill banked the aircraft over to the west, towards the port of Haiphong. There below was a wonderful view of Ha Long Bay which she remembered being taken to as a child. How she would love to show it to Justine.

As they lost altitude, Hanoi appeared in the distance and she remembered that the farms and villages around it were now under the influence of the Vietminh. Ho Chi Minh's people were infiltrating everywhere, and she'd heard the French only controlled either side of the highway to Haiphong. Ka knew it was just a matter of time until the Viet forces marched into the city. She must persuade her parents to move now.

Landing at Hanoi's Bach Mai military airfield, Ka was amazed at the number of aircraft on the ground. She was told this was the most important airbase for supplying Dien Bien Phu. With the airfield there closed by enemy gunfire, all supplies were being parachuted in. There were Dakotas, Flying Boxcars, and fighter bombers everywhere. Maybe that's where the napalm was to be dropped.

―――

It was a dramatic homecoming. Ka was overwhelmed by the outflow of love from her parents and brother. They treated her like a hero returning from another world. Her brother was now a strong young man, recovered from the affliction that was threatening his life. Her father still working for the French army, her mother teaching again at the convent school Ka attended before leaving for university in France.

She waited for the second day before referring to the imminent defeat of the French army at Dien Pien Phu. When she did, putting it in the context of the peace conference opening in Geneva, it was clear that they would take a lot of convincing before her gentle suggestion of a move to the south would be taken seriously.

Ka and Bill were to meet up on the third day. He wanted to introduce Ka to his old schoolfriend Leo who was also in Hanoi with his girlfriend Theresa. There was a connection with Justine that he would explain.

'We're going to the Metropole,' he said when he picked her up in a borrowed jeep. 'Leo and Theresa will meet us there.'

'So what's the connection with Justine?' asked Ka.

'I don't know how much Justine's told you about her experience in the war in Europe,' said Bill.

'Only that she was beaten up and sent to the camps. That's enough.'

'Yes, we met in a concentration camp called Buchenwald. Vile, vile place. I had flown her out of France earlier in the war when she came to Britain for training, so we recognised one another. We managed to escape from that camp together.'

'Must be quite a story,' said Ka.

'It is. We reached Freiburg, that's when our luck ran out, or at least Justine's. She was taken by the SS, although I escaped thanks to my old schoolfriend Leo. Even though, as a German, he was on the other side.'

'I see, sounds unusual and yet wonderful. I certainly look forward to meeting him and his Theresa.

Bill pulled up in front of a large colonial style building and gave the keys of the jeep to the doorman. They walked through the lobby and found Leo and Theresa at a table in a quiet corner of the garden area beyond.

Theresa told Ka how much she admired Schiaparelli clothes when she lived in Paris, doing her training to become a nurse.

Then the story came out of Theresa and Bill being stranded in Dien Bien Phu just before General Giap's massive attack, when their Dakota was shot up. Theresa added that since there were no more medivac flights, she was temporarily helping in the production of parachutes there in Hanoi.

'We have a problem,' said Theresa. 'Silk is an important industry in Vietnam. It's logical therefore that we make parachutes, the fabric for the canopies being silk. The demand is very high because very few parachutes are recovered. There are thousands required every week. You can imagine, fifty transport planes a day parachuting into Dien Bien Phu thirty canisters from each aircraft, some needing four parachutes each.

Leo interrupted. 'The problem is there's been a fire at the main manufacturing facility for parachute production, just on the outskirts of Hanoi. We think it was arson.' He paused, then added, 'The fire was almost certainly started by Viet infiltrators. We're looking for an alternative site, to re-start production. Also there's need for an expert seamstress to do the final inspection,' he said pointedly. 'The correct sewing of each silk canopy is all important. So is the quality of the silk from which the canopy is to be made.'

'Okay, I will come over and see what I can do to help,' said Ka.

'Why you?' exclaimed Bill.

'Because I sew silk as well as the best in Paris couture,' laughed Ka.

'Security is tight,' said Theresa. 'We have to prevent the Viets from stopping production again.'

'What about staffing?' asked Ka. 'I heard that people are no longer willing to work here on French war materials. They're scared they will be singled out for punishment if the Viets take over?'

'That's right, it is a problem and it's growing.'

Ka was thinking. 'I have an idea. What about my old school? It's a Catholic convent school. There must be thirty or forty nuns there, and I bet they can all sew,' said Ka. 'What's more, there's space, several big rooms and a hall. You could establish fabrication of the parachutes right there. And no problem with internal security, the nuns are very much with the French.'

'Would they agree?' said Theresa, surprised by Ka's inventiveness.

'I think so. If the Viets take Hanoi, the nuns are going to be in trouble anyway. The Catholic Church regards Communism as a global threat. She paused, thinking how to move the idea forward. 'I think we should have a word with Reverend Mother. My mother still teaches there. We could go with her.'

Leo was looking on in astonishment. 'Bill and I were educated by the Benedictines. I'm sure they would support the idea.' Everyone laughed. 'You're right to sound out the nuns first. All being well, we can move quickly to bring the authorities in and get things moving. I guess you should ask for a month. After that, a more permanent facility should be ready.'

Ka said, 'I will speak to my mother right away.'

⋯⋯

Ka's mother didn't hesitate when they put the plan to her that evening. The best time to approach Reverend Mother was in the staff coffee break in the morning, and Bill agreed to collect Ka and the three of them would meet at the school then.

60

Convent of Sisters of St Paul de Chartres, Hanoi, April 1954

Memories flooded back to Ka as she watched the children streaming out of their classes, shepherded by the nuns in their flowing white habits. Easter was at the end of the week and the school would become deserted for a fortnight. Little had changed since her days there.

'Ka, I remember you so well,' said Reverend Mother when Ka's own mother introduced her. 'It's wonderful that you are back. What can I do for you?'

Theresa was with them, wearing her uniform of a Foreign Legion nurse, and Ka introduced her.

They explained the urgent need for a facility to handle parachute production, following the fire. Reverend Mother's response was that Easter was late that year, on the eighteenth, and the school would be empty from Thursday the fifteenth for a fortnight. That would provide time to set up the fabrication of the silk canopies in the main hall which could be made available right away. The nuns would be pleased to help in any way. Many would volunteer to assist in the sewing process.

Theresa was thrilled with the news. It was agreed that nothing would be publicly announced. The need was urgent and production would be kept secret. They didn't want any leakage to Viet sympathisers.

She would go straight to the authorities and pass on the Convent's offer.

The response of the authorities was immediate. How quickly could they start? The target was to commence production by the coming Easter weekend. Ka was to train the volunteer nuns, after Theresa showed her the sewing process for the parachute canopies.

'The news from Dien Bien Phu is not good at all,' said Theresa, as she and Ka made their way into the Convent for the first day of production. 'They can't hold out for much longer. Leo says the Viets are likely to launch a final overwhelming attack by the end of the month.'

'Is there nothing new that can be done?' said Ka.

'He's screening the volunteers who want to be dropped into the zone to fight alongside the garrison. Over a thousand volunteers so far, remarkable when you think they will either be killed or taken prisoner, in all likelihood.'

Ka nodded. She was already running an expert eye over the bales of silk arriving and being unloaded. Work surfaces were in place in the hall. The nuns to be trained by her were on one side of the hall, and the experienced staff from the burnt out factory were in two large groups, those sewing the canopies and those on final assembly of cords and harness.

Leo turned up at that moment, bringing with him a contact from the Sûreté whose concern was security at the new facility.

'They burned down the factory. What's to stop them burning down the Convent?' he said to Leo.

'That's the risk,' replied Leo. 'There are Viet sympathisers everywhere. Just a word to one of them and Ho Chi Minh will know what's going on here.'

'This woman, Ka. What do you know about her?'

'She's from a Paris couture house. Came over to see her family. She's concerned about their future should the Viets take over in the north.'

'I don't blame her. Frankly, if the peace conference gives Ho Chi Minh the northern part of Vietnam, everyone connected with the French establishment will be wanting to get out in a rush. There won't be enough ships to take them off. Better they get ahead of the game.'

'As you know, I work closely with the Deuxième Bureau,' said Leo. Their listening posts have been picking up more non-military radio traffic in the past month. The sign is that underground activity is being stepped up, pointing to sabotage of the infrastructure.'

'And burning down factories,' said the man from the Sûreté.

Ka felt like she did that terrible day in Paris when she was followed. The day she was taken to the rue du Bac. She was sure someone was on her trail. It must have started as she was leaving the Convent for her parents' home a few days after parachute production restarted. That feeling of being watched. It became a sixth sense ever since that experience in Paris.

She was now sure. Just a trick or two, and she saw in the reflection of a shop window a man in civilian clothes and sunglasses. Her protector, Justine, was on the other side of the world. She thought of Theresa who'd become a good friend. Ka would tell her about her pursuer as soon as she could.

'I will stick with you,' was Theresa's response.

The next evening Theresa hung back behind her at some distance as she headed for home. Ka was able to check from time to time that she was there from her distinctive clothing and tall silhouette. If her tail latched on again, her friend would have a better view of him from behind, and whether there was more than one.

As she was crossing the large square in the Hoàn Kiếm district, she realised Theresa was longer in view. Why should she have left her? It didn't make sense.

Then it happened. As she entered a small street on the far side, a man leapt from a shopfront and took hold of her with both arms. A second man, also young, grabbed her by the legs. No one else was close by. She was about to shout when they forced a gag into her mouth and a blindfold over her eyes. Ka felt herself bundled into a bicycle rickshaw. One man sat beside her in the back, holding a gun against her neck. He said nothing. She felt the other leap on the machine in front and pedal furiously.

Their surveillance skills were more professional than she thought. Who were they? Possibly the Sûreté, although unlikely. It must be the Viets. Why have they chosen us? Must stay calm.

The rickshaw bumped and jerked through the streets. Eventually, it swung to the right and stopped. They manhandled her up some steps and into a room, taking off the blindfold. It was a large room with only small windows. A Vietnamese man sat opposite her, the usual white shirt open at the neck, lit cigarette in his hand. He didn't move, just watched her. He looked older than the young men who brought her in, perhaps in his forties. To Ka, he gave the impression of authority although she wasn't sure why.

Suddenly he spoke. 'I know who you are. You are known as Ka, and you only recently arrived in Hanoi. We have been watching you since your plane landed from Saigon. Your mother works at the Convent of St Paul of Chartres. That is all correct, isn't it?'

'Yes,' said Ka. There was no point in pretending otherwise or in refusing to respond, at least at this stage.

'You arrived on a C47 flight from Saigon seven days ago. Why did you come?'

'I came to visit my parents and my brother who has been ill.'

'He looked down at the table and she realised for the first time that her identity card and the Schiap letter were lying in front of him.'

'I see you are a French national and you live and work in Paris.'

'Yes.'

'Tell me why you came all this way, from France.'

Ka felt she should be as helpful as possible at this point in the interrogation, and gave him a full explanation of why Schiap sent her to Saigon.

'Very well. Now tell me what you know about the cargo carried in the Dakota plane you flew in to Hanoi.'

So that was it. They knew about the cargo of Napalm B. The silver eggs. They must want to know how much of it was being shipped to the north for the defence of Dien Bien Phu. Napalm, particularly the slow-burning variant, terrified the Viet soldiers. Justine told her. Now what should she say?

Ka remained silent, still thinking through how to respond.

The interrogator looked down again at some papers in front of him. 'Take a look at this, Mademoiselle Ka.' He passed her an enlarged photograph. She looked at the picture and caught her breath. That must be napalm in use. There was a short line of Viet soldiers in their conical helmets, advancing crouched down in a trench. A flood of fire was coming down the trench towards them.

'Now look at the next one,' he said as he passed another photograph over to her. In the second picture, the fire had engulfed the first three or so soldiers. Those behind them were turning back, trying to escape.

'And this one.' Ka saw a line of bodies flat on the ground, perhaps twenty of them. Each corpse was burnt to a skeleton.

The interrogator lit another cigarette. 'That was Napalm B. The jellified petroleum that stuck to those men's bodies went on burning for several minutes.'

Silence. Then he added, 'That's what you were transporting in the aircraft.'

Ka thought she was going to be sick. She said nothing.

The interrogator now pushed towards her a small photograph. 'I think you know this woman.'

Ka looked closely at the image of a woman walking on a sidewalk, in Place Vendôme by the look of it. The shock of recognition rushed through Ka. There was no doubt, it was Madame X.

He said slowly, 'You know who this is, don't you? You see, we know all about this client of yours, and her father.'

Ka was staggered. How could the Viets be on the trail of Madame X's father, the link in the supply of Napalm B? She couldn't get a word out, even if she'd wanted to.

The interrogator leant forward, his head resting on his hands. 'Mademoiselle Ka, you are in serious trouble. We intend to learn everything you know about this woman and her father. They connect you to the supply of a weapon which is being banned by the United Nations. A weapon which is brutalising our gallant soldiers fighting for the independence of our country.'

A long silence, then the interrogator rose from his chair.

'We will take a short break. Then you will tell me the whole story.' With that, he stood up, brushed the ash off his shirt, and walked out of the room.

The one guard in the room showed Ka into a small bathroom just outside, and turned the lock. Ka's mind was racing.

What did they think they would learn from her? Their aim must be somehow to interrupt the supply of Napalm B from the United States to French forces here. How should she play it? What advice would Justine give her if she was here?

When she was brought back into the room, there was Theresa, still in her uniform dress. She was strapped face up on a bed against the far wall. They glanced at one another before Ka sat down in her chair.

The interrogator entered and took his seat opposite Ka.

'The whole story, Mademoiselle Ka, tell me everything you know about the woman in the photograph, and about the supply chain for Napalm B.'

'I was just doing my job. I don't deny that the woman in the photograph looks like one of the clients I did sewing for. I know nothing about napalm or how it gets here.'

The interrogator nodded to the other man in the room, whom she noticed was wearing rubber gloves. That was the signal for the gloved man to go across to Theresa.

'Mademoiselle Ka. You have misunderstood me. If you continue to do so, your friend here is going to suffer terribly.'

A surge of terror swept through Ka. What were they going to do to Theresa?

'Have you heard of the *Gégène*?'

'No.'

'The *Gégène* is an apparatus introduced to us by the French colonial Sûreté. Many Vietminh heroes have suffered under its murderous treatment. Even the regiment your friend here serves in, the Foreign Legion, are known to have used it to obtain information in the battlefield.'

'Corporal,' he said, 'bring in our female assistant.'

A middle-aged Vietnamese woman entered the room, expressionless face, and walked over to the bed on which Theresa lay.

'Let us have a demonstration, not too strong an electric current to start with. Mademoiselle Ka, turn around so you can see the effect on you friend.'

Ka focused for the first time on the electrical apparatus on a table beside the bed. The woman was connecting an electrode from it, underneath Theresa's skirt, attaching another electrode to her chest. The Corporal looked across and the interrogator nodded. Ka watched in horror as Theresa's body contorted under the shock applied and a terrible howling cry filled the room.

'Enough.' The man turned back to Ka. 'You see, Mademoiselle, the effect this machine can have. If the treatment continues long enough, the patient usually dies.'

Ka's mind was working furiously, searching for a solution to this terrifying predicament she found herself in. She couldn't let Theresa suffer in such devastating fashion. At that moment, she heard the wail of a siren in the street outside. The interrogator ordered the other two to find out what was going on. As they left the room, he rose and went over to the small window behind him.

Ka's hand went to the seam of her light khaki jacket, ripping it open deftly with a sharp thumbnail. Her hand linked onto the coil of piano wire and ripped it out.

There was shouting in the street as the interrogator leant over the window sill. Ka moved silently round the desk, making a double coil in the wire as she crept towards the man's back. In a sudden movement she had the coil over his head and down around his neck, above the open shirt collar.

His hands flew up to the wire as she pulled both ends with the passionate strength flooding through her. He tore at the wire with his fingers and as she continued to pull the ends, the wire bit tighter into the flesh, closing the supply of air to his head. Ka found strength she never knew she had. On and on they struggled until the interrogator started to go limp, slowly sliding to the floor.

Ka was across to the bed in a flash, her delicate fingers undoing the fixations around Theresa's arms and legs.

At that moment Leo burst into the room.

Dien Bien Phu, late April 1954

Where was Bernard Fall? Henri warned him against heading for 13 DBLE's remaining 1st Battalion, now at the Huguette strongpoint. The Viets were attacking the hedgehogs in the complex, some already overwhelmed. Almost dusk and less risk of sniper fire, Henri's jeep was making heavy going in the mud of the track leading to Huguette 6, close to the north-western end of the airfield.

What was that? The unmistakeable thwack of a Sikorsky coming in for the seriously wounded. That happened rarely, given only a handful of helicopters were operating from Muong Sai in northern Laos. Some said that Secretary of State John Foster Dulles was holding back on America supplying much-needed helicopters to the French. They would help the seriously wounded but not alter the outcome, in Henri's view.

An intelligence overview from Hanoi was reporting a big fall in Viet morale after continued heavy casualties and the disruption that monsoon rains were bringing to their supply lines. Little hope in Henri's view, that such news would bring any withdrawal. Much more likely that General Giap would launch a final devastating offensive very soon. Then what? Talk of a relief force breaking through from Laos must be wishful thinking. Even if it did traverse the impossible terrain, surely Giap's divisions would annihilate it.

Henri didn't want to speculate about becoming a prisoner of the Viets. There was still a battle to be fought. He was brought back to reality by running into Fall coming the other way. Bernard said he never reached Huguette 6. He was with a party and strong escort dispatched to re-supply the strongpoint with water and ammunition. It was held by two companies of 13 DBLE's 1st Battalion and some colonial paras. A Viet shell killed two of the defending officers as he approached in one of the communication trenches, and although some of the supplies found a way through, he was ordered back.

By then it was Good Friday. Huguette 6 became impossible to hold. That evening, orders were received by the defenders to pull back. Could Bernard begin to understand what Henri was thinking? The 1st Battalion's tenacious defence of the Huguettes, after the 3rd Battalion was wiped out at Beatrice, was another chapter 13 DBLE was writing in the short but illustrious history of that Legion half brigade, formed in 1939 and famous for its defence against Rommel at Bir Hakeim.

'The end must be close,' said Henri. He and Bernard were up late in a corner of the HQ bunker, a few days later.

'So much for the optimism that the Americans might send in their heavy bombers, or that a relief force would fight its way through from Laos. Never figured in my book,' said Fall. 'After Giap's latest offensive to take out the Eliane complex, it will be impossible to recover any of the air drops. No more supplies means no more fighting.' Bernard said it with a degree of finality.

'What will you do when the Viets appear in the doorway?'

'Offer them a copy of the *Tribune*, and my press card,' said Fall.

61

Justine was out buying her breakfast when she noticed more people than usual outside the *tabac*, reading the front pages for free. Only one headline that morning, the fall of Dien Bien Phu. Immediately, the drama burst upon her. Ka and her family. She'd heard nothing except a teleprinter message from Jean who met her flight two weeks ago, saying she was in Bill's safe hands and on the way to Hanoi. She must go to Jean's office and ask for news.

She purchased a copy of *Le Monde*. A fight to the end, when the remaining defences were overrun. Thousands of casualties. Thousands of French and colonial troops taken prisoner. The lead article referred to the impact of the French defeat on the peace conference just starting in Geneva.

Justine remembered she was due to meet Kim that evening. She wanted to know how the journalist was finding work on the Paris *Herald Tribune*. She would see what the latest American view was on the peace conference and the future of Indochina. After all, Kim was originally from Cambodia.

⚬━━◎ ◎━━⚬

They met over bowls of onion soup in the marketplace of Les Halles, the hot sticky cheese surface of the soup making it a meal in itself.

'Any news from Ka?' asked Kim, who was very interested when Justine mentioned her friend's mission to Vietnam. 'I ask because I just heard from Madame X about her father.'

'What news?'

'He's dead. Cause unknown. He went missing, and they found him in the Seine. It's been kept out of the French press, so far.'

'He's a controversial figure among those on the inside,' said Justine, 'having escaped the *épuration* in spite of collaboration.'

'He was close to being in the news a few months ago, when our paper ran a syndicated article originating with the *New York Herald Tribune*.'

'The transfer of Napalm B from a United States vessel in Marseille port, to a French ship bound for Saigon,' said Justine.

'Exactly.' Kim paused, looking hard at Justine. 'If you want my view as an enlightened Cambodian, the Viets did him in.'

On her way to Jean's office to see if there was any reply to her teleprinter message to Saigon, Justine remembered Ka's last few words before she left. 'I'll be back as soon as arrangements are made for my parents to move south. We mustn't let your politics come between us, Justine. You're not often at Schiap nowadays. I couldn't survive without your love and friendship.' And how she replied. 'Ka, ma chère amie, my career is one thing. My life outside has room for whatever I want. To remain close to you is at the top of that list.'

62

They were marching, thousands of them. The survivors, now prisoners. Marching in columns to the camps. Three hundred kilometres' distance away, they said. At least twenty kilometres every day. The Viets weren't sadistic like the Japanese, his mates told him. They didn't hold them in contempt for not dying in action. They seldom beat them, except for attempted escape. It was the near-starvation that was slowly killing Henri. Rice with its husks. The very occasional vegetable. Disease rampant, particularly dysentery from untreated water. Their own doctors were made to stay with the officers, refused access to the men who were sick. Those too sick to undertake tasks on the way, were left behind.

Bernard Fall? Not seen him since the day the central camp was overrun, the day they were captured. He should be okay. With the peace conference under way, Ho Chi Minh wouldn't want to upset the international press corps.

What of himself? If he were leaving school again with Leo and Bill, would he have done the same thing? Not much choice at the time, with the war in Europe beginning. He could have changed course afterwards. Staying in the Legion was like living in a second family. He wasn't a natural soldier, he just grew into it. The friendships, they wouldn't be the same in civilian life. The downside was obvious, he wasn't married, no children. So often one was posted out of reach of French society. Vietnam was a typical example. If he survived and was ever released, he would think seriously about a new start.

Now was the immediate challenge. When they reached the camp, he'd heard, the indoctrination began, intensive if you were an officer. What should he expect? Reports from the few prisoners repatriated in the past were their source of information on camp life. The Viet interrogators attacked your self-respect, disorientated you, broke you down. That was the first stage. Then they brainwashed you in Communist ideology. Always the threats that you might be executed, hung over you though it rarely happened. Their aim was to recruit you into their cause. How long that took depended on the person. The more simple-minded, just a few months. The stronger, those who resolutely resisted, much longer. They never relented.

63

Bordeaux, June 1954

Justine remembered the house so well as she walked the last few yards to the front door. She'd dashed down from Paris on the train as soon as she'd received the call from Françoise. Before leaving, a teleprinter message came in saying that Ka was safe and that Jean was staying with her. Through her *lycée* years, she and Françoise spent most of their time together, and this was like a second home. The door opened without her having to knock, and she fell into the arms of Madame de Rochefort. 'I'm so terribly sorry, Madame. It is a tragedy for you.'

'Come on in and join everyone, Justine. I'm so happy you've come.'

She knew the geography of the house as though she'd always lived there. Little was changed as they walked over to the salon, through the double doors. Her gaze fell on Françoise who was sitting on the window seat close to Monsieur de Rochefort in the same chair he always used. She gave both of them a kiss on each cheek, before looking up at Leo and then Bill, standing next to one another by the piano. They'd just flown in.

She'd only met Leo once before, years ago in Freiburg when the SS took her. Bill told her how Leo rescued him and Theresa after they were stranded in Bien Dien Phu, what Leo called the *Kessel*. He said she'd been lucky to survive her flights to the front as a *convoyeuse*, and now had her feet firmly on the ground.

The conversation was muted. They spoke sparingly. There was only one subject but no one wanted to mention it. Madame de Rochefort wiped away a tear, and started to pour out the tea. 'Missing in action', that ever so familiar term. There it was in the cable which lay on the table by the cups and saucers. Justine was the last to read it, but she knew already.

Monsieur de Rochefort's face was ashen when at last he spoke. 'It's so good of you all to come. It's not just those of us here who are in mourning for Henri, France is mourning for a dead army. You know the losses at Dien Bien Phu as well as I do. The world knows. They held on to the last, then defeat and tragedy, coming just as the Geneva peace conference opens. The weeks ahead will be hard to bear, for this family and for France as it sits at the table opposite Ho Chi Minh and General Giap.'

'We must be strong,' said Madame. 'France is still France. There is the will to continue her recovery, even after losing her empire.'

Suddenly the telephone rang. Françoise was on it in a second. 'Allô, oui, de Rochefort à l'appareil. Oui, ce n'est pas possible! Je vous remercie de votre appel, Monsieur.'

She turned round towards everyone, her face alight. 'He's alive. He's believed to have been taken prisoner.'

Everyone rose and embraced one another. No one wanted to ask what being a prisoner of the Viets meant. It was enough to know Henri was alive.

'We'll find him,' both Leo and Bill said, almost together.

'And after that?' said Monsieur de Rochefort, with the first grin on his face for a long time.

'Algeria,' said Leo. 'More trouble,' said Bill.

There was silence. Now is the moment, Justine thought, pulling the *Paris-Soir* evening newspaper from her bag. 'Have you seen this? It reads, "PMF wins vote in the Assembly." My boss Pierre Mendès France is the new prime minister.'

Author's note

Elsa Schiaparelli, more than any other designer during the first half of the last century, stood out in Paris haute couture because of the individuality and style of the clothes. Her clients were challenged by her maxim 'Never fit the dress to the body, but train the body to fit the dress.' During the Second World War, Elsa worked in the United States on relief programmes to help French people suffering under the Occupation. After the Liberation, new designers such as Dior and Balenciaga took up the leadership mantle and when her old rival Coco Chanel returned from exile in Switzerland, Schiap closed the doors of her couture business at 21 Place Vendôme.

Bernard Fall became a leading political scientist and war correspondent. He predicted the failure of France and later the United States in their conflicts against the Vietminh, due to their lack of understanding of the people and how to conduct their campaigns. In February 1967, while accompanying a company of US Marines in Vietnam, he stepped on a landmine and was killed. Colin Powell, former US National Security Advisor, said 'I recently re-read Bernard Fall's book on Vietnam, *Street Without Joy*. Fall makes painfully clear that we had almost no understanding of what we had gotten ourselves into. I cannot help thinking that if President Kennedy or President Johnson had spent a quiet weekend at Camp David reading that perceptive book, they would have returned to the White House Monday morning and immediately started to figure out a way to extricate ourselves from the quicksand of Vietnam.'

Geneviève de Galard stayed on site after the fall of Dien Bien Phu to continue to treat the wounded, being released and sent back to Hanoi three weeks later. Her heroic efforts to assist Dr Grauwin and his team of surgeons in the field hospitals received worldwide acclaim. From the cover of *Paris Match* to a parade down Broadway attended by a quarter of a million New Yorkers, to the award of the Presidential Medal of Freedom by President Eisenhower at the White House.

Henri's regiment, 13 DBLE, was the sole formation on the French side at Dien Bien Phu that saved its colours. The *guidon* of the 3rd Battalion was taken by the enemy during the attack on strongpoint Beatrice on 13 March. While the enemy were celebrating the birthday of Ho Chi Minh on 19 March, a legionnaire NCO of the Legion's 1st Parachute Battalion penetrated the Viet command post and took back the flag. Seriously wounded, the NCO was helicoptered out of Dien Bien Phu shortly afterwards with the *guidon* concealed under his clothing. As to the fate of Henri de Rochefort himself, well, time will tell.

About the Author

David Longridge moved to Paris after becoming a chartered accountant, CPA as it is known in the United States and expert comptable in France. For the first six months he lived with the widow and family of French Lieutenant General François de Linares. The General had commanded French forces in northern Vietnam from 1951 to 1953 during the French war in Indochina. It was from this beginning that David's interest in French politics and military matters grew to the point where he took to writing historical fiction in that genre.

Polka Dots and Moonbeams is perhaps an unusual title for David's latest novel, but in fact is also the title of a song which he heard played by the American jazz pianist Bud Powell at his favourite jazz club in Paris, the Blue Note.

Central to this story is Justine Müller, whom readers of David's previous two novels will recognise and who has returned to her role of mannequin, as fashion models were known in those days, at the house of Schiaparelli in Place Vendôme. The haute couture industry in France had recovered from the war and Occupation, to become a powerhouse among France's exporting industries. The excitement, glamour and intrigue that went with this renaissance comes alive in this story.

Few of the younger Anglo-Saxon generation these days have heard of the titanic struggle the French nation had on its hands in Vietnam from 1950 to 1954, before the American nation found itself similarly involved. Their common enemy was the Vietminh, led by Ho Chi Minh and his General Nguyen Giap.

David has sought to capture the challenge and horror of this odyssey as a graphic contrast to the luxury of haute couture at a time when France and its people were desperately short of money.

This novel invokes the spirit of a remarkable period in French life when a proud nation was struggling to grow out of poverty and depression at a time when its young men were dying in their thousands in a costly colonial war of scale and intensity not seen since Britain's South African colonial war against the Boers fifty years before.

Other novels by David Longridge in the de Rochefort series:

In Youth, in Fear, in War
Silence in the Desert

Acknowledgements

I remember well the political and military drama that unfolded in Paris and French Indochina during my last years at school, and the contrast between that and the breath-taking beauty to be seen through the windows of the great couturiers as one walked down rue du Faubourg St Honoré. Nevertheless, having an interest in the historical background to what one is writing is not enough. Happily, I have been able to draw on the knowledge of good friends. In particular, my great thanks to Sally Eyre for her insight, through close friends of hers, into the life of a mannequin in haute couture in the fifties. Equally, thank you Eddy Shah for sharing your views on the work as a whole, they've been of immeasurable value.

Four books have been an Aladdin's Cave of inside information: Clare Wilcox's 'The Golden Age of Couture', Martin Windrow's 'The Last Valley', Frederik Logevall's 'Embers of War', and Bernard Fall's 'Hell in a Very Small Place'. I recommend all of them to anyone wishing to learn more.

Imogen Robertson, through The Literary Consultancy, reviewed the manuscript at an interim stage, and proved again how perceptive a gifted writer of fiction can be in adding value to one's efforts. Kim McSweeney at Mach 3 Solutions Ltd and Graham Frankland displayed exactly the level of understanding and efficient execution that I looked for in typesetting and proof editing, respectively. My sincere thanks to you all.

Throughout, I have enjoyed the added advantage of my tenacious wife's input on all matters French. An avid reader in that language ever since her education at the University of Pau, Anna has assisted me at every turn in the writing of this book. My greatest thanks to her, not least for her patience as the unrelenting literary endeavour proceeded apace in the room next door.